MISTAKEN

A DJINN WARS NOVEL

CHRISTINE POPE

DARK VALENTINE PRESS

MISTAKEN

Copyright © 2024 by Christine Pope

ISBN: 978-1-946435-78-1

Published by Dark Valentine Press

Cover design by Indie Author Services

Ebook formatting by Indie Author Services

Chapter 1

"Do you know what this is about?" Monica Weiss asked, and Sarah Wolfe shook her head.

"Not a clue," she replied. "But I've mostly been working at Pajarito's or the co-op this week, so I probably missed out on any gossip that might have been circulating at City Hall."

The two women had just entered the auditorium at the high school, the usual place for these sorts of gatherings in post-Dying Los Alamos. The world's only all-human community was nominally run by a city council made up of five members, but most of the time, the councilmembers—Miles Odekirk, his wife Lindsay, Brent Sutherland, Shawn Gutierrez, and Nora Almeida—were pretty much content to let the people in the town do their own thing.

Well, besides strictly following each week's duty rosters, an institution born out of the chaos immediately following the plague that had killed off most of the world's population, a disease created by the djinn so they could claim the earth as their own after millennia of watching it be ravaged by humans. The rosters were a way of making sure everyone in the community pulled their own weight—and learned as much as they could about the individual tasks required to keep them thriving, whether that was installing solar panels or harvesting corn—which was the reason why Sarah had split her time this past week between the co-op that supplied the town's food and Pajarito's, the restaurant on Trinity Boulevard that was a holdover from the time before the Heat and had only become more popular since.

"And I've been out weeding and watering the community garden," Monica said. She was a pretty woman a few years older than Sarah's own twenty-eight, married but without any children so far. Her fair skin was now tanned a few shades darker than it had been a couple of weeks ago, before summer had begun in earnest, which bore out her comment about spending most of her time doing garden work.

"I suppose we'll find out soon enough," Sarah replied.

Dylan, Monica's husband, waved to them from

one of the rear rows in the auditorium, and the two women headed over so they could seat themselves in the folding chairs he'd saved. He was in his mid-thirties, a man who'd lost his family during the Dying and had finally decided it was time to move forward, marrying Monica only a few months earlier. As far as Sarah could tell, he seemed like a decent person, and she could only wish them well.

God knows her own romantic life hadn't been so great lately.

Her own fault, she knew; she'd dated a few survivors who were close to her age, and had even moved in with a guy she thought was compatible enough, only to realize after six months that their relationship definitely wasn't meant for the long haul. Just one of the many problems involved in living in such a small community; the dating pool wasn't very big, and Sarah realized she'd tried to settle because she knew her prospects for finding the man of her dreams were virtually nil.

Not that she'd ever even had a man of her dreams. Not really. Back in the before time, she'd been far too focused on what had seemed like an exciting, burgeoning career to worry about seriously dating someone, let alone marriage or kids.

And then everything had changed, and even now, almost five years after the horrible sickness everyone called the Heat had almost annihilated human life on earth, Sarah still wasn't sure what she was supposed to do with herself.

She stared down at her hands, which once had been pretty and graceful and now seemed already worn and older than their true age, fingernails cut short and several scars from grease burns and random cuts marring her skin. Maybe the scars would fade eventually, and maybe they wouldn't. It didn't really matter, since she knew she'd only acquire new ones.

The murmurs in the crowd quieted down as the five councilmembers made their way onto the stage and seated themselves in the folding chairs that had been set up behind the long table placed near the front. Sarah studied them as they went—gawky mad genius Miles; handsome and perpetually unruffled Shawn Gutierrez; gorgeous Lindsay with her long dark blonde hair and green eyes; Nora Almeida, plump and motherly; Brent, who always seemed a little unsure of himself, as if he thought someone would surely come along at some point and tell him that he had no right being a member of the group that kept Los Alamos running.

It was a habit Sarah had acquired a long time ago, to watch people carefully, to see how they moved their hands and their bodies, to note the subtle shifts in their expressions. Her coach had told her once that acting was all about absorbing what people did and reflecting it in a way that an audience would immediately recognize, and she found herself still falling into that same habit even though there was no chance of her ever gracing a stage again.

If nothing else, her quiet observations of those around her helped to prevent her from being surprised by very much.

It seemed that Lindsay—who was generally the one who ran these meetings—thought everyone in the audience had quieted down enough, because she leaned forward and spoke into her microphone.

"Thanks for coming tonight," she said. "We have a few pieces of business we wanted to get out of the way, and it just seemed easier to have everyone gather here rather than trying to get the news out through the bulletin board or the intranet."

Because Miles and several other technically minded people had managed to get a sort of limited internet running in the town, just simple email and a few sites that posted community information, but still way better than what they'd had before, which was basically nothing. Sarah wasn't at all technical, so she had no idea how they'd accomplished such a feat, but she had to admit it was nice to simply boot up her laptop each morning to check that week's duty roster rather than having to go to City Hall to take a look at the physical one posted there.

Lindsay glanced at her husband then, and Miles nodded. Even after all this time, he still didn't seem all that comfortable speaking in front of crowds, and right now, he mostly looked resigned, as if he knew he was the one who needed to talk next but wasn't very happy about it.

"A bit of news about the Millerite," he said, naming the odd mineral that had been found on a farm in Cedar Crest about six months back. The farm had once belonged to a family named the Millers, hence its name. The pyrite-looking crystals had strange properties and could block a djinn's powers in a way that wasn't physically debilitating like the devices Miles had created so many years ago, those odd little boxes that had been the only thing between them and destruction for much of that time. As everyone in the audience seemed to perk up at his words, he went on, "Months of experimenting appear to have confirmed that its half-life is approximately thirty hours. This makes it still useful, of course, but it also limits what we can do with it. For now, we will have to continue to rely on our devices to keep us safe."

A murmur went through the crowd, although no one seemed inclined to speak up to ask any further questions. Sarah supposed she could under-stand that; while it might have been nice to have a way to block the djinns' powers without making them drained and weak, it also wasn't as though the immortal elementals had much to do with day-to-day operations here in Los Alamos. The community was friendly enough with the djinn/Chosen population in Santa Fe—the former state capital was home to those elementals who'd disagreed with the decision to spread the Heat, along with the human partners they'd saved—but they certainly didn't rely on the djinn to keep things running.

Well, except for a few special cases, like getting insulin for Nora Almeida when Los Alamos' one and only nurse practitioner discovered the council-woman had diabetes, or providing the heat pumps they were using to slowly replace the much more energy-wasteful air conditioning units in town. Summers now were cooler than they'd been even a few years ago, but there were still stretches where temperatures were downright uncomfortable without some form of cooling.

And really, Sarah couldn't even say for sure whether the elemental-repelling devices were necessary anymore. The djinn had all settled down in the houses their elders had assigned them, and even the few bloodthirsty types who'd made it their mission to hunt down immune humans and kill them had also appeared to have laid down their swords, so to speak. After years of tumult, the world seemed ready to settle into a new pattern, one where the djinn went their way and the humans went theirs, and never the twain should meet...well, except for communities like Santa Fe, of course.

But she supposed it was up to wiser minds than hers to decide when it was time to turn off the devices and trust that there was no longer any reason for enmity between the two races. To be honest, she'd gotten so used to knowing that Los Alamos and the countryside around it—stretching into Española and the Rio Grande valley, where they did most of their farming—were protected by the devices that she barely thought about them from day to day.

"That said," Lindsay put in, taking up the thread of the topic from her husband, "we also think it's time to begin expanding northward. We've done great work in Española and its environs, but there's a lot of good country up near Abiquiu and Ghost Ranch—fields that could be made fertile again, not to mention the Rio Chama and Abiquiu Lake, both of which would help us supplement our food supply with fresh fish."

Sarah found her eyebrows lifting slightly at those comments. It wasn't that the area Lindsay was talking about was off-limits, but the people in Los Alamos also hadn't made much effort to expand in that direction, either. There was some fertile land up there, true, and yet the country was also rough and difficult to navigate, especially with the way many roads—other than the ones they used regularly—were beginning to buckle and fail after years of neglect.

On the other hand, Los Alamos kept growing... and growing. Some of the people who'd gotten started early already had three or four kids, and although there was still plenty of housing to accommodate them, it wasn't only about keeping roofs over people's heads. You also had to find a way to feed them all.

"We don't have any recent surveys of that area," Miles added. "And that's why we're looking for a couple of volunteers to go scouting. We'd like one person to go to Ghost Ranch, and another to head over to Abiquiu Lake and the Rio Chama and see what the local trout population looks like. It should be an easy enough expedition, just a day in either direction, since we'll drive you to the northernmost point along Highway 285 before we send you on your way."

For a moment, no one seemed inclined to say anything. As far as Sarah could tell, the expedition didn't seem especially dangerous, not when the volunteers would have a companion for the first part of their trek before heading off in different directions.

And it wasn't as if she hadn't spent plenty of time in Española, helping with the gleaning operations intended to collect every even slightly useful item from the abandoned houses and businesses in the small town. With a pang, she thought of her friend...well, more like good acquaintance...Isla, who'd also been an enthusiastic gleaner. One of those expeditions had gotten her a lot more than she'd bargained for, since she'd encountered a djinn who'd captured her, but that had all turned out fine in the end. They'd fallen in love, and Isla was now Aamir's Chosen and living a life of luxury in Santa Fe.

Sarah kind of doubted the same kind of fate awaited her, and yet she had to believe that a few days hiking around Abiquiu and Ghost Ranch would be infinitely preferable to another week of stocking the refrigerated cases at the co-op or scrubbing down tables and pouring beer at Pajarito's.

Almost of its own volition, her hand shot into the air.

"I'll go," she said.

The three djinn elders stood in front of Abdul, none of them looking particularly pleased with him.

"It is time for you to leave," Ibram, the eldest of them, said.

Abdul crossed his arms. Not for the first time, he was glad of the long black robe he wore, a garment that had done well to shield his face for countless millennia because of the way the hood dropped far forward, casting deep shadows. It did an excellent job of concealing the frown he knew pulled at his brow.

"Why now?" he asked, doing his best to keep his tone mild. "For I see little that has changed between yesterday and today."

Istar, the only woman among the elders, surprised him by smiling. Like all djinn women, she was strikingly lovely, with red hair that fell to her waist and emerald-hued eyes, but she also had a certain whimsy about her, as if she possessed knowledge that no one else did...and was amused by it.

"Nothing has changed," she said. "Except perhaps that our patience has finally worn thin. It has been some months since the last of our people abandoned their palaces here in the otherworld. You are the only one remaining."

"Not precisely true," he countered. "For I know that Lyanna al-Syan still maintains her palace on this plane."

Idris and Ibram flickered a glance at one another. Abdul knew they could speak non-vocally, but although he was not precisely the same as all the other djinn, neither was he an elder, and so he had no idea what the two men standing a few paces away had been saying in their thoughts.

"That is not the same, and you know it," Ibram said. An edge had entered his voice, one that Abdul had heard several times before over the centuries, although it had been a long while since the elder's irritation had been directed at him. "For Lyanna al-Syan has been sentenced to remain here alone for all eternity, thanks to her crimes against Zahrias al-Harith and his Chosen. You, my friend, have committed no such crimes, and therefore must also remove yourself to a new life on Earth."

Perhaps he had not engaged in the same crimes as Lyanna, but he knew he had committed countless others. Crimes in service to his people, true, and yet he doubted humans would have the same understanding view of the situation.

"This palace pleases me," he said, more to use up a bit more time than because he thought he could bend the three elders to his way of thinking.

"And you will find a place on Earth that pleases you as well," Istar responded easily. "For no palace, no matter how beautiful, can possibly compare to the beauties of Earth."

Unlike many of the djinn, Abdul had not spent any great amount of time on the mortals' plane. However, he had been there enough to know that, on the surface, Istar's assertion was mostly valid. Except....

"There is still a great deal about it that is decidedly *not* beautiful," he said. "For I know that, even though our people have been busy, it is going to require a great deal of time to rid the place of all the ugly works of men."

This time, it was Istar and Ibram who exchanged a glance. Idris, on the other hand, appeared annoyed, as if he believed Abdul was wasting their time.

Perhaps. After all, Idris had taken a human woman for a companion, one who was reputed to be quite beautiful, and no doubt he would much rather be spending time in her company than standing here and arguing with an obstinate not-quite djinn reluctant to abandon the only world he had ever known.

"We understand the service you have done for us," Istar said, the smile she had been wearing a moment earlier gone as if it had never been. "And we also understand that sometimes it is difficult to give up places that are familiar, even beloved. But you will make a new home on Earth, just as the rest of us have."

Although her expression was serious, it was impossible to ignore the warmth in her voice. It seemed clear enough to Abdul that she was happy in her new home...and she expected him to be as well.

"Surely you must have given it some thought,"

Ibram said. "For while we have been patient with you, we all knew that the time must come when even you abandoned the otherworld and joined the rest of us in the place that had been denied us for so long."

Yes, that had been the dream—to eradicate humankind so the djinn could lay claim to Earth and all its beauties, beauties that should have been theirs countless millennia ago.

Certainly, they would have been much better stewards of the place than humans ever were.

And he would not lie. While he had lingered here far longer than any of the djinn—except, of course, for the hot-headed Lyanna al-Syan, made a prisoner by her own exceedingly bad decisions— Abdul had still known the time would come when he would also have to leave the palace he had constructed for himself over the years, a towering edifice of basalt and obsidian, whose shadowed hallways had served very well to conceal who he was.

What he had done.

No palace for him on Earth, however. He wanted his destination to be someplace remote, a location where he could be certain that no one... human or djinn...would have any reason to stumble across his sanctuary. If that meant he must live humbly—at least at first—then so be it. Let the djinn live in their palaces and mansions, their ocean-front properties that had once been the playgrounds of humanity's wealthy and notorious. He would take refuge in the natural world and hope its much simpler beauties might help soothe some of the darkness in his soul.

For a moment, though, he was silent. If he uttered the name of his new home aloud, then that would make it real, would tell him that his time in the otherworld and the palace he had built would at last be at an end.

No help for it, unfortunately. Even if he kept his plans to himself, he knew the elders would discover his destination soon enough. That was their way, after all—they saw and understood far more than any ordinary djinn.

Including someone like himself, who was not ordinary at all.

"Very well," he said, knowing how heavy his voice sounded. "It is a place in northern New Mexico, quiet and isolated."

He paused there.

"It is called Ghost Ranch."

Chapter 2

Sitting next to her in her folding chair, Monica looked shocked, and Sarah couldn't really blame the other woman. Until the instant when she'd raised her hand and volunteered for the Ghost Ranch mission, she herself hadn't known that was what she truly intended to do.

In the next moment, though, someone in the audience stood.

"I'll go," the man said.

Sarah bit back a groan. Although he'd been sitting on the other side of the auditorium from her, she knew that voice all too well.

Carson Mailer, the guy she'd lived with for six months before she broke things off, knowing there was no way in the world she could spend the rest of her life with him...or even another year.

Or even one more damn day.

Had he volunteered out of some sense of misguided chivalry, thinking he needed to protect her, keep her safe out there in the wilderness?

She kind of doubted it. He certainly hadn't shown much chivalry in the time they'd been together. No, he'd been just nice enough at the beginning to convince her he was worth being with, and as soon as their relationship had been more or less settled, he became demanding and needy, wanting to know how she spent every hour of her day. Not that it was too hard to discover that information, considering how everyone's schedule was dictated by the duty roster and it was public record, but still, she'd never been with anyone like that before, and it drove her crazy.

No, it seemed much more likely to her that he'd volunteered now because he thought going on this expedition together would allow him to spend more time around her, and maybe convince her that she'd made a horrible mistake by walking out.

Fat chance of that happening. The only mistake she'd made had been moving in with him in the first place.

Maybe she should try to back out.

No, that would look terrible. Although she'd done her best to maintain a low profile during her time here in Los Alamos, she still didn't want all these people to think she was a coward.

Before she could even stop to think how she

might try to fix this, Lindsay said into her microphone, "Great—we have two volunteers. Can you stay behind so we can discuss logistics?"

Unable to do much of anything else, Sarah nodded weakly, while on the other side of the auditorium, Carson said, voice carrying clear and sure over the crowd, "Absolutely."

Well, that seemed to be that.

There wasn't any real business to be discussed afterward, only Lindsay thanking everyone for coming, while the rest of the people on the council —her husband included—just looked happy that the matter at hand had been settled so easily.

Monica, on the other hand, didn't seem quite so certain. "Are you sure about this?" she asked in an undertone as she and her husband got up from their seats. "I mean, with Carson volunteering, too—"

"It's fine," Sarah cut in, also keeping her voice low...even though she didn't know for sure whether it really was. "We're both adults. Anyway, we won't be working together the whole time. He can go count trout or whatever, and I can poke around Ghost Ranch."

In a way, it would be fun. She'd visited the retreat once when she was a kid and her father had brought her to Abiquiu as part of a weeklong trip exploring the northern parts of the state, and even at eleven, she'd been struck by how beautiful the country there was. It would be good to go back as an adult and explore, to be away from people for a while and maybe...just maybe...find some inner peace.

Maybe that was asking a lot, but still, she couldn't see why a change of scenery might not do her a whole lot of good. Lately, she couldn't help thinking she'd fallen into a rut, one she'd felt powerless to change.

That could be why she'd volunteered without even stopping to think about what she was doing.

Monica nodded, although her expression was still dubious, and then she and her husband joined the rest of the crowd that flowed through the auditorium's doors and into the warm, breezy evening outside. Moving against the clumps of chattering people, Sarah made her way to the stage at the front of the auditorium, where Lindsay and Miles and the other council members had already descended to the floor so they could talk.

Carson hadn't needed to travel as far, so he was already there, chatting with Lindsay and the rest of the group as though he didn't have a care in the world. "Oh, yeah, I used to fish there with my dad and big brother," he was saying as Sarah approached.

As far as she knew, that was a flat-out lie. Like her, Carson was from Albuquerque, but in all the time they'd been together, he'd never once mentioned going fishing with his family at Abiquiu Lake— or fishing anywhere at all, as far as she'd been able to tell. Back in the before times, he'd worked as a retirement fund manager for a big national bank and, judging by the stories he'd told her about going to local clubs on the weekend and flying to Vegas with his buddies when he had the chance, hadn't seemed the slightest bit outdoorsy. Now, of course, he didn't have much choice, since everyone got rotated in and out of assignments that could involve planting crops one week and hauling lumber the next.

She wouldn't call out the lie, though. By this point, Carson had enough experience hiking and being in the great outdoors that she doubted he could get himself into too much trouble while wandering around the Rio Chama or Abiquiu Lake.

"Hi, Sarah," Lindsay said, looking almost relieved to see her approach. After all these years being married to someone as cerebral and nononsense as Miles Odekirk, she probably had a low tolerance for Carson's finance-bro schtick. "Thanks for volunteering."

"No problem," Sarah responded, even as she hoped it truly wouldn't turn out to be too much of an issue. Since she didn't want to sound like her ex and start recounting childhood tales of roaming around the area...even if her stories at least were true...she just added, "It's beautiful country up there, and this is a great time of year to go exploring."

"It is," Lindsay agreed. They were now in the last week of May, well past any chance of snow or frost, even with the weather being kind of strange these past couple of years, wetter, and with summer rains coming earlier than the onset of the monsoons in late June or early July that they were all used to. "But still, we appreciate it. None of us have really poked around up there lately, so it's good to know what we're getting into before we start making serious plans to settle that area."

"Sarah and I will find anything you need to know," Carson said, and slid a glance at her that was almost but not quite leering.

What, did he think she was going to jump into his sleeping bag at the first hoot of an owl or crack of a twig under a coyote's foot?

Possibly. She'd been quiet Sarah around him, the Sarah she'd turned into after the world ended and she'd done everything she could to hide the person she used to be, so he didn't know her very well despite the six months or so they'd spent together.

No wonder he'd been so utterly shocked when she announced that she was walking out. He probably didn't think she had the guts for that kind of maneuver.

"It's too bad none of our people here had pilot training," Miles remarked. "Then we could have done some aerial reconnaissance first. But having you go in on foot will still be invaluable."

She supposed some might have thought that a little strange, that no one out of the thousand-plus survivors who'd made it to Los Alamos could fly a plane. Then again, New Mexico always had been a poor state, with probably a lower percentage of people who could afford to keep a small plane as a hobby. Add to that the Heat's 99.8%—give or take —mortality rate, and then maybe the situation didn't look quite so odd.

"I know it will be fine," she said stoutly, making sure to keep her gaze fixed on Lindsay and Miles, and trying her best not to give Carson any encouragement. "It's not as if no one has gone that way since...well, since."

"But it's still been a couple of years," Lindsay replied. "Which is why we need to do this at all. I assume both of you are okay with setting out tomorrow morning?"

"As long as we're off the duty roster," Carson said with a grin, the kind that should have been ingratiating but sometimes had felt like nails on a chalkboard, even back when Sarah thought she actually cared for him.

"Not a problem," Nora Almeida, who'd been listening to the entire exchange, said briskly. "Since

I'm in charge of setting it up this month. I'll make sure both you and Sarah are off the roster for the rest of the week."

"This fact-finding mission isn't going to take that long," Miles protested, but Nora only shook her head.

"Maybe not, but it's probably better to have a buffer in there anyway, just in case. Besides, that's a long way to walk. Even if everything goes smooth as butter, they're going to be tired when they get back."

Her tone was cheerful but firm, and Sarah guessed that even Miles—who was notoriously bad at picking up on social cues—got the message.

"I suppose that's for the best," he allowed.

"Great," Lindsay said. "How about we all meet at City Hall at nine tomorrow morning? I'll give you some maps and a list of things to look out for, and then I'll drive you as far as La Chuachia, where Highway 285 and Highway 84 branch. That's the northwest boundary of the safe zone in Española. From there, you'll need to go on foot."

"Will we have devices to take with us?" Carson asked. His voice sounded a little too deliberately casual, telling Sarah he wasn't too thrilled about the possibility of facing the wilderness without that extra bit of defense.

"Of course," Miles replied, and Carson appeared to perceptibly relax. "Too many unknowns to have you go out there without them, although the djinn threat does seem to be reduced to almost nothing these days. But we have plenty to spare, so there's no point in taking chances."

That was one bit of good news. As Miles had said, there was no reason to believe any djinn would attack her and Carson as they made their way toward Ghost Ranch or the Rio Chama, but on the other hand, they'd been churning out the things for years now, which meant there were plenty to go around.

"It's too bad the Millerite has such limited use, though," the scientist went on. "Otherwise, we'd each give you a piece to carry with you, since it's much less bulky."

Well, that was true. The devices weren't huge, but even a four-inch cube could take up a lot of space in a backpack when you compared it to a hunk of mineral you could slip into your pocket.

"We'll manage," Sarah said. "But since it sounds like we have a big day ahead of us tomorrow, it's probably better if I go home and get to sleep early."

"Good idea," Lindsay agreed. "I'll see you tomorrow."

Avoiding eye contact with Carson—Sarah knew looking at him directly would be a bad idea —she tilted her head briefly in farewell before heading for the door. Even though she walked quickly, it wasn't quite fast enough to prevent him from catching up to her.

"Hey," he said, and she slowed down, knowing that to do anything else would be rude. "I hope you don't mind me volunteering, too."

She glanced up at him, doing her best to keep her expression blank. While she was forced to admit that Carson was one of the better-looking guys in the Los Alamos group, with his dirty blond hair, bright blue eyes, and regular features, now she could only reflect that it was too bad his inside didn't match his outside.

"Why should I mind?" she said carelessly. "I mean, they needed volunteers, and they got two. All good, right?"

He gazed back at her for a moment, probably doing his best to see if he could detect anything in her expression that would signal her words weren't exactly the truth.

Good luck with that. If nothing else, her early training had made her extremely good at keeping what she was thinking well away from her face... unless she wanted it to show, of course.

The nonchalant act must have worked, because after a second or two, he shrugged and said, "Yeah, it's all good. See you tomorrow morning."

He turned and exited through the door, clearly wanting to be the one who ended the conversation.

Too little, too late. Whatever he did now, he'd

never be able to completely forget that last winter, she'd been the one to walk away from him.

———

The land here was beautiful. Breathtaking rock formations that shaded from rust red to sand to striking ochre, with a green river bottom to the west and blue skies dotted with clouds above. In the distance, Abdul could see the flat-topped rock formation known as Cerro Pedernal, once beloved by the human artist Georgia O'Keeffe.

Ghost Ranch itself...well, he could see why the elders had been somewhat concerned that he had chosen this place as his new home.

To a human, the ranch would have seemed normal enough. Modest, of course, with its series of low-slung buildings and odd little nooks and corners, specifically designed so that one might easily find a place to be quiet and meditate. However, djinn had much loftier notions of what constituted a proper house, and Abdul had to admit to himself...even if he would never make such an admission to anyone else...that this place was going to require a great deal of work to make it habitable.

Small buildings dotted the property, many of them obviously used as guesthouses back when the place functioned as a retreat. None of them were at all suitable for his purposes, although he refrained from knocking them down. Perhaps at some point, he would still decide to do so, but for now, it was better to go to the only structure he thought at all viable as his future residence, an L-shaped building situated well away from the main campus, with a spectacular view of Chimney Rock in the background.

In the otherworld, djinn residences towered many stories, reaching into the brooding sky with fanciful spires and turrets, but Abdul knew at once that such a structure would not work in his new home and would obstruct the very view that was the main part of the reason why he had come here in the first place.

No, the outer appearance of the building would remain much the same, albeit with all the dirt and abrasions and scars from almost five years of vacancy swept away. Inside, though, it was utterly different, with the mixture of wood and Saltillo tile floors changed to all solid oak, the kitchen hugely enlarged, and the living area made much bigger as well, encompassing several of the former bedrooms so its dimensions might better suit his tastes.

All this was done in the djinn way, of course, with not even a snap of his fingers required to make the necessary changes. The furniture was upgraded as well, although he kept the style similar, plain dark oak and simple lines, with Navajo rugs on the floors and wrought iron fixtures hanging from the ceiling. No reason to fight the pueblo aesthetic of the place, or he might as well have taken an empty Bavarian castle for his use rather than this lonely slice of northern New Mexico.

With all that accomplished, he summoned a glass of wine and walked out into the courtyard so he might take a seat in one of the tall Adirondack chairs placed there. They faced south, directly toward the Pedernal, and he thought it would be good to sit there and breathe in the air and allow himself to relax into the space.

He was not the first person to have had this idea, of course; the chair he lowered himself into was merely a replacement for the battered ones that had been placed in this spot long before the Heat came along and changed the world forever. No one who had ever seen this view would want to do anything other than sit here so they might admire it at their leisure.

It was very quiet, with only the rustle of the wind in the grass and the far-off cry of a hawk to tell him all this was real, rather than an extremely detailed picture. Despite the near-silence, he could feel how intensely alive this place was, from the scent of sun-warmed earth in his nostrils to the bright blooms of the orange-hued penstemon wildflowers growing only a few feet away from where he sat.

So very different from the otherworld. Nothing grew there, save the plants the djinn had carefully cultivated in their palaces and courtyards, knowing that the terrestrial flora would surely die if it were ever exposed to the harsh conditions of that other plane. The sky had been an unsettling miasma of shifting colors, rather than this cool, serene blue.

Abdul breathed in and then breathed out again. Yes, this was good. He might have fought the elders, might have done his best to cling to a world the rest of them had abandoned, but now that he was here, he wondered why he had been so stubborn. It was not as though there was anyone living anywhere close to here, no one who would intrude on his solitude.

No one who would come near to poke and prod at the burden he had been forced to carry eternally.

Yes, there were the djinn and their Chosen in Santa Fe, but they had no reason to come to Ghost Ranch. Likewise, the community of surviving humans in Los Alamos might have spread into Española, and yet Abdul doubted they would have any need to explore this part of the world. There had been some agriculture here, true, spread along the valley of the Rio Chama. Still, probably not enough to pique their interest, not when they had so many matters to occupy themselves so much closer to home.

He lifted the glass of wine to his lips and drank slowly, savoring the taste of dark fruit and the warm, rich earth that had nourished it. Perhaps it was something of a pity that this wine would never be made again, for the people who had grown the cabernet grapes and bottled this particular vintage had perished nearly five years earlier. Then again, he could re-create it whenever he wished, so he would not allow himself to be too saddened by the thought.

However, he somehow knew that whatever he conjured wouldn't be quite the same.

Chapter 3

SARAH ALLOWED HERSELF A SMALL measure of satisfaction when she saw she was the first one to arrive at City Hall that morning. True, Lindsay Odekirk had a three-year-old to wrangle, so she could be excused for not being exactly on time. Carson definitely didn't have that same excuse, but he'd never been on time for anything the entire six months they'd lived together...or even during the couple of months he and Sarah had dated before that, when you would have thought he'd be on his best behavior.

The hour probably didn't matter too much, though. It wasn't as if anyone was expecting her at Ghost Ranch.

Lindsay came hurrying up about five minutes after Sarah arrived, looking breathless, her dark gold hair pulled back into a messy bun.

"I am so sorry," she said. "Mandy Miller was supposed to watch Dylan this morning, but she forgot to set her alarm clock and was still asleep when I called. I hope you weren't waiting too long."

"Only a couple of minutes," Sarah replied, then decided against commenting on the way Carson hadn't even shown up yet. His absence was obvious, and she didn't want to sound petty. As far as she knew, Lindsay had no idea that she and Carson had even been a couple for a while. Their community was small, but Sarah had realized long ago that she was a very insignificant cog in it, and there was no reason for someone who carried the double burden of serving on the town council while also assisting her scientist husband with his research to have paid any attention to the romantic entanglements of Los Alamos' residents.

"Good," Lindsay said.

The night before, she'd sent Sarah and Carson a quick email to meet in the downstairs conference room in the building, so that was where they stood now. Lying on the table in front of them were several folded pieces of paper, ancient Triple-A maps that must have been scrounged from Española during a gleaning mission.

She reached for one of them now and opened it on the tabletop. "Have you ever been to Ghost Ranch?"

"Once, when I was around eleven," Sarah said. "My dad and I stayed at the Abiquiu Inn and spent about a couple of days exploring the area."

The worried expression Lindsay had been wearing ever since she arrived at City Hall eased itself somewhat. "Oh, that's good," she replied. "Then at least it won't be totally brand-new for you." She paused there, because Carson had finally deigned to show up and had paused in the doorway to the conference room. Tone growing a little sharp, she added, "Nice of you to drop in."

He'd been smiling faintly, and his expression didn't slip even the slightest bit as he replied, "Sorry I'm a little late. Things got away from me this morning."

Considering how perfectly styled his hair looked, Sarah guessed that his lateness had everything to do with his elaborate grooming habits and not any kind of external complications. He'd been like that the entire time they'd been together, always hogging their small home's single bathroom, taking what felt like ungodly amounts of time to get ready for the day.

Why he'd felt the need to look so polished for their mission, she had absolutely no idea. Most days, she just pulled her long brown hair back into a ponytail because she didn't see the need to do anything more with it...especially since she was working all the time and needed to keep it out of the way. Back in the before time, she'd taken a lot more care with her appearance, obviously, because she'd never known when she might bump into someone who was connected to a casting director or even active in local community theater. Granted, the chances of that happening in Albuquerque were a lot lower than they would have been in L.A., but still, she'd never wanted to waste an opportunity.

And it had paid off at least once, as she'd gotten a part in a local commercial just because she'd run into the producer while waiting in line at the co-op in Nob Hill.

Sometimes, you just never knew.

"It's fine," Lindsay said, although something in her tone let Sarah know that it actually wasn't all that fine. "Here's a map you can use to help you get around."

She picked up the map that was still folded and handed it over to Carson, who didn't even bother to open it up, but merely stuck it in the backpack he had slung over one shoulder.

Well, it wasn't as though he was going to need the thing right away, not with Lindsay driving them to La Chuachia so they'd only have to walk for about a day before they reached their respective destinations.

"And also trail rations for five days, and some

canteens," she went on, pointing toward the supplies that had also been stacked on the table.

Carson and Sarah both moved forward to take their share, although she found herself hoping she wouldn't need quite as much as Lindsay had provided. True, it would take one day to hike in and another to hike out, with one sandwiched in between for exploring and taking notes, but five days' worth of supplies seemed a little excessive.

Then again, they were going into territory that, if not precisely uncharted, still hadn't been explored for several years, and there was no way of knowing exactly what they might encounter. Better to play it safe.

"We might as well get going," Lindsay continued after the two volunteers had stuffed their backpacks, although this time she kept her attention more on Sarah than she did on Carson, another sign that she wasn't too thrilled with the way he'd sauntered in here so late. "Miles had to take Dylan to the lab because I couldn't find anyone else to watch him on such short notice, and I don't even want to think what kind of trouble those two could get into."

Sarah managed to keep her mouth from twitching. Although she'd never been asked to watch Miles and Lindsay's young son, she'd heard horror stories. Or rather, he seemed like a pretty typical three-year-old...well, an exceptionally smart typical three-year-old...and that was enough to convince her she wanted to stay far away. It wasn't that she had a problem with anyone who was doing their best to repopulate the world, but rather that, as an only child, she didn't have much experience with little kids and was just fine with keeping it that way for the time being.

And although it seemed as though Miles was a very good father—something Sarah found a little surprising, considering how focused he was on his work—she had to admit that leaving the two of them unsupervised in the lab for any length of time probably wasn't a good idea.

Even Carson seemed to realize it was better not to comment, because he kept his mouth shut as they walked out to the parking lot, where Lindsay's Volvo SUV was waiting for them. He went straight for the front passenger seat, and once again, Sarah found herself trying her hardest not to roll her eyes. True, he was much taller than she and therefore should have been the one to ride shotgun, but he could have at least asked.

That wasn't really his style, though, so she allowed herself an inner sigh of resignation as she got into the back seat and buckled her seatbelt. At least she'd sat down behind Lindsay and had more legroom than she would have if she'd taken the position directly behind Carson.

With them all strapped in, Lindsay pulled out

of the parking lot and headed down Highway 30 toward Española. Rather than follow the route they usually took, however, going into the heart of town, she followed 285 along its outskirts, positioning them to head roughly northwest toward Abiquiu.

Sarah hadn't gone this way for quite a while, and she found herself scanning her surroundings with interest. True, there wasn't a huge amount to see, only shabby houses and businesses that hadn't improved much after five years of standing empty.

That wasn't entirely fair, though. In empty lots, community gardens were green with young corn and squash and beans, and some of the homes had obviously been worked on, too, with fresh paint and newly mended fences. It would take years for an appreciable number of houses here to be occupied, but she could tell that the Los Alamos community was taking its expansion plans seriously.

Which made her wonder why moving out toward Abiquiu and Ghost Ranch was even that necessary, considering how many homes were available in Española. Then again, this wasn't only about housing, but also increasing arable land so food would never be an issue...and that didn't even take into account the fishing the Rio Chama would provide to supplement what they already caught in the Rio Grande.

Sooner than Sarah would have liked, Lindsay stopped in La Chuachia, right where the two highways diverged from one another. "I'll be back here on Saturday morning," she said, then reached into her vehicle's console so she could extract a pair of walkie-talkies. "These are fully charged, and they should last for up to forty-eight hours or even more if you don't use them too much."

She handed one to Carson and the other to Sarah, who took it with some reluctance. While she understood the need to keep in contact with her fellow volunteer, she still didn't like the idea of him calling and bugging her whenever he felt like it.

On the other hand, she'd probably be pretty glad to have the thing if she slipped and fell, or ran into a pack of coyotes or something.

Not that coyotes were usually too much to worry about. However, there had been a couple of wolf sightings in the area this past winter, and while the animals might have ranged farther north with the approach of summer—no one had seen any wolves for months now—that still didn't mean she should let down her guard.

Well, she had a large hunting knife on her belt, and while she hadn't brought a gun along...mostly because she knew she wasn't a very good shot and had decided carrying might be inviting trouble...it also wasn't as though she was completely defenseless.

Carson was smiling as he thanked Lindsay and put the walkie-talkie in his backpack. No doubt he was already thinking about how he could use it to bother her during her hike, and Sarah knew she'd have to resist the temptation to turn hers off entirely.

"We'll meet you back here around ten on Saturday, then," she said, after a glance down at her watch to double-check the time. Back in the day, she hadn't worn a watch very much because she'd used her phone to see what time it was, but in this post-Dying world, cell phones were pretty paperweights and not much more.

"Good luck," Lindsay said. "If you encounter anything weird, though, come back early. It'll be more of a hike for you, but someone in Española will be able to patch a call through to City Hall. No point in using the walkie-talkies—they don't have the range."

Definitely not, since even Abiquiu was more than fifty miles away from Los Alamos, and Ghost Ranch farther still.

"I'm sure there won't be anything weird," Carson replied, clearly unconcerned. "So we'll see you here on Saturday."

Lindsay nodded. "Okay. Be safe, you two."

"We will," Sarah said. Or at least, she knew she'd be cautious. She couldn't vouch for her companion's actions.

But Carson had a pretty strong sense of self-preservation, so she kind of doubted he'd do anything to put himself in danger. No, he'd probably hotfoot it out of there at the first sign of trouble.

The two of them got out of Lindsay's Volvo and began walking north on Highway 84. To either side were small ranches and farms, their outbuildings already falling apart from exposure to the wind and weather, fences sagging, private access roads cracked and buckled. A line of cottonwoods on the right picked out the path of the Rio Chama as it meandered through the valley, and thanks to the rain they'd gotten lately, everything was green and lush.

Yes, this was good land. It would be a shame to let it go to waste.

"Nice day," Carson commented, and Sarah nodded.

"I suppose that's one good thing about the world as it is now," she said. "The weather's gotten cooler and wetter. I remember when things wouldn't be this green until late July or early August, depending on what the monsoons were doing that year."

Talking about the weather was safe enough, right?

"Yeah, I guess so," Carson replied. "I suppose I haven't really thought about it too much."

No, he probably wouldn't. With hindsight, Sarah knew he was the kind of person who didn't pay much attention to anything outside himself.

As best she could, she shoved the thought away. She didn't like the guy, but she needed to be civil to him for at least the next couple of hours until they reached the spot where he'd turn off to go to the lake and she'd keep heading north to Ghost Ranch.

"It'll make farming a lot easier," she said. "And it looks like there's already plenty to work with along here. The houses will need to be fixed up, and some of these barns probably would be easier to pull down than try to repair, but—"

"I wasn't aware you were so into farming," Carson cut in, a not entirely pleasant smile tugging at his lips.

She really wasn't. Or rather, while she knew agriculture was important for the continuation of their community, she hadn't put a whole lot of thought into the nuts and bolts involved and had been fine with working where she was told to work and not much more.

Come to think of it, she herself hadn't put a lot of thought into much of anything lately, either. It was easier to cruise through this new life while at least partially checked out...which might have been a large part of the reason why she'd hooked up with Carson in the first place.

"Well, it's important to the community," she

said, knowing how unconvincing the words sounded even as they left her lips.

One of Carson's sandy-brown eyebrows lifted. To her relief, though, he didn't challenge her statement, and instead only responded, "I guess that's why we're both here, right? So we can do something for the community?"

"Exactly," Sarah said, glad that he seemed willing to take her words at face value. But then, he'd never been the type to probe too deeply.

They walked in silence for a while after that, for which she was extremely grateful. The night before, she'd manufactured all sorts of awkward scenarios as to what might happen today, with most of them having Carson grill her over their break-up and demand to have her explain why she'd ever thought leaving someone as awesome as him would be a good idea.

However, he seemed willing to let it alone. For all she knew, he was already seeing someone else. She thought she would have heard about something like that, mostly because it was very difficult to keep secrets in a community as small and interconnected as theirs, but she supposed it was possible that even if one of her friends—and by "friend," she meant the people she was friendly with, since she didn't have anything close to a confidant—had heard the news, they might have decided not to pass it along to her.

Whatever the reason, the quiet between her and Carson was almost companionable as they followed Highway 84 along its various curves and bends, until a few hours later, they arrived in Abiquiu. The little town wasn't much more than a wide spot in the road, with the Abiquiu Inn being one of its main landmarks, but at least it let them know they weren't too far from the place where they'd have to part ways.

As they walked past the Inn, Sarah couldn't help feeling a little pang of something that might have been nostalgia, or possibly just simple regret that the place was shuttered and dark and left to decay. She remembered lunch there with her father, how she'd thought the smoked chicken quesadillas were the best thing she'd ever tasted. Even now, she had to admit that she hadn't eaten many meals that surpassed that one, simple as it might have seemed in retrospect.

Something must have shifted in her expression, because Carson hitched a shoulder in the direction of the low adobe building and said, "You ever stay there?"

"When I was a kid," she replied. "It was a long time ago."

A stupid thing to say, she supposed. While she still had a couple of years before she hit thirty, she hadn't been anything close to a kid for more than a decade, so of course her stay at the Inn would have taken place years earlier.

Carson only nodded, though, and they continued in the same silence that had accompanied them for the past couple of hours. Another forty-five minutes or so of walking, and then they paused by the turn-off for Abiquiu Lake and its recreation areas.

"Guess this is my stop," he said.

Something about him seemed almost nervous, which felt very out of character. Was he having second thoughts about bravely hiking off into the wilderness?

If that was the case, they'd gone way too far for him to change his mind now.

"Guess so," she said, doing her best to sound casual. "Don't go crazy with any abandoned speed-boats you might find."

The comment made him crack a grin, as she'd hoped it would. "I wish," he replied. "But I'm pretty sure the gas would be totally stale by now."

He had a point there. "Or kayaks," she added with a smile.

"Yeah, I don't think that'll be a problem." He paused and looked down at his watch. "You should make it to Ghost Ranch before nightfall, so that's good." Another hesitation, and then he added in an echo of Lindsay's words, "Be safe."

"You too."

Nothing left to say, so he turned away from her and began striding along the road that led to the lake, while Sarah made herself head northward again.

She wasn't sure what she would find at Ghost Ranch, but better to get there while the sun still shone.

Chapter 4

So much to do here. While the building that would be his main residence was now mostly in order, this new day presented its own set of challenges. Ghost Ranch had become a sort of retreat space in its latter years, and had dormitories, a visitors center, and several different museums. While he would leave the museums alone—the largest space housed a fine collection of art and relics related to Georgia O'Keeffe's tenure here, while others contained Native American artifacts and fossils discovered on the grounds of the facility —he certainly had no need for all those other structures with their small rooms and communal bathrooms that had once catered to the budget-conscious traveler who had come to this place.

After walking the property from end to end

and surveying everything with narrowed eyes, he concluded that most of it should go. His house and the museums would stay, and for now he would also keep the library and the building that was obviously some sort of center of worship, but all the guest rooms should be removed. However, he was happy to keep the pool, as well as the lovely labyrinth and Zen garden, both of which offered additional locations where he could be alone with his thoughts.

A wave of his hand, and the collection of buildings was gone. The result was a much barer landscape than he would have preferred, and his eyes narrowed. Something would need to be done about that.

In the next instant, a large pond filled some of the space next to the house, with cottonwoods and willows growing along its banks. Stands of ponderosa and piñon pines helped to fill in the rest of the landscape, along with artfully arranged sandstone boulders and graceful plantings of wildflowers such as penstemon and Indian paintbrush.

Much better. Now his immediate surroundings were a better complement to the majestic rock formations that had first drawn him to this location. Perhaps in time he would decide to get rid of more of the buildings, but this was a good start.

And while he had no reason to believe the elders would pay him a visit any time soon—it seemed enough that he had agreed to take up residence here—he could not help thinking that if they were to see the changes he had wrought, they would understand he truly was doing what he could to make Ghost Ranch his home.

All this had come much more easily to him than it would have for a regular djinn. While he was not precisely an elder, like them he had control of all four elements, allowing him to work with earth and water, fire and air.

Sometimes, though, he preferred to use his hands, as he would now to make some coffee and a fine breakfast.

Feeling lighter of heart than he had in years, he headed back up to the house that was his new home, already dreaming of bacon and fresh-baked scones, and perhaps some eggs and fruit.

As she slogged along Highway 84, Sarah couldn't help thinking that Carson had gotten the better part of this bargain. She'd never come this way on foot before, and her childhood memories hadn't adequately prepared her for just how steep the hill leading away from the lake truly was.

But because there wasn't much she could do about it now, she knew she could only forge ahead. Assuming that everything at Ghost Ranch still more or less stood, she'd at least be able to sleep with a roof over her head tonight. Yes, she had a tightly rolled sleeping bag stashed in her pack, but she should be able to spread it out across a bed rather than on the floor...or worse, out in the open somewhere. She'd never been much of one for camping, and she didn't intend to start now.

Despite the slog up this hill, she couldn't quite ignore the feeling of lightness that seemed to over-take her as she realized she was utterly alone here, with Carson now miles behind. Maybe to some people, the thought of being so completely by themselves might have been terrifying, but to Sarah, it only meant she was in a place where she could at last be herself.

She crested the hill and pulled in a relieved breath—not the least because she also spied a sign that told her the exit to Ghost Ranch was only two miles away.

Almost there.

In fact, now she could see the trio of slender lodgepoles that formed a frame for the entrance to the ranch, as well as the dirt road that ran beneath them. Her pace quickened a little, although she told herself there was no real need to hurry. The main part of the day had come and gone while she made her way along Highway 84, but there was still an hour or so until sundown, giving her plenty of time to get settled before night fell.

When she arrived at the entrance, she paused there so she could reach inside her backpack to get out the stainless steel container of water she'd stowed there. As usually seemed to happen, it had migrated to the bottom of her pack, and she had to dig past all the other items stowed in there—several changes of underwear, her toothbrush and a travel-sized tube of toothpaste, various other odds and ends—to reach it.

One of those items was the device Lindsay had given her. Sarah began to lift it out of the way, only to have it tumble from her fingers and fall onto the rocks that had been stacked around the base of one of the lodgepoles that marked the entrance to the ranch.

Oh, no.

The crunch of glass on stone hit her ears, and she immediately dropped the backpack and reached for the thing—only to stop once she realized the touchscreens on two sides had shattered, and she'd only risk cutting her fingers if she tried to pick it up.

Shit, shit, shit, went through her mind, but she knew there wasn't anything she could do to salvage the situation. While the devices were great at their job, they were also notoriously fragile, which was part of the reason why they were constantly being repaired and replaced.

No hope of either fixing it or getting a new

one, not out here in the middle of nowhere. About all Sarah could do now was reassure herself that there were no djinn reavers left, and therefore she didn't need that device.

Or at least, that was what she tried to tell herself. Considering the circumstances, there wasn't much else she could do.

She used the toe of her hiking boot to nudge the shattered device closer to the rocks, just so it wouldn't be so obvious.

And then she kept going.

The landscape didn't materially change once she'd passed through the entrance to the ranch—the same chaparral on either side, the same scrubby shapes of junipers and piñon pines. As she'd already noted, the landscape was much greener than it normally would have been at this time of year, but still, her surroundings felt mostly familiar, with only the contours of the hillsides different from those that surrounded Española.

Despite the loss of her device, that same sensation of lightness from a few minutes before filled her, a sensation she'd only been able to experience during the times when she was away from the people in Los Alamos. It wasn't that she didn't like her fellow survivors—well, most of them, anyway—or that she didn't want them all to thrive and be happy.

No, it was more that, even after all this time,

she didn't want to talk about her past, about what the Heat had taken away from her. Saying it out loud would only make her concerns sound selfish and petty compared to all the losses everyone in her community had suffered.

Here, though...here, she was completely alone. And that meant she could do the thing she always consciously avoided when she was in Los Alamos. She only allowed herself to be utterly free during the times when the duty roster sent her foraging in Española on her own, with no one else around.

She began to sing.

The song was an old, old English folk tune she'd learned a million years ago when she was in her high school's madrigal group.

Early one morning
Just as the sun was rising
I heard a maid singing in the valley below
O don't deceive me
O never leave me
How could you use a poor maiden so?

True, it was late in the afternoon and not early in the morning, and at twenty-eight and with a couple of long-term relationships under her belt, probably no one would have ever referred to her as a "maid," but still, Sarah couldn't help thinking the song somehow fit her situation anyway. She was definitely in a valley, and she was certainly singing her heart out in a way she very rarely had a chance to.

The wind seemed to catch her voice and carry it along, allowing it to echo off the canyon walls. Not so long ago, it hadn't been so strong, had been soft and breathy after years of ignoring her instrument, but now it was almost back to what it had been five years earlier, when she thought she'd gotten her big break at last and everything was going to change.

Oh, it had changed, all right...just not the way she or anyone else had suspected.

In late August, only a month before the Heat came along, her agent had called her with the big news. The producers of the revival touring company of *The Phantom of the Opera* had listened to her tapes, and they wanted her to come to New York to audition in person.

No time to think about anything except booking a flight and a hotel room, using the money she'd earned from one of the commercials she'd filmed six months earlier. A week of auditions and callbacks and waiting, and then she got the news.

She'd been given the role of Christine's understudy, and would sing and dance in the chorus as well. It was a lot more than she'd been expecting, considering she'd only performed in local productions and dinner theater before that. Even better, she'd be able to perform the lead role in alternating Sunday matinees...and the producers had hinted she might be given an even bigger part if their regular Christine had to drop out for some reason.

A mad rush to rearrange her life so she could be in New York for a month of rehearsals soon followed. And then, only two days before she was due to board her flight, she got a call from the hospital at UNM. Her father had collapsed at work, and she needed to come see him right away.

Of course she'd rushed over, even as a small, selfish part of her kept praying that it was something minor, maybe low blood pressure or low blood sugar. Patrick Wolfe had always pushed himself too hard, had never questioned the sometimes punishing hours required for his high-level job at Sandia Labs. Sarah still didn't know exactly what that job involved, except it was nuclear in nature and highly classified. The work had allowed him to provide a good home for her, to make sure there were always nannies and caregivers to be at the house around the clock, to drive her to school and piano lessons...and later, voice lessons...and anything else she needed or could possibly desire.

What she'd really wanted was for him to be there for her, but she never made the request. Even when she was very young, she understood that when her mother died, she'd taken a piece of him with her, and he would spend the rest of his life trying to compensate for that part of himself he'd lost.

The test results came back quickly.

Stage IV pancreatic cancer.

Even now, she couldn't completely piece together what had happened after the diagnosis. More tests, discussion of possible treatment...the realization that hospice was the only thing anyone could truly offer with his disease so advanced.

No thought of going to New York after that. She'd called the producers directly and let them know what had happened, made her apologies. They'd sounded sympathetic and had even told her that perhaps there would be a place for her in the production later on.

Maybe that had been a kind lie, and maybe it hadn't.

All Sarah knew was that none of it really mattered, because several weeks later, her father passed while she sat at his bedside and held his hand. And a few days after that, stories of a terrible fever began to circulate on the news, and within another thirty-six hours, most of the world's population was dead.

But she wasn't.

Not that it seemed as if she would be alive for very long after that, considering the way the djinn appeared soon afterward, hunting anyone who'd managed to survive the terrible fever. She'd hidden in her father's house for a few days, but then a group of fellow survivors had come along and told her they were heading to Los Alamos, that a scientist there claimed to have created some sort of device that would protect them from the bloodthirsty elementals.

She'd gone along because right then, she hadn't known what else to do.

When she got to Los Alamos, though, she said nothing about her background in music. It seemed horrible that she still mourned what might have been when it was only a silly role in a musical, after all.

Or maybe it had been easier to let herself hurt over that than come to terms with losing her father in such a way, with it happening so fast, she'd barely had time to absorb what was happening before he was gone forever. Maybe some people might have said cancer was still better than the Heat, but Sarah wasn't so sure. She supposed the only good thing about the situation was that at least she'd been able to properly say goodbye to him.

That was something most of her fellow survivors in Los Alamos hadn't been able to do.

Even when opportunities to sing came along— like when Nora Almeida had organized a caroling group their first Christmas after the Dying in an effort to cheer everyone up—Sarah had demurred. It was easier to pretend she couldn't sing at all than to have to tell people about the way she'd almost had her dream finally come true...only to have it snatched away by the cruel hand of fate.

The first time she'd sung had been almost two years after her escape from Albuquerque. The town council had decided there was enough coverage by the devices in Española that it was all right to let people go foraging there on their own, and Sarah had been sent off with a pickup truck and an admonishment to find whatever she could but to make sure to be back before sundown.

That part was easy enough; no chance that she'd allow herself to get caught away from Los Alamos when night fell. What had shocked her, though, was how she seemed to relax once she was finally by herself, and how she'd started humming as she picked through an abandoned barn on the north end of town...and then finally lifted her voice and sang.

It was like being able to breathe again after being held underwater for too long.

She still had made sure not to request too many solo assignments, just in case someone noticed that she was a little too interested in being out on her own. Even so, over time her voice had come back to her, had almost returned to what it had been when she'd stood in front of those New York producers and sung "Think of Me," Christine's opening piece from *Phantom*.

And that was why she used it now, knowing

that Carson was miles and miles away, and her friends and acquaintances in Los Alamos even farther.

Out here in Ghost Ranch, she wouldn't have to explain herself to anyone.

Abdul paused just as he was about to clip a branch of Indian paintbrush so he could place it in a hand-made ceramic vase he'd found in the gift shop earlier that day. Sweet sound drifted on the wind, something so unexpected, he had to take a moment to analyze what it could possibly be.

Was someone *singing?*

He wanted to tell himself that was impossible. Perhaps someone had left a music player of some sort behind in one of the buildings he had yet to raze, and it had come to life through a kind of glitch.

But no, this didn't sound like a recording. It was far too real.

He set the clippers down on a nearby boulder and lifted his head into the breeze so he might get a better idea of where the sound had originated. Yes, definitely a woman's voice, clear and bright and lovely, so entrancing in its perfection that for a moment, he could only stand there and drink it in.

Reason kicked in a moment later, of course,

telling him that no matter how pure and perfect those tones might be, they had to belong to a human...a human who must be uncomfortably nearby.

The voice was drifting to him from the west, toward the dirt road that led into the property. That made sense—there was only one true way in and out of here, unless someone was prepared to do some fairly serious rock-climbing.

And he found himself doubting that anyone would be able to maintain that kind of breath control while scaling down a sheer rock face.

Now he was glad he hadn't yet torn down the visitor's center or the museums, as they provided ample cover for him to take to the shadows and get a good look at the intruder.

Yes, there she was, walking along the dirt road, long brown ponytail caught in the wind even as she sang some sort of sprightly song about a corner of the sky, or some such. He was not very good at estimating human ages, for he had never spent any time among mortals, but she seemed fairly young, perhaps somewhere in her twenties. Middle height, slender, and...pretty. Or at least, he assumed most people would have thought her even features and oval face were attractive, although he had never been in a position to evaluate a mortal woman's looks in such a way.

She wore serviceable clothing, jeans and hiking

boots, with a denim jacket tied around her waist and a large backpack hanging from her shoulders. Her stride was neither fast nor slow, but measured, as though she'd come a long way already and intended to continue at that steady pace until she reached her destination.

Which he assumed had to be somewhere here on the grounds. Why she had come to such a remote place—and unaccompanied—he had no idea. And that meant he needed to remain in hiding while he watched her movements and decided what to do next.

The easiest thing, of course, would be for her to complete a survey of the property and then leave, but Abdul doubted he would be given such a simple outcome. It was far too close to the end of the day for her to turn around and head back to wherever she'd come from, which meant she surely planned to spend the night here.

That would never do.

He watched her as she paused in front of the welcome center, a frown plucking at the clear skin of her brow even as the song she had been singing cut off abruptly. It seemed she was disturbed by something, for even from where he lurked in the shadows of a clump of junipers and a sheltering boulder, he could see the way she glanced from the welcome center and up the hill, then back again, as if attempting to compare the scene before her with something she held only in her memory.

Could it be that she had been here once upon a time, and was trying to reconcile the highly altered layout of the campus with what it had been before? Abdul wanted to curse himself for his haste in altering the landscape to something he found more aesthetically pleasing, although he had to admit that he could never have known his sanctuary might have been intruded upon by a mere mortal. Humans hadn't ventured here in years and hadn't shown any sign that they wished to return.

What possible reason could she have for coming here now?

A visible lift of her shoulders, and then she kept moving past the visitor's center, along the path that led upward to the house of worship and the labyrinth...and to the long, low home he had taken for his own.

His first impulse was to hurry out, grab her, and blink her back to the road before disappearing. However, while doing so would certainly remove her from his property, such actions would only let her know that something unearthly lurked nearby. She might go back to Los Alamos—for he could not think where else she might have come from—and return with reinforcements.

But if she went inside his house, she would see right away that it was occupied. Everything was clean and new, not covered in dust the way it should be if it truly had been sitting here empty for nearly five years.

The frown he wore mirrored the one on the strange woman's face, although even if she had been close enough to see him, the hooded cloak that was his perpetual outer garment would have kept his expression hidden from her.

For now, he decided, he would only observe. It was possible that she wanted to conduct a brief survey of the buildings and afterward would return whence she had come.

If she made a move to go inside...well, then he would decide what to do.

The place was different. Sarah wouldn't flatter herself into believing that she remembered every single nook and cranny of Ghost Ranch, not when it had been almost twenty years since she'd come here with her father, but still, she knew there should have been many more buildings scattered around the property. Also, it hadn't felt this...manicured...for lack of a better term. Still wild and lovely, but more like someone's carefully xeriscaped backyard than a location that had always had a lot of weeds and rocks to give it character.

True, the big open field across from the visitors

center looked familiar, although greener and not as overgrown as she remembered. But there had been lots of smaller buildings in various shapes and sizes, and almost all of those were gone now, replaced by careful groupings of native plants and some pretty spectacular boulders.

Maybe a survivor of the Heat had made their way here and then decided to turn the Ghost Ranch campus into something that more closely matched their tastes. All this work would have taken a lot of time, but then, it had been nearly five years since the Dying. Even a single person could accomplish a good deal in that sort of span, especially if they didn't have any other projects to keep them occupied. But if that was the case, where were they? She hadn't detected a single whisper of anyone else's presence here, and surely they would have heard her and come to investigate who was singing as she trespassed on their property.

Farther up the hill was a low house with more trees clustered around it, some of them cotton-woods and weeping willows, signaling there must be some kind of water there. It seemed as good a place as any to check out, so that was where Sarah headed now.

Besides, the sun kept slipping farther and farther to the west, and since she had to crash somewhere around here, it might as well be the one structure that looked as if it might have a real bed inside.

Trudging uphill at the end of such a long walk wasn't much fun, and her calf muscles told her exactly what they thought of the additional exertion. She kept going, though, knowing there wasn't any point in stopping until she'd reached her destination. Without a device to protect her, it seemed even more important to find some kind of shelter.

Yes, that was a small pond located next to the house, with willows drooping graceful branches into the water and cottonwoods whose leaves fluttered with the slightest breeze. Sarah couldn't remember seeing anything like that when she visited Ghost Ranch all those years ago, but then again, she didn't think she and her dad had explored the various casitas and guesthouses. She supposed it was possible that the pond had been here all along.

The L-shaped house overlooked a large courtyard set with brick in a basketweave pattern, and at the front of the courtyard were several sets of Adirondack chairs obviously placed there so they could take advantage of the magnificent view, which was pretty much due south, with Georgia O'Keeffe's beloved Pedernal centered in the middle of the scene.

A gorgeous setup, but Sarah couldn't stop herself from frowning at the big wooden chairs, all of which had been painted a cheerful turquoise that was a perfect contrast to the red brick beneath and the warm adobe of the house behind them. If those chairs had been sitting here since the Dying, the paint should have been flaking off, and at least one of them probably should have also been knocked over by the wind.

But everything looked peaceful and tidy and well-cared for, and she frowned again.

A little shiver went down her spine.

Even though she still felt utterly alone, she couldn't help wondering if someone was lurking nearby, watching her.

"Hello?" she ventured, hoping she didn't sound as small and frightened as she felt.

No response. Was that better or worse?

Even so, she waited there for a moment, gaze scanning the courtyard and the trees that sheltered the house. Nothing moved except branches swaying in the wind.

She had to be alone here, right? Anyone who was watching would have responded to her greeting...wouldn't they?

Part of her wanted to turn and run back to the highway, but she knew that was no solution. There was no way in the world she could make it back to the turn-off for Abiquiu Lake before night fell, and even if she did decide to go blundering around in the darkness, she would have to hope that Carson had left his walkie-talkie on so she could reach out to him. That didn't seem very likely, not when he wouldn't expect to meet up with her until some-time tomorrow afternoon and probably had shut the thing off to conserve the batteries.

Well, damn.

You're here, she told herself. *So you might as well go inside and take a look around.*

Fine.

She reached up to adjust the backpack she wore, then made herself walk over to the nearest of the several sets of French doors that opened onto the patio. The handle turned easily when she wrapped her fingers around it, so it clearly wasn't locked.

A deep breath, and then she headed inside.

The place looked like something out of a maga-zine, or maybe a travel brochure. Smooth oak floors, rough-troweled plaster walls, expensive Navajo rugs underfoot, and a large wagon wheel of a wrought-iron fixture overhead.

She had no idea the accommodations here at Ghost Ranch had been so fancy.

And just like the meticulously tended grounds she'd walked through to get here, this place looked way too clean to have stood empty for the past four and a half years. Not a speck of dust anywhere that she could see, and when she left the large living room and passed through the dining area, it was to find a kitchen that again looked like it should have been in *House Beautiful* or something, or maybe one of those home improvement shows her father liked to watch when he was trying to relax after yet another ten-hour day at the labs. Fabulous counter-tops that she thought might be quartzite or soap-stone, an enormous copper hood over the eight-burner stove, backsplash of the same pale stone with greenish veining that covered the counters.

Maybe this house hadn't been intended for guests at all. Sarah supposed this might have been where Ghost Ranch's director had lived, or someone else high up in the organization. It had been so long since she'd been here that she couldn't even begin to guess.

A peek inside the refrigerator showed that it was empty, although it was definitely on, the interior cool and ready to accommodate whatever food needed to be stored there.

And that was also weird. Yes, the place probably had solar panels to keep things going, but still, if the house had been empty all this time, you'd think there would be long-spoiled food remaining inside the fridge.

None of this made any sense.

She turned away from the refrigerator and let out a shocked gasp. Standing a few feet away was a tall man, his face and form completely hidden by the long robe he wore, which had a hood so deep that it concealed everything within it. The getup looked like something a medieval monk might have worn, and she couldn't help gaping at the apparition.

Despite the way the hood fell forward and shadowed his face, she fancied she saw a glitter of eyes from inside the hood as he demanded, "What are you doing in my house?"

Chapter 5

At first, Abdul hadn't intended to confront the woman. He'd held himself back as he watched her enter the house, then seem to hesitate as she glanced around the living room.

But when she opened the refrigerator door, he'd had enough. It wasn't as though there was anything to see in there—he hadn't yet gotten around to stocking the thing, and only summoned the raw ingredients he needed when it came time to prepare his meals—but something about the casual way she'd looked inside the refrigerator angered him, as though she thought she had every right to poke around as she liked.

And so he'd removed the veil of invisibility he'd wrapped around himself, and asked her to tell him what she was doing.

Her face immediately paled under its light

golden tan, but although he could see the way she swallowed, she didn't turn and flee. Instead, she stared directly back at him and said, "Who are you?"

"I am the one who owns this house," he replied. "A house where you are trespassing, I might add."

Now she looked almost guilty, her gaze moving away from him to somewhere nearer the floor. In the late afternoon light streaming through the kitchen window, her eyes looked almost golden, although he guessed they would be more of a greenish blue in illumination that wasn't quite so warm.

"I didn't know anyone lived here," she said. Her voice as she spoke was as clear and as pure as the singing he'd heard earlier, although pitched slightly lower. "I thought Ghost Ranch was just as deserted as the rest of this part of New Mexico." She stopped there, and now her eyes came back up again to meet his. "Are you—are you a djinn?"

The easiest way to answer her was to say yes, and that this place had been granted to him by the elders and therefore was nowhere she should be.

But that would not have been precisely the truth. Also, while he might have wished fervently that she had come nowhere near here, now that she had seen him, matters were a bit more complicated than they had been a few moments earlier.

"That does not matter," he said. "What matters is that you have come to my home, unbidden, and seen what you should not have seen."

Now one of her well-arched brows lifted slightly. This close, Abdul could see that his earlier estimation of her had been accurate, that her features were regular and well-shaped, her skin smooth and without blemish. And although she did not seem to wear any cosmetics—wise, he supposed, for someone who clearly had spent the day walking—both her cheeks and her lips were rosy with color.

"Considering that robe you're wearing, I haven't seen a whole lot," she remarked. Her lips parted again—perhaps to inquire why he covered himself in such a fashion—but then she seemed to think better of the question, for she only said, "I'm really sorry that I barged in here like this. If I'd known the place was occupied, I would have left it alone. So I guess all I can do is offer my apologies and get on the road."

She did sound genuinely contrite...but also troubled. Was it fear over how he might respond, or simple worry about heading back to the highway with nightfall so near?

Not that it mattered. She had seen him, and that meant he could only respond in one way if he wished to preserve the safe, quiet world he'd created for himself here.

"I'm afraid it isn't quite so simple," he said, and her brows drew together. Before she could say anything in response to his comment, however, he went on, "For now that you have seen me, I cannot allow you to leave this place."

A horrible second or two passed while Sarah stared back at the man...djinn...whatever he was. Was this some kind of a horrible joke?

What did he mean? He couldn't actually be saying that he planned to keep her *trapped* here, could he?

Apparently so, because he seemed to interpret her horrified silence and continued. "You see, this house—all of Ghost Ranch, really—is my sanctuary. I assume you must have come here to explore, to gather information. But I cannot let you take the knowledge of my presence here back to your people."

The way he phrased those words made it pretty clear to her that he must be a djinn. Why he was covered up in that hooded robe, though, she had no idea. Although she'd never seen a djinn in person—she'd managed to evade them during her escape from Albuquerque, and she'd never gone on one of her town's expeditions to Santa Fe where the conscientious objector djinn lived with their human partners—she'd always heard that the immortal elementals were supposed to be almost supernaturally good-looking.

If the weather had been colder, she might have told herself he was merely trying to stay warm, but since the weather had been utterly beautiful lately, with highs floating in the upper seventies, she didn't see any reason why he'd need to bundle up.

"I won't tell anyone," she said quickly. "Really. Besides, we know to stay away from djinn houses unless we've been given an actual invitation. No one is going to bother you here."

"No one is going to bother me because they will not know I am here at all," the djinn said, his tone almost mild...but implacable nonetheless. "Tell me, why did you come to Ghost Ranch in the first place?"

Sarah wanted to lie, to give him an explanation that seemed utterly harmless. Problem was, she had a feeling he'd be able to figure it out right away if she told him anything less than the truth. And even though she didn't know his name or anything about him, something about the quiet strength of his tall, lean body, the dark glimmer of eyes within the hood, seemed to signal he was not the sort of person to put up with that sort of prevarication.

"I'm from Los Alamos," she said, although that should have been obvious. It wasn't as if there was anyplace else on the planet where humans were allowed to live in peace. "We're scouting areas north of there to see if they're viable for expanding our community."

"I see," the djinn replied, which didn't tell her much of anything.

How she wished she could see his face! All her skill at reading people's expressions was utterly worthless in this particular situation.

However, his tone was studiously neutral, which experience told her was not a good thing. No, he didn't like the idea of humans coming around here, not at all.

Which she kind of understood. If she'd chosen an isolated spot like this to make her home, only to be faced with the prospect of having it overrun by a bunch of humans trying to find new places to live, she probably wouldn't have been too thrilled, either.

"But now that we know someone is living at Ghost Ranch, obviously we'll give it a wide berth," she said quickly.

His hooded head tilted to one side. "You just said you wouldn't tell anyone I was here."

Oh, right. She wanted to berate herself for making such a stupid comment, but she knew she was tired and probably had low blood sugar to boot. If she hadn't been so tense, she might have also sensed she was hungry and not at her best, even if food was pretty much the farthest thing from her mind right now.

"Of course," she replied. "I meant, now that *I* know you're here, I'll just make up some kind of story about how this place won't work for us."

No response at first. But then he said, "No, I fear that is not a good enough solution. I know all too well how driven humans can be when they decide they want something, how they allow very little to stand in their way when they are determined upon a course of action. And that means you must remain here."

What, did he think he could keep her a prisoner in Ghost Ranch indefinitely? Her brain wanted to laugh at the notion, except she knew that djinn could do pretty much whatever they wanted to do. Yes, the djinn elders appeared to be the elementals' nominal rulers, but they didn't seem to step in and lay down the law unless a situation was particularly fraught.

And somehow she couldn't help thinking that they most likely wouldn't consider the fate of one lone human to be their problem. No, they'd probably say she'd asked for her current trouble by coming here in the first place and trespassing on land that had been given to one of their kind, and then they would wash their hands of the matter.

The whole situation was so surreal that her

brain didn't want to accept it. There had to be some way to get out of this mess.

"Can't you, I don't know, erase my memories of being here or something?" she asked, even though she realized at once how crazy...and desperate...her question must have sounded.

She couldn't see his face, but she got the impression he smiled under the hood.

"The djinn control many things," he replied. "But even we are not capable of altering a human's memories. So you see that it is not safe for me to let you go."

Impasse. Sarah stared at the djinn, mind flitting from one possibility to the next, wondering if any of those hypothetical options could give her the key she needed to extricate herself from this situation.

Well, when all else failed, it was time to go on pure instinct.

She slipped the heavy pack from her back and slung it at the djinn. It caught him square across the chest, causing him to stumble backward a pace or two.

Would it be enough?

She supposed she'd find out...much sooner than she'd like.

Even as the backpack smashed into her would-be captor, she bolted for the door. She'd heard that some djinn could fly, but not all of them. Her luck had been so spectacularly bad so far that she could only hope it would finally turn, and he would be an elemental of the earth or of water, and therefore would be forced to pursue her on foot.

Looking back would only slow her down, so she resolutely kept her gaze forward as she grabbed the door handle and lifted it, then made a gazelle leap through the front door that would have made her dance instructors proud.

All for nothing, though, as the hooded djinn immediately appeared in front of her, blocking her way.

"That was...not a very good idea," he said. His words sounded slightly winded, so it seemed her attack with the backpack had had some effect. Djinn could be wounded, she knew that much, although they healed very quickly and were almost impossible to kill.

But she hadn't hurt him enough to stop him, and now she guessed he was even less disposed to think kindly of her.

"Sorry about that," she said with a disingenuous smile. "But I had to try."

"I suppose you did," he responded. He reached out and grasped her by the arm, fingers like steel around her bicep.

She didn't wince, though. The last thing she wanted was to let him see he was hurting her.

No other comment, though, and immediately they whirled away through a terrible shifting darkness that lasted for less than a second even though it also felt as though it went on forever. Through it all, the strange djinn maintained his grip on her arm. Sarah knew this was the way the elementals traveled, bending space to get to their destination, although she'd heard that usually, a human traveled with their arms around the djinn's waist so there was no chance of being separated, or getting lost in that terrible other plane.

She hadn't been lost, though. Barely before she had a chance to process what was happening, they appeared in a large room that, if not part of the same house, had been decorated pretty much the same way, with wide-plank oak floors and white plaster walls. Up against the wall opposite was a canopy bed with a black iron frame, and a chandelier of the same dark metal hung from the ceiling overhead.

"This is where you will stay," the djinn told her, and Sarah stared at him blankly for a second or two before the words sank in.

Well, she supposed it was better than a prison cell, especially when she spied a large, luxurious bathroom through the partially open door off to one side. Still, she didn't plan to stay here any longer than she had to.

He'd loosened his grip on her bicep just enough that she was able to pull her arm away.

"Nice," she said. "Does it come with room service?"

His head tilted toward her. "You will not starve," he said.

And then he disappeared.

Sarah couldn't help blinking, even though she knew that was how djinn came and went. Really, it had been stupid to try to get away from him. He was probably angrier than ever with her, thanks to the way she'd assaulted him with her backpack.

What the hell was she supposed to do now?

Wait and hope for rescue. What else was there to do? She wasn't under any illusions that Carson would come riding to her aid, her knight in shining armor, but surely after he realized she'd missed their rendezvous, he'd head back to meet with Lindsay and let her know what was going on. Lindsay Odekirk was a very capable woman, and Sarah knew she'd mount a search party right away, just like she'd done when Sarah's friend Isla had gone missing last fall.

This time around, though, Sarah knew she stood on much thinner ice. Isla had been actively kidnapped by a djinn, whereas she'd made the mistake of stumbling onto one of the elementals' properties. It was entirely possible there wasn't much Lindsay or anyone else in Los Alamos could do, except maybe appeal to the elders to see if they would step in.

Whatever ended up happening, Sarah had a feeling it was going to take a while, and that meant she might as well explore her prison cell.

As she'd thought, the bathroom was huge, almost the size of the bedroom in the house where she'd grown up and had still been living when the Heat came along. When her father passed away, she dimly realized that she'd inherited that house, but there hadn't been any opportunity to do anything about it, not with the world ending just a few days later.

And she had to admit this suite was absolutely gorgeous. A free-standing tub sat under one window that offered an amazing view of the tall red rocks only a few hundred yards away, and the glass-enclosed shower had vertical subway tile in a moody shade somewhere between deep green and teal. The floors under her feet were also tile, large-format pieces in a soft beige that she thought might be travertine.

Clearly, no expense had been spared here. Who had designed this place, though—someone from Ghost Ranch, or the djinn himself? Sarah had heard they could make their houses look pretty much any way they wanted, so she thought it wasn't too improbable to believe that he'd remodeled this house to suit his own particular tastes and needs.

All the drawers were empty, as was the enormous walk-in closet she'd passed on her way to the bathroom. Good thing she had a change of clothes and some basic toiletries in her pack.

Except that her pack was still lying in the middle of the living room where it had fallen after her aborted escape attempt. About all she could do now was hope that the djinn would show her a little mercy and blink it into the bedroom after he realized she needed it.

And that, she thought, was expecting a level of forbearance she wasn't quite sure she deserved. It was wrong for him to hold her here like this, but on the other hand, she'd been trespassing...had been poking around in his refrigerator, for God's sake.

No wonder he was so annoyed with her.

Well, there wasn't much she could do now, so she went over to the little sitting area near one of the windows, which also looked south toward the Pedernal, although part of the view was obstructed by a corner of the low-slung house. Still, she could see how the sun had now truly set, and long shadows stretched across the landscape. Off in the distance, the flat-topped peak that had been the subject of so many Georgia O'Keeffe paintings turned dusky purple.

Sarah sat down and watched the world turn dimmer and dimmer.

What else could she do?

No sound from the woman's bedroom, which told Abdul that she had—so far, at any rate—not attempted to escape. Perhaps she had learned her lesson.

He frowned as he extended a hand to have the lights turn themselves on, for the drapes to draw closed and hide the darkening landscape outside. It felt odd to have a human here in the house, albeit in one of the secondary bedrooms. An irony, he supposed, when he had always intended to live here alone.

In hindsight, it might not have been entirely wise for him to pull down all the guesthouses and casitas, for if even one of them still stood, he could have put the intrusive human female in that structure rather than under his own roof. At the time, though, he had only thought of the aesthetics of his surroundings. Certainly there was no reason for him to believe his sanctuary here would be intruded upon by a mortal interloper.

Grudgingly, he had to admit that she'd shown some spirit by hurling her backpack at him, even though she must have known such a gambit was doomed to failure. His gaze moved to the spot where the pack still sat in the middle of the living room rug.

Should he give it to her?

Still wearing a small frown, he lifted a finger, and the backpack floated across the room and into his hands. A quick inspection of the contents told him she had packed light for her expedition—a change of shirt and underwear and socks, but not a second pair of jeans. A few meager toiletries, and a lightweight bag of some kind of synthetic material rolled around itself, clearly intended for sleeping.

Nothing in there that was anything she needed, not when he could provide items that were much higher quality.

Only an intention in his mind, and the bathroom drawers were filled with makeup and toiletries, the closet full of clothing he thought would be more comfortable and becoming than her current denim and hiking boots.

Not, of course, that he cared what she looked like, but more that those plain, ugly human clothes offended his sensibilities.

That task done, he blinked her backpack away into the hall closet and pondered what he should do for supper. He would have to feed the woman, of course, but should he compel her to come out and sit down at the table with him, or would it be better to have a tray appear in her room?

A tray, he decided. While he guessed that making her share a meal with him in the dining room would be far more uncomfortable for her, bad enough that she'd trespassed in the way she had. Why on earth would he discommode himself further by inflicting any more of her company on him than he absolutely had to?

But if you ate together, you could ask her why she sang, passed through his mind then, even as he tried to brush the thought away.

There was no reason for him to know anything more about her. True, she had the voice of an angel, but still, she needed to suffer the consequences of her actions.

And that meant a solitary existence...for as long as it pleased him.

Chapter 6

THE LANDSCAPE WAS UTTERLY DARK NOW, and Sarah pondered whether she should pull the drapes closed or whether she should continue to sit here until the moon rose. Whenever that might be; she had to admit she didn't pay a lot of attention to such things, especially since the townhouse she'd been given to live in was located in a complex with lots of tall pine trees and she couldn't even see the moon day to day unless she had a late shift at Pajarito's and spied it as she was walking home.

Probably better to close the drapes. She didn't think the djinn would lurk outside and spy on her through the windows, but still, why take the chance?

She'd just risen from her chair when a knock came at the door.

What the hell did he want now? Wasn't the

whole point of this little exercise to leave her to rot in this admittedly very nice bedroom suite?

"Yes?" she called out.

His voice came to her, slightly muffled by the thick pine door. "I wanted to know if you had any restrictions on your diet."

How...accommodating of him. She really didn't, mostly because survivors in this post-Dying world couldn't afford to be picky about what they ate. There were a couple of people in Los Alamos who were vegetarian, although their food wasn't varied enough to support a true vegan lifestyle.

Sarah, on the other hand, had always been an omnivore, although back before the world changed, she hadn't eaten a lot of red meat. Now, though, she consumed what was available, whether rabbit or venison or elk or the rare chicken. They'd just recently begun to have enough of a spare poultry population that chicken had started to show up on the menu at Pajarito's from time to time, but it wasn't anything she could count on.

"No restrictions," she said. Then she couldn't help smiling as a certain thought occurred to her. "But I'd kill for some pepperoni pizza."

Because, while there were several decent pizza makers in Los Alamos, no one had come up with a way to make pepperoni yet. It had been years and years since she'd had such an indulgence.

"I am sure killing will not be necessary," the djinn replied.

Before she could even blink, a freshly baked personal-size pizza appeared on the small table in the sitting area, along with what she thought might be a glass of chianti. Not that it mattered. It was red wine, and she knew she could use a drink after the day she'd had.

"Um...thanks," she told the door.

"It is nothing."

That seemed to be that, because he didn't say anything else. Which was fine by her, since trying to carry on a conversation through a door was just a wee bit awkward.

She went over to the table and sat down on the chair she'd occupied only a few minutes earlier. The scent of the pizza rose to her nostrils, warm and rich and spicy, and her stomach growled.

Even as she began to reach for a piece, however, she hesitated.

What if he'd drugged the food or something?

Don't be ridiculous, she told herself. *He already has the upper hand here. Why would he need to drug you when he's already got you locked up right where he wants you?*

Good question. But maybe he had other, darker designs on her, even though so far he hadn't shown a single hint that he even recognized she was female.

No, that was also ridiculous. Sarah knew she was pretty enough, in a kind of girl-next-door way that had allowed her to land those local commercials back in the day, but she didn't have the model-perfect looks of a woman who would have attracted a djinn, like Julia Innes, who'd once been the main administrator in Los Alamos, or even Lindsay Odekirk, who'd been with one of the elementals before he was murdered by a bunch of rogue djinn.

Obviously, she hadn't been pretty enough to be Chosen, which meant there was no reason in the world for her captor to have any designs on her person. He had her locked up because she'd trespassed, and that was it.

Satisfied with her logic, she went ahead and pulled a piece loose from the pizza, trailing wonderfully gooey mozzarella along with it. That first bite was amazing, rich and tangy at the same time, while the crust had wonderful char and crunched as she bit into it.

Who knew a djinn could be so good at making pizza?

Something so amazing should be savored, so she slowed down after the first two bites, punctuating the remainder of the slice with sips of chianti. That, too, was incredible; she'd never been a wine expert, but she knew whatever he'd provided, it wasn't some supermarket brand.

Well, at least she wouldn't starve while she was trapped here.

Go crazy from boredom? Sure.

And she'd need to find some way to stay active if she kept eating like this. Yoga every morning would help, and possibly some dance exercises. The room was big enough for that kind of activity, especially if she rolled up the rug to get it out of the way.

Maybe it was crazy to be making contingency plans like this when she didn't even know how long the djinn intended to keep her captive. For all she knew, he was only trying to frighten her, and once she'd been thoroughly cowed, he'd send her on her merry way.

Not the most likely of scenarios, but better to think that than to allow herself to wonder if he truly intended to keep her trapped here until she died of old age.

Suddenly, the pizza didn't taste so good. However, she made herself eat two more pieces and drink the rest of the wine, mostly because she knew she'd exerted herself today and her body needed the nourishment.

What she was supposed to do with the dirty plate and glass, she wasn't sure. Then again, the djinn had blinked them in here, and she assumed he could blink them right back out when he decided she was finished with everything.

A peek outside the curtains told her the night was now utterly black, without a single sign that the moon intended to rise any time soon. Not quite sighing, Sarah let the drapery fall from her fingers and wondered what she should do next. It wasn't as if there was anything in here to entertain her—no TV or books or tablet.

And because he hadn't returned her backpack to her, she wasn't sure how she was supposed to get ready for bed.

Well, she'd splash some water on her face and scrub a washcloth across her teeth. Better than nothing, she supposed, although she would definitely let him know tomorrow morning that he needed to provide at least a few amenities if he planned to keep her here.

She went into the bathroom and blinked. When she'd come in here earlier, the large quartz-topped vanity had been empty except for a set of folded hand towels. Now, though, a dark metal toothbrush holder flaunted a brand-new brush, and several small jars with iron lids held cotton balls and Q-tips.

Startled, she opened the drawer next to her and saw that it contained toothpaste and floss. A quick inspection of the medicine cabinet revealed all sorts of moisturizers and serums, the kind of stuff she'd spent money on back in the day because she knew it was important to keep up her appearance, even though lately she'd been getting by with a single jar of Oil of Olay intended to last her for at least six months if not more. There was a small group of people in Los Alamos working hard on concocting alternatives to those beauty treatments based on the supplies they had readily available—namely, goat's milk and various local flowers and herbs— but they still couldn't make enough to supply everyone.

Where had all this come from? Obviously, the djinn had blinked it here, but had he found a cache in an abandoned department store somewhere, or had he simply conjured it into existence?

Hard to say; Sarah hadn't spent any time around the elementals, but she'd heard that sometimes they simply grabbed what they needed from already available supplies elsewhere in the world, while on other occasions, they basically manufactured an item from the atomic level up.

Either way, she didn't need to worry about washing her face or brushing her teeth.

And when she went to the closet, it was to find the previously empty space full of clothes so gorgeous, they looked more like something out of a costume house than regular everyday clothing. Long silk tunics with matching pants, airy dresses and skirts and blouses in equally luxurious fabrics.

No jeans or T-shirts, though, nothing that looked remotely practical.

Was this the djinn's way of telling her she might as well wear something decorative since he wasn't letting her out into the wild any time soon?

Well, she'd worry about that later. It was enough to know she wouldn't be stuck in the same dirty clothes day after day.

Besides, she'd always loved getting dressed up. Life after the Dying had been hard in all sorts of new and uncomfortable ways, but one of the things she'd hated the most—shallow as it felt to her—was never having a reason to put on a pretty dress. And that ignored the way she'd never again need to wear a gorgeous costume like one of Christine's from *Phantom,* or the glorious ballgown that had been part of her wardrobe when she'd played Belle in a production of *Beauty and the Beast* at a local theater a few years before the Heat went on its tour of destruction across the planet.

No elaborate gowns among the clothing the djinn had given her, and Sarah supposed that was probably a good thing. She couldn't really imagine him twirling her around in an oversized ballroom. He didn't seem the type.

Besides, she knew she would never allow herself to dance with him.

Not after what he'd done to her.

All seemed quiet behind the door of the woman's room, so Abdul guessed she must have resigned herself to her situation and had sat down to eat the food he'd provided for her. Once he was seated at the dining room table and consuming his own very different meal—he'd conjured *osso bucco* on a bed of orzo pasta, washed down with a very fine Aglianico —he found himself wondering if he had done the right thing by keeping her confined in the guest suite rather than forcing her to come out here and eat with him. For some reason, this room felt quite empty when he knew there was another living, breathing being only a few yards away.

But no, that was ridiculous. She was not his guest, but a prisoner, one whose tenure here might be of some duration. At least it seemed that she was not inclined toward any other escape attempts.

Unless she was acting quiescent now in order to lure him into a false sense of security.

Frowning, he set down his fork so he might listen more closely to the sounds in the rest of the house. All seemed utterly silent, so he knew she could not be attempting to force open a window or fiddle with the lock in the hope that it might give way.

So it seemed she was ready to accept her captivity...for now, at least.

Somewhat reassured, he consumed the rest of this meal, then snapped his fingers to have the empty plate and glass disappear. A completely unnecessary gesture, and yet it was something he did on occasion just because it gave him a sense of completion. Enough time had elapsed that he thought the woman should also have finished her food, so he did the same thing with her dinner dishes.

No sounds of protest came from her room, which seemed to signal she was now somewhat used to the way he could make her food come and go.

Had she spent any time around djinn?

He somehow doubted it, but that was hard to say. The djinn in Santa Fe had some traffic with the humans in Los Alamos, so he supposed she might have had some exposure to them while on a visit to the former capital city. Even if she had not, she would at least have heard some tales about djinn powers, which meant none of this should have been a huge surprise to her.

The quiet of the house seemed almost oppressive. If he had been alone, he might have chosen a favorite piece to play on the unobtrusive but very expensive sound system he'd summoned with the rest of the home's furnishings, but now he wasn't sure. Would she be soothed by hearing music in another room, or would it keep her from sleeping?

Impossible to say. Clearly, she was of a musical nature, or she would not have been able to sing so effortlessly, so beautifully. Abdul had listened to countless hours of recorded music ever since it became available, but nothing was quite the same as hearing it come directly from the throat of the person performing it.

Would she sing for him if he asked?

Somehow, he doubted it.

For now, he thought it better to leave listening to Mozart or Rachmaninoff for another evening. Instead, he let himself out the front door and walked through the courtyard, finally pausing near one of the Adirondack chairs placed there. Off to his left, the faintest pale smudge behind the mountains told him the moon was beginning to rise, although it would not reach its zenith for many more hours. Otherwise, the sky was utterly black, the stars like scattered diamonds across its vast expanse, with the mist of the Milky Way a soft glow in the background.

Yes, it was very beautiful here.

The only fly in this ointment was the presence of the woman in the guest suite. Abdul realized that he had never asked her name, and decided he would have to correct that oversight tomorrow.

If, of course, she even deigned to speak to him.

But while he understood her anger, he would not allow it to move him. He absolutely could not risk the rest of the mortals discovering his sanctuary, and especially could not allow them to learn the truth about him. It was a truth he had kept hidden from everyone save the elders, and he meant to keep it that way. Some might have argued that there was very little the humans could even do against one such as he, but Abdul knew the barriers he had erected existed both without and within, and he would do whatever he must to keep them in place.

Sarah opened her eyes the next morning as pale light stole past the heavy linen drapes, then allowed herself a luxurious stretch, the kind that seemed to pull her taut from the tips of her fingers all the way down to her toes. Maybe she shouldn't have been feeling quite so comfortable, considering where she was and why she was here, but she couldn't quite help herself. This bed was the most comfortable one she'd ever slept in, even better than the fancy Saatva pillow-top model she'd bought for herself to replace the mattress she'd had since junior high. Since she'd still been living at home and didn't have to pay rent or a mortgage, she could justify the expense, but the Saatva still hadn't been as good as this one.

Well, from everything she'd heard, djinn were extremely adept at providing themselves with the finer things in life, and she supposed high-end mattresses should be included among those luxuries.

And speaking of luxuries, she was more than ready to try out the spa-like shower in the bathroom.

It was everything she'd expected and more, including the neverending flow of warm water. Back in Los Alamos, everyone had learned to take fast showers so as not to use up too much energy, but that definitely wasn't a problem here. She'd heard how djinn used some of their power to heat water and run furnaces and air conditioning, so she assumed that must be what her captor was doing here as well.

That thought made her a wee bit uncomfortable...but not so much that she sped up the rest of her shower. It just felt too good to indulge herself with all that hot water, and to use shampoo and conditioner that seemed as though they'd come straight from a high-end salon rather than the drugstore stuff she'd been using for the past four-plus years.

Afterward, she dressed herself in fresh underwear...that part did feel a little weird, but again, not so weird that she was going to scruple at putting on a pretty lace bra and matching panties...and then chose one of the dresses her captor had provided for her, made of deep red silk, with a high waist and what felt like yards of fabric in the skirt. The whole thing made her want to twirl around like a little girl playing dress-up, but she managed to keep control of herself and instead slid her feet into a pair of pewter-hued thongs that were neutral enough to go with pretty much anything.

As far as she could tell, he hadn't summoned any jewelry, but that was all right. She'd been wearing a pair of small silver hoops when she was captured, and they were better than nothing.

To be honest, she wasn't sure whether it mattered what she looked like, since it didn't seem as though she'd be getting out of this room any time soon.

She went to the window to take a look at the day. The sun had been up for a while, and the sky overhead was its usual gorgeous sapphire. Some clouds were building to the south and east, however, telling her they might be in for some weather by the time late afternoon rolled around.

Nothing she needed to worry about, though, because again, she had no reason to believe her captor would even allow her to go outside at all.

Just as that thought passed through her mind, he knocked at the door. She went over to it and said, "Yes?"

"Would you like coffee or tea? Do you have any preferences for breakfast?"

"Tea," she said at once. For some reason, she

wanted to smile. If nothing else, she had to admit that the djinn was a very polite jailer.

And although everyone else she'd known in the theater community had been a fiend for coffee, she'd never acquired a taste for it.

"For breakfast...." She paused, wondering what she wanted. In the past, she'd never been much of a breakfast person, and she'd continued that practice in Los Alamos, thinking she was doing her part by not consuming very much for her first meal of the day. Sure, the djinn could probably get her anything she wanted, including fancy omelets or Belgian waffles, but she didn't see the point in pushing things. "Just a blueberry muffin or something."

He didn't respond right away, and she wondered if he was going to try to urge her to eat more than that. However, he only said, "Of course."

Movement out of the corner of her eye made her turn away from the door. Sure enough, a small lacquer tray had appeared with an adorable little brown-glazed teapot and matching mug, along with a gorgeous blueberry muffin that sat on a plate of the same thick stoneware.

It seemed her joke about room service hadn't been too far off the mark.

"Thank you," she called out to the closed door,

but because there was no reply, she guessed that he'd already gone.

All right, then. She sat down on the chair and poured herself some tea. The djinn hadn't asked what she wanted, but this tasted like it was probably English Breakfast or some other mild black tea, and that was fine by her. A small bowl of sugar and a matching baby-sized pitcher filled with milk had come along with the teapot and mug. Nice of him, she supposed, but she always drank her tea plain.

Well, unless she was indulging herself in a Thai iced tea, although she had to admit she hadn't had one of those for several years even before the Heat came along.

The muffin was delectable, moist and with the blueberries so large and juicy, they almost didn't seem real. Sarah supposed the ingredients were like the mattress and all the other items that had come with this room, everything the best it could be because that was just how the djinn rolled.

After she was done eating, she went and brushed her teeth, and then put on a little of the makeup she'd found in one of the other drawers, a hint of blush and some rosy-toned gloss, a flick of mascara. Her reflection as it stared back at her from the mirror now looked quite polished, a definite change from the simple, outdoorsy image she'd been cultivating ever since she got to Los Alamos.

No, she almost looked like the Sarah Wolfe she'd been before, a woman who'd tried to take good care of herself so she'd always present her best face no matter who she might encounter.

Too bad no one was around to see her.

She went to the door, putting her ear against it so she could get an idea as to what her captor might be doing right now, but she didn't hear anything.

For all she knew, he wasn't even inside the house. With the door and the windows of her suite locked down tight, it wasn't as though he needed to be right there to keep an eye on her.

She'd tried all of them the night before, not jiggling them so hard that he would hear what she was doing, but enough to tell her there was no way she was getting out of that room unless he came by and unlocked the door for her. Likewise, she'd gone over to the kiva-style fireplace in the corner and tried peering inside the chimney, but it quickly became obvious to her that nothing bigger than a cat was getting up there.

The utter silence outside her suite didn't prevent her from calling out, "Hey!"

Almost at once, she heard him respond, "What is it you need?"

To get the hell out of here, she thought. However, since she doubted he'd comply with that request, she didn't even bother to ask.

"Something to keep myself from going crazy

with boredom," she said at once. "Books. An iPad. A computer. Anything."

"I see," he said politely. A pause so long that for a moment, she thought he'd gone away, but then he added, "And what is your name? I realize I did not ask."

Took you long enough. But again, she kept the thought to herself and instead responded, "Sarah. Sarah Wolfe. And you?"

"Abdul," he said briefly.

"Abdul what?" Because even she knew that djinn names had a patronymic kind of surname, with everyone being "al-this" and "al-that."

"Only Abdul. I will see about getting you some form of entertainment."

For a moment, she wondered if she should press him further about his name. But she once again caught movement out of the corner of her eye, and saw that an iPad had materialized on the chair opposite the one where she'd sat and eaten her breakfast.

The tablet wasn't password-protected, so when she woke it up, she saw at once that it had been loaded with a veritable library of popular books, and that it also was stocked with movies and music and games. Maybe it wasn't quite the same as the gorgeous multi-story library the Beast had given Belle in the movie, but it should still keep her occupied for quite some time.

"Thank you," she called out.

No answer. By now she was beginning to get used to the way Abdul would provide her with something she'd requested and then leave, so she wasn't quite as surprised by the lack of response as she might have been even the night before.

All right. She still had every intention of getting out of here, but at least in the meantime, she wouldn't drive herself mad by pacing around her luxurious prison.

Tablet in hand, she sat down and began to read.

Chapter 7

As far as he could tell, the tablet computer he'd provided for Sarah was keeping her occupied, for he heard no further sounds from her that morning. But even though he'd done as she asked and should have been able to dismiss her from his thoughts until it was time to inquire as to her lunch preferences, she lingered in his mind nonetheless, like the faint traces of a perfume left behind even after its wearer had long since left the room.

She seemed to have accepted her captivity with some equanimity after her initial protests, although he thought that wasn't so strange. After all, she was a human, and, as far as she knew, he was a djinn, and therefore she did not have many options for escape, not when she was so grossly outmatched.

If he had no need to fear any further escape

attempts, Abdul was not quite sure why he should continue to feel unsettled. After a while spent in contemplation of the situation—a time during which he wandered out to the pond he had created near the house, and was gratified to see that a family of ducks had already taken up residence there—he realized there was a perfectly plausible reason as to why Sarah Wolfe would continue to linger in this thoughts.

This was the first time in his very long existence that he'd had another person dwelling in his home. Unlike the djinn, who generally had many partners during their long lifetimes, he had lived alone, apart. And unlike Ibram and Istar, who had found solace in a relationship with another of their kind, there was no one in the world precisely like Abdul. He had made his peace with the situation millennia ago, but still, he had to admit that the current situation was a novel one for him.

Not that he had any romantic designs on his prisoner. She was an inconvenience to be dealt with and nothing more. He was forced to admit to himself that he understood deep down he could not keep her here forever, and that this was a temporary measure at best, but he also didn't think she could be trusted to keep his secrets. True, he could always go to the elders and ask them to tell the humans in Los Alamos that Ghost Ranch and its environs were strictly off-limits, and yet he wasn't sure whether he could trust the mortals to respect such an edict. They definitely had a penchant for sticking their noses where they didn't belong...and probably thought their devices would be sufficient to protect them should they attempt to encroach on his lands.

In which case, they might suffer quite the shock to find out how wrong they were.

No, he would keep Sarah here until he could think of a better solution to the problem. However, he also realized it was perhaps not optimal for her to be always trapped in her room. Even if he let her out so she could enjoy some fresh air, it wasn't as if she could get away. The road was several miles from his house, and she would never reach it before he stopped her.

Also, if he showed her some hints of mercy, then it seemed likely she would be less inclined to make another escape attempt. She seemed meek enough now, but that didn't mean she might not be secretly plotting something.

Humans were devious that way.

Sarah was a little surprised to hear Abdul knock at the door; while she couldn't be sure that the time on the iPad he'd given her was at all accurate, she also knew it was nowhere close to noon, the hour when she'd expected him to come back and ask her what she wanted for lunch.

So she set down the tablet and went to the door. "Yes?"

"I wondered if you might like some fresh air."

She blinked, trying to decide whether this was some kind of joke. "Um...sure," she said after a pause.

At once, the door opened. Abdul stood just outside, wearing the same black hooded robe he'd had on the day before. Idly, Sarah wondered if he had only the one garment and used djinn magic to keep it perpetually clean, or whether he had a closet full of the same outfit and just rotated through the robes as necessary.

"It is a fine day," he said, as though it wasn't just a little nuts that he'd offered to let her go outside after making it seem as if she was going to be locked in her room forever. "You may go out in the courtyard. Do not venture any farther than that, however."

"Not even to look at the pond?" she asked, surprising herself. It might have been wiser to accept the small gift of freedom he'd offered, but she wanted to see how he would react to her pushing the boundaries, if only the tiniest bit.

His eyes glinted within the hood. "You may go to the pond," he allowed. "But no further. Understood?"

"Yes," she said. He'd given her that one conces-
sion, but his firm tone...underlaid with just the
slightest hint of annoyance...told her she'd better
not push for anything else.

That was fine. To be honest, it wasn't as if she
could have gone much farther than that, not
without trading the thong sandals she wore for
something a lot sturdier.

He went to the front door and she followed,
guessing that he wanted to be the one to open it for
her in order to show his dominance. Under other
circumstances, she might have been annoyed by
that kind of flex, but now she was only glad that
this didn't seem to be some kind of mind game and
that he really did appear to be willing to allow her
outside.

As she'd seen from her bedroom window, the
day was sunny and clear, although the bank of
clouds to the southeast was larger now, getting
closer. If she'd been back in Los Alamos, she would
have looked forward to a monsoon storm, to being
safely inside while the thunder boomed and the
lightning crashed. Here, though...here she couldn't
help thinking Abdul might not be the most
comforting companion in such a scenario.

But the storm clouds were still far off, and right
now the sun was clear and bright, warm but not
hot. The morning breeze caught her hair, which
was still slightly damp underneath. Because it

always went straight even without the help of a blow dryer or flat iron, she'd let it dry on its own... not that she had much choice, since her captor had provided a comb and brush but nothing that would allow her to actually style her long locks.

"It's beautiful here," she said, not looking at Abdul. He hadn't gone back inside but had stopped a yard or so behind her, as if he intended to keep an eye on her the whole time.

Well, she hadn't planned to bolt anyway. Not now. Yesterday's little incident had shown her there was no way she could outrun him, which meant she needed to come up with a different kind of plan. In the meantime, she'd play along and do her best to make him think she'd resigned herself to the situation.

"I can see why you'd want to settle in Ghost Ranch," she went on, since he didn't seem inclined to respond to her first comment. It was harder than she thought to force the conversation like this, mostly because she'd been so withdrawn the past few years, not wanting to reveal much about her past or what had happened in those last days leading up to the Heat. Once upon a time, she'd been outgoing, even gregarious, but the passage of those months and years seemed to have ensured that the social butterfly she'd been had slid right back into its cocoon.

Abdul shifted, moving a little closer, although

he still paused several feet away from the spot where she stood near one of the Adirondack chairs. "Yes, this land has its beauties," he said. "And it is isolated, which has a charm of its own."

His voice had taken on a disapproving tinge, and Sarah could see why. He'd thought he could live here alone without interference from humans... and maybe djinn...and then she'd come blundering onto his property without a care in the world.

Rather than address his comment directly, however, she only said, "That's New Mexico for you. We've got miles and miles of empty land. I'm sure thousands of djinn could settle here and not see each other for weeks."

Was that a chuckle that had just emerged from within his hood? If it was, it had an odd, rusty sound to it, as if he didn't laugh very often.

And even though Sarah had absolutely no first-hand knowledge of the djinn race and could only go on what other people had told her, she was starting to think that Abdul was different from the rest of them in some way she couldn't exactly explain.

She wouldn't even try to ask him any personal questions, though. Since she didn't appreciate those sorts of intrusions herself, she knew she should do what she could to respect his privacy.

"The djinn have the entire world to choose from," he told her. "A world with many beauties.

There are far fewer than the number you mentioned who have made this state their home, as many would rather have their residences on a beach, or perhaps in a castle or country estate."

Yes, she could see why a djinn might want a castle. Hadn't they lived in palaces in that weird plane that had formerly been their home?

"I'm surprised you kept the original house here, then," she said. "It's kind of modest by djinn standards, isn't it?"

The robes he wore hid a great deal of his body language, but Sarah still got the impression that Abdul stiffened. "It suits me well enough," he replied.

Clearly, she'd misstepped, but any attempt to backtrack would sound even worse, so she decided to let it go. "But that's why you got rid of so many outbuildings, isn't it? So the view would be nicer?"

"I did not need them," he said, his tone almost dismissive. "And yes, I think this place is more pleasing now that there aren't so many structures to clutter it up."

She had to admit he was right. Her memories from her trip here so many years ago were a little hazy, but she still could recall more buildings than she'd expected when she visited with her father, thinking that the ranch should have been all open fields, maybe with horses and cattle grazing on the dry grass.

"It was a lot different when I was here," she commented, and Abdul's head tilted, as though he was surprised.

"You have been here before?"

"Once, when I was eleven," Sarah replied. "My father and I spent some time exploring northern New Mexico, and we stayed a night in Abiquiu and came to visit Ghost Ranch the next day. We went horseback riding," she added, realizing she hadn't seen a single horse since she'd come here.

Well, maybe that wasn't so strange. She knew that the djinn had made their own odd provisions for all the pets and domesticated animals left behind after the Dying, had used their powers to ensure those animals would have ample food and shelter. Any horses that had been kept at the ranch would now be long gone.

"I hope the changes I have made weren't too shocking," he said, and now she grinned.

"'Shocking' probably isn't the right word. It's just...different."

Another tilt of his head. "Perhaps you would like to see the pond?"

Was that his attempt to change the subject? She couldn't tell for certain, and decided it probably didn't matter so much. After all, she was the one who'd brought up going to look at the pond he'd created, so it would seem odd if she wasn't eager to see it now.

"Sure."

He lifted a hand, as if beckoning her to follow him, and she trailed along in his wake as they left the brick-paved courtyard and made their way over to the pond. The going wasn't as rough as she'd feared it might be, since there was a smooth path covered in pea gravel that led the way, and soft grass grew around the perimeter of the small body of water that definitely hadn't been there when Sarah visited this place almost two decades earlier.

Not that anyone would have been able to tell that the pond hadn't been a fixture of Ghost Ranch for decades, with the tall cottonwoods clustered around its border and the graceful weeping willows whose lacy branches trailed along its surface. At the far side of the pond, a family of ducks was just launching themselves for a morning swim, with the parents leading five fuzzy little brown ducklings into the calm, deep green water.

"It's amazing," Sarah said, then glanced up at Abdul. As before, he'd stopped a few feet away from her, as though he wanted to make sure he didn't intrude on her personal space.

Very polite for someone who seemed bent on keeping her prisoner for an unspecified amount of time.

"How do you do it?" she went on, and the hood dipped slightly, as though he was puzzled by her question.

"Do what?"

"All this," she said, extending a hand to indicate the pond and the graceful trees that surrounded it, their leaves shimmering in the morning breeze. "I mean, it looks like it's been here for decades or even more. I know that djinn can summon all sorts of stuff, but to make the landscape seem as if it's been this way forever?"

For a moment, he didn't answer. When he spoke, though, his voice sounded almost amused.

"As you said, we djinn can call many things into existence. It is not all that different to make a pond appear or to summon a set of trees of a particular height or age. I wished for the landscape to feel established, and not like something carelessly brought into being on a whim."

Sarah supposed she could see that. At the same time, she couldn't help thinking he must have something of an artist's eye, even though she'd heard that djinn in general weren't all that creative, and were instead consumers of human-created art rather than making anything of their own.

But still, even though she somehow doubted Abdul would pick up a paintbrush and start creating his own renderings of the beauty that surrounded him, she couldn't help thinking that he'd made his own form of art, starting with the new fields of wildflowers and carefully arranged rock formations she'd noted down by the visitors center, and ending with this pond and the trees that grew around it, as thoughtful and lovely as a Japanese garden.

"It's very beautiful," she said, an echo of her words just a few minutes earlier. Somehow, the moment felt almost too solemn, and she found herself smiling as she added, "And it definitely looks as though the ducks like it."

Had he smiled as well under his hood? Sarah couldn't detect even the slightest flash of teeth in there, so it was impossible to say.

"Yes," Abdul replied. His tone sounded friendly enough, but there was also something almost guarded about it, as if he thought they'd begun to develop some kind of rapport and now needed to draw back so she wouldn't get the wrong impression. "And I hope it will attract other forms of wildlife as the word gets out, so to speak. For now, though, I will leave you here to enjoy this place. You may come back inside when you are ready."

She blinked at him. "You're just going to...let me stay out here on my own?"

"I am," he said, apparently unperturbed. "I can sense your presence, and I will know if you try to wander away from this spot to anywhere other than the house. Besides," he went on, his voice turning dry, "I doubt you will get very far in that footwear."

Since she'd thought pretty much the same thing only a little while earlier, she didn't bother to protest. "No, I wouldn't," she said cheerfully. "But thank you for letting me stay out here for a while."

He only nodded, then turned and walked away down the path. Sarah knew he could have blinked himself back inside if he'd wanted to, and guessed that he, too, wished to stay outside in the bright morning for as long as he could, even if he'd decided it was a good idea to give her some time alone.

For a moment, she stood there as she watched him disappear around a corner of the house, then shook her head.

He's an odd one, she thought.

Even for a djinn.

⸻

The fresh air had been welcome, but now Abdul found himself glad that he was back inside, and alone. He had not thought it any great thing to let Sarah out of her room and to allow her to taste a small measure of freedom, and yet—even though he was the one who had provided the clothing—he had not been prepared for the vision she presented when she emerged from her suite after he opened the door. Her hair, which had been pulled back in a tight ponytail the day before, had lain, lush and full and just the slightest bit damp, against her bare shoulders, and everything about her appeared far more polished than he'd expected, from the faint hint of cosmetics on her face to the way the red silk gown he'd supplied had seemed to caress her body, hinting at the graceful form beneath even while revealing very little.

Perhaps it had been a mistake to provide her with pretty clothes. At the time, he had only thought that he did not want to look at his prisoner in the drab, unappealing garb that humans seemed to favor. He truly hadn't believed that a dress would have made such a transformation in the woman who'd stumbled into his sanctuary.

No, he reminded himself, she had not stumbled. She had come here with a purpose in mind, one that was directly opposed to his plans for this place. Although she seemed friendly enough... perhaps too friendly, if he wanted to put a point on it...he could never forget that her people wanted to seize this land for their own, to very likely ruin it with their buildings and their vehicles and their ravening desire to take ever more and more from this world.

He would do whatever he must to prevent that from happening.

But still, he couldn't quite ignore how lovely she'd looked as she stood there in the morning sunshine, hair glinting with hints of copper and gold against the deeper brown, or the way she'd smiled as she watched the ducks venture into the cool waters of the pond. There was something about her that seemed far more alive than anyone else he'd ever encountered, as if she needed to drink in everything and everyone around her.

And that was without bringing her voice into the discussion. They had carefully spoken about externals and nothing more, for he had no desire to share intimacies. However, even as he listened to her speak, his mind kept moving back to the preceding afternoon when he'd heard her sing as she made her way onto the property, trained and yet effortless at the same time, like a falcon diving from a great height as it returned to its master's arm. While he certainly could not count himself an expert, he also knew enough to understand that people did not sing in such a way without a great deal of training.

Who had she been in the world before?

He was not sure whether he would ever find the courage to ask.

Some people might have taken off the sandals, hitched up their skirt, and made a break for it anyway, but Sarah knew that wasn't a possibility. Sooner rather than later, her feet would be bruised and bleeding from walking on the rocky ground, and she doubted there was any way in the world she could make it far enough before Abdul caught up with her.

No, she had to be careful about this. Besides, her planned rendezvous with Lindsay and Carson was coming up the next morning. When she didn't show, they'd certainly come in search of her.

Or…would they? Not that Sarah thought they'd abandon her—at least, Lindsay wouldn't—but it seemed much more likely that they'd return to Los Alamos for reinforcements rather than go looking for her on their own. It just made sense to be careful, especially when dealing with the unknown.

So she knew she'd be here for at least a couple more days, maybe longer. That was all right. Abdul seemed to have backed down from his plan to keep her locked in her room at all times, and she supposed there were worse fates than being confined to a gorgeous property like this one and being fed whatever she liked…and getting to wear pretty clothes, the sort of stuff that hadn't been on her back for almost five years.

Maybe that was shallow, but after all this time scrapping and working hard and not having much beauty in her life, she thought she'd roll with it for the time being. She could think of her captivity here as being on vacation, a sort of mini-retreat.

True, a retreat that was watched over by a hooded djinn who was on guard for a single misstep, but still, things could have been worse.

It wasn't as if he'd locked her in a dungeon or something.

When she came back inside, she didn't see him anywhere, which didn't mean much. She hadn't explored the whole house when she first came here, only the great room and the attached kitchen and dining area, so she thought he was probably either in his suite or maybe one of the secondary living spaces. From what she'd seen of the exterior, she guessed this place had to be at least three thousand square feet minimum, maybe a lot more.

And that meant Abdul would have plenty of places to hang out where she couldn't see him.

Just in case this was a test of some sort, she headed back to her room, although she left the door standing open. If he preferred for her to keep it closed, then he could come along and shut it himself—and lock it, although she didn't much see the point when he'd already made it seem as though he was all right with her coming and going as long as she stuck close to the house.

After that time spent outside, it felt a little strange to pick up the iPad and settle herself back in the chair where she'd been sitting when Abdul came along, but she told herself that it wasn't as though she could spend all day outdoors. No, it was better to know that she could read for a while and then venture back out to the courtyard or even the pond when she felt as if she needed a break.

He didn't allow her even that much time, though, because after some fifteen or twenty minutes had passed, he returned, pausing just outside the door rather than attempting to enter the bedroom.

"Perhaps you would like some lunch?"

At once, she set the iPad down on the table in front of her. Although the blueberry muffin he'd provided for breakfast had been amazing, all the fresh air had done its job, and now she knew she needed something a little more substantial.

"That would be great," she said, and couldn't help smiling. "What did you have in mind?"

Oddly, Abdul found himself more at ease with Sarah than he'd been expecting, and, rather than informing her that he'd conjure a tray of food for her, asked if she would like to have their midday meal in the courtyard.

She slanted a look up at him, expression a little startled. However, when she replied, it wasn't to demur, as he'd halfway expected, but to ask, "Is there a place to sit down and eat out there? All I saw were those Adirondack chairs."

"I can summon whatever we need," he said, which was only the truth.

So she smiled, expression sunny as the day outside, and replied, "Oh, right. I need to remember that stuff. I've just never been around a djinn before."

"You never met with any of the elementals from Santa Fe?" he inquired as he led her outside.

She shook her head. "No, I never had any reason to. Or at least, when groups from Los Alamos went there to talk to the djinn for one reason or another, I wasn't included. You're my first," she added, still smiling.

The old protest rose to his mind—*I am not precisely a djinn*—but he of course did not utter the words aloud. Doing so would have required far too many explanations. Better for her to think he was one of the elementals she already had some knowledge of, even if he might be one with an odd preference for completely hiding his person.

A wave of a hand summoned a handsome wrought-iron patio set, and another called into being an enormous sun sail that stretched across half the courtyard, sheltering them from the sun overhead, which had only grown warmer as the day progressed. Not exactly hot yet, but he knew that sitting out there with absolutely no shielding would have become uncomfortable soon enough.

Sarah blinked, although she didn't say

anything. In fact, her expression turned almost wistful, and he wondered if she was thinking about how much easier life was for the djinn, who could summon just about anything they might need.

Well, it was easier for them in some ways, he supposed.

However, he also remained silent as he seated himself and she followed suit. If they had been dining out the way mortals used to, then this would have been the time when a server approached them to take their orders—or at least, Abdul assumed that was what should have happened. Since he had never interacted with human society the way so many djinn had over the centuries, he couldn't say for sure.

"Iced tea?" he asked. "Or perhaps lemonade or water?"

"Tea," Sarah responded immediately.

As that was also his preferred drink for his noontime meal, he summoned a large pitcher for them to share, along with a set of tall glasses. He poured some for her and then filled his own glass, and she murmured a thank-you.

"What would you like?" he inquired. She hadn't eaten very much for breakfast, although he couldn't say whether such behavior was typical of her or whether she didn't have much of an appetite due to being locked up in that suite.

He'd expected her to make a specific request

the way she had the night before, when she'd asked for pepperoni pizza. However, she surprised him by asking, "What are you having?"

Because it was a bright, warm day, he'd already decided to have some sort of salad. When he told her that, she nodded.

"That sounds good. I'd like a salad as well."

Of course, he hadn't told her what kind of salad, but decided that something he'd had once, with mixed greens and chunks of chicken and bleu cheese and cranberries and candied walnuts, seemed like it would be a good choice. Immediately, a pair of identical salads appeared in front of them, and Sarah gave an approving nod.

"This looks really good. I haven't had cranberries like this since...."

The words trailed off, but he knew what she was trying to say. Although certain canned and dried foods had survived the Dying, the human survivors in Los Alamos probably would have already consumed whatever stores they had on hand, and cranberries were nothing they could grow themselves, not with the terrain here so very different from the bogs of New England.

"I am glad I could provide something you like," he said, knowing it would probably be better not to acknowledge the reason why Sarah would not have eaten anything similar to this meal for a very long time.

She also seemed to realize they'd been treading on delicate ground, because she only nodded and reached for her fork, then speared some chicken and dried cranberries before popping them in her mouth.

Afterward, they ate quietly enough, for which he was glad. He knew that djinn and mortals alike often conversed during their meals, making them last much longer than they needed to, but it appeared Sarah understood he had no need for idle chatter.

When she was done, though, she set down her fork and looked up at him. "Thank you," she said, and something in the timbre of her voice seemed to tell him she was expressing gratitude for more than merely the salad.

Was she also thankful for the way he'd allowed her to leave her room today?

Perhaps. Since it seemed she had no immediate plans to flee, he thought it better to leave matters as they were. This way, she could come out to the courtyard or the pond when she wished and perhaps would not feel quite so much like a prisoner.

Even if that was exactly what she was.

Chapter 8

DINNER THAT NIGHT WAS SIMILARLY LOW-key, so much so that Sarah wondered if she was actually getting used to being here with Abdul. They didn't eat in the courtyard that evening, but rather in the dining room, and they had chicken again, only this time not in a salad, but some of the best cacciatore she'd ever had. He hadn't consulted her about the food, instead seeming to take her comment about not having any real dietary restrictions to heart.

It had been another mostly silent meal, though, with her only making a few comments about the dish and the wine that accompanied it, and then shutting up when the djinn didn't seem inclined to talk. Awkward for sure, but she survived, and thanked him afterward before returning to her room.

Again, she shut the door but didn't lock it. She'd already heard from the other survivors in Los Alamos that door locks didn't matter much to djinn...and neither did most other human inventions.

If Abdul wanted to get into her room, he could.

She didn't get that vibe from him at all, though. If her door was going to be locked, it was because he'd done it to keep her in and not vice versa.

Even though the food had been delicious, anxiety still knotted her stomach. It was one thing to tell herself to be chill about her stay here, that sooner or later the cavalry would come to get her at some point, and quite another to look at the time stamp on the iPad she held and know that in about twelve hours or so, she was supposed to show up at the rendezvous point in La Chuachia.

That definitely wasn't going to happen.

Or at least, she couldn't think of a way she could get out of here.

Unless....

Had Abdul been lying to her when he'd said he could sense her presence, that he'd know if she was no longer somewhere close to the house?

Hard to say. She wracked her brain, trying to recall every single scrap of information or gossip she'd heard about the djinn. There were four kinds, corresponding to the four elements, although the only way to know which power a djinn commanded was to see him or her using it. They lived for what felt like forever, but they could be wounded. Problem was, any injuries they suffered healed in almost no time, which meant they were almost impossible to kill.

Not that she would ever try to hurt Abdul. Yes, he was holding her captive here, but he'd been almost courteous the whole time, and she knew she just didn't have it in her to creep up on him in his sleep and stick a butcher knife in his neck or something.

Even if she was that murderous, she doubted she'd be able to get close enough to indulge in that kind of carnage.

Anyway, as much as she pummeled her brain, she couldn't remember anyone saying anything about djinn having a sixth sense about whether a human was nearby, which didn't help at all. Maybe Abdul was lying...or maybe she'd never heard about that particular djinn gift simply because no one she knew had ever mentioned it.

Either way, she didn't think it was anything she wanted to put to the test.

And that meant all she could do now was try to sleep and see what the next day might bring. For the moment, she had a measure of freedom, and throwing that away on a half-baked plan to escape didn't seem like a very good idea.

Like it or not, she knew she would have to sit tight and wait for the cavalry to arrive.

Sarah appeared composed enough the next morning when she emerged from her room—this time in an outfit of the djinn-style flowing tunics and slim pants he'd provided—but something about her seemed almost subdued, as if a second night spent here had convinced her that her captivity was going to be of some duration.

Good. She needed to face her new reality, however unpleasant it might be.

Then again, he thought it was equally unpleasant for him. He had expected to spend days of quiet solitude here, and not have to worry about the emotional vagaries of some human female. Yes, the current situation was his doing, for quite a few djinn would have simply tossed her over a cliff and been done with her, and he knew he was not quite that bloodthirsty.

At any rate, not on such an individual level.

She ate a little more this morning, though, consuming the vegetable frittata and bowl of fresh fruit he'd conjured for their breakfast. As he watched her—or rather, did his best not to seem as though he was observing her while regarding her from behind the drooping edge of his hood—a sudden thought struck him.

"You said you went riding here when you visited as a child," he said. "Would you be interested in a ride today?"

Her startled gaze met his. Now, after a few days spent in her presence, he knew her eyes weren't precisely hazel, but an odd, deep tone somewhere between green and blue, so dark that good lighting was required to see they were not brown at all. "Horseback riding?" she responded, tone just as hesitant as her expression.

"Yes," he said. "I can summon mounts that would be suitable for both of us. It would allow you to see more of Ghost Ranch."

"More places that you've altered?" she asked, her full mouth quirking a little.

"No," he replied, his tone a bit more severe than he had intended. "I have only touched the more public spaces here at the ranch. There was no need to do anything more than that, for the majority of these lands had been left unspoiled, save for riding and hiking trails."

She appeared cheered by that prospect. "Then that sounds like a great idea, except...."

"Except what?" he asked.

"That ride here at Ghost Ranch when I was eleven was the last time I was on a horse," she replied, expression now somewhat rueful. "I'm not exactly what you could call an expert rider."

"That is fine," he said, and knew it was. He would make sure one of the horses he summoned was gentle and biddable, and safe for an inexperienced horsewoman. Now he smiled a little under his hood, and added, "You have nothing to fear from a horse conjured for you by a djinn."

Lindsay Odekirk looked at the clock on her Volvo's dashboard and frowned. While she knew it was asking a lot to expect Carson and Sarah to have been here right on the dot, they'd all agreed to be back here as close to the time when she'd dropped them off two days ago as they could. That had been around ten in the morning, and now it was past eleven.

Worry crept up in her, adding an extra layer of unease to the overall queasiness she'd been battling for the past week. She and Miles hadn't said anything to anyone yet—well, except Ellen O'Dell, the nurse practitioner who'd helped her through her pregnancy with Dylan—because she was still barely ten weeks along, but as far as Lindsay could tell, everything seemed pretty normal. Maybe a little more morning sickness than she'd had last

time, although nothing she could call incapac-
itating.

It also hadn't helped that Miles didn't want her
coming out here at all, arguing that she could send
someone else and she shouldn't be taking any
unnecessary risks. She'd brushed off his objections,
telling him she'd driven to the drop-off point several
days ago and everything had gone like clockwork.

Except it definitely wasn't clockwork today, not
with her two volunteers more than an hour late.

Hers was the kind of brain that liked to manu-
facture worst-case scenarios, and the current situation was no different. What if one of them had
fallen and sprained an ankle or broken a leg? What
if they'd been attacked by wild animals? What if
there really were still rogue djinn out there, and
Sarah and Carson had been taken and killed?

All right, that last scenario was probably a bit
far-fetched. The three al-Qadir brothers had been
the last of the reavers, and since they were now all
happily settled down with mortal women, it didn't
seem as if the djinn threat was anything she needed
to worry about.

Besides, both Sarah and Carson had a device
with them. Even if a few bloodthirsty djinn whose
only desire was to wipe all humanity off the map
still existed, they wouldn't have been able to get
within a quarter-mile of the two explorers without

having all their powers erased as if they had never been.

Lindsay settled against the seatback and let out a breath, then reached for the tumbler of water she'd brought with her and took a long sip. Some pregnant women couldn't stand the taste of water, but it had always helped settle her stomach.

And wait—was that movement far up ahead, just around the curve in the highway?

She returned the tumbler to its cupholder and lowered her sunglasses to get a better look.

Yes, that was definitely Carson Mailer, now looking a little more disheveled than he had when he first set out a couple of days ago. Not, as he got closer, that it seemed as if he'd suffered any kind of injury, but only that his hair wasn't nearly as perfect, and stubble darkened his chin and jaw.

Her brows pulled together. Where was Sarah? The plan had been for the two of them to meet up after they'd individually explored Lake Abiquiu and Ghost Ranch, and yet it seemed pretty obvious that Sarah Wolfe was nowhere to be seen.

Lindsay fumbled for the door handle and then pushed it open so she could climb out of the Volvo. As soon as Carson was a few yards away, she said, "Where's Sarah?"

He pushed a lock of hair away from his forehead. On most people, Lindsay would have thought that wayward piece of hair was nothing more than that—something overgrown because he hadn't gotten it cut lately. With Carson, though, she got the feeling he wore it that way on purpose so he could draw attention to himself by continually shoving it back.

"I don't know," he replied. To be fair, he actually sounded worried. "I waited and waited for her at the spot where we were supposed to meet, but she never showed up. Then I walked about a mile up the highway, just in case I'd gotten confused about the actual location. But I didn't see any sign of her, and I knew if I kept going all the way to Ghost Ranch, then I'd never make it back here on time."

None of this sounded very good. "And you tried contacting her with the walkie-talkie?"

Now Carson's expression grew pained, as if he couldn't believe she'd asked him such a stupid question. "Of course I did. She never answered. But if she was still up at Ghost Ranch somewhere, then she would have been out of range anyway."

True. The walkies were there more to facilitate their meet-up and not to maintain communications, since they would have been too far apart for that to work.

Lindsay set her hands on her hips and gazed at the highway ahead of them, gauging all the various cracks and potholes, and trying to figure out whether her Volvo could handle such rough terrain. It had all-wheel-drive, but that was intended for maintaining traction on icy surfaces, not white-knuckling it across country roads that had never been that well-kept in the first place and certainly hadn't improved after nearly five years of neglect.

Miles, she thought, would kill her if she tried to take the little SUV crossover all the way to Ghost Ranch, even if she had Carson Mailer's dubious assistance and wouldn't be going alone.

Should they wait a while longer? Yes, the original meet-up time had come and gone more than an hour earlier, but Lindsay knew she'd hate herself if she learned later on that Sarah had turned up only a few minutes or even a half hour after she and Carson had headed back to Los Alamos.

On the other hand, it wasn't as if she planned to simply let this go. No, she was going to head home, tell Miles and everyone else on the town council what had happened, and then immediately organize a search party, one that was armed and driving one of their four-wheel-drive vehicles so they could go wherever they needed to go. The worst that would happen was that Sarah would have to wait a couple of hours while they got themselves together. She'd been given food for five days and there was a river full of fresh-flowing water only a hundred yards away, so she should be fine on that front.

That seemed to decide things. All the same, Lindsay kind of hated herself for saying, "Okay, let's head back to Los Alamos."

Yes, this had definitely been a good idea. As Abdul had promised, the horse Sarah was riding, a beautiful blood bay with a strikingly long tail, seemed to be utterly calm and ready to follow the big black stallion the djinn had chosen for himself. That horse seemed a lot more strong-willed, but Abdul managed his mount with surprising skill.

The horses had appeared out of nowhere and had been waiting for them when they emerged from the house after breakfast. Sarah had been a bit concerned about riding in these clothes—she could tell as soon as she put them on that they were real silk—but her companion had brushed those worries aside.

"They will be quite comfortable for riding," he told her. "And if you should stain them somehow, that is easy enough to fix."

Yes, she supposed cleaning clothes would only be a finger snap to a djinn. Also, the tunic and slim pants were extremely comfortable, and allowed her to climb up into the saddle without any worries about something being too tight. She'd switched out her sandals for a pair of flats, and Abdul had conjured a hat and a pair of sunglasses for her, so she was about as well-outfitted for the ride as she was going to be, even if the ensemble might have looked a little funny to any onlookers.

But she and Abdul were here alone, so she knew she didn't need to worry about any outside observers.

Now they'd ranged far beyond his house, following a trail that led into the hills and sloped upward, although not at a steep enough angle that the horses seemed to be getting winded. From here, she could see almost all of the ranch, including the dirt road that led in from the highway. She stared off into that distance, wondering if she might be able to catch any sign of Carson coming this way... and what in the world she would do if she did manage to spot him.

However, the highway appeared utterly empty, so it sure didn't look as though he had decided to come and investigate her absence. She wasn't completely sure of the time, but she guessed it had to be past eleven or maybe even a little later, and that meant she was horribly overdue for their meet-up. And, in true Carson Mailer fashion, he hadn't even tried to come and find her, but instead had headed down to La Chuachia to meet with Lindsay.

All right, that wasn't completely fair. While he had one of the devices with him and a knife similar to the one she'd carried, it wasn't as if he was prepared to fight off a bear or a contingent of djinn, or whatever else he might think had delayed her here in Ghost Ranch. Honestly, the smart thing to do would be to regroup and figure out the best way to go looking for her.

"Do you see something?" Abdul asked, and Sarah immediately wrenched her attention away from the road and back to the trail before her...and the djinn who rode only a few yards ahead.

"No," she said hastily. "I guess I was just trying to see if I could figure out how big Ghost Ranch is."

"Well over a thousand acres," he supplied, which surprised her a little. Or maybe not. After all, this was his land, so it seemed logical that he would have learned as much as he could about it. "From this trail to the highway, it is around four miles."

Not an impossibly huge distance under normal circumstances. But when she had no idea how she would even get away from Abdul, let alone cover those four miles on foot before he realized she'd gone, her prospects for escape seemed pretty dismal.

She nodded, then said, "Have you ridden up here a lot?"

"Several times," he replied. "When I came here and saw there were stables, I realized this must be a good place for riding. This horse and I have begun to know one another."

In response, the stallion tossed his mane—not, Sarah thought, because he was fighting against the reins Abdul held, but almost as a way to confirm what the djinn had just said.

"Do you keep the horses in the stables?" she asked, now curious. Her blood bay and the stallion Abdul was riding had appeared out of nowhere, but she supposed they could have been kept somewhere nearby on the property rather than being conjured out of thin air.

"No," he replied. "That is, they roam free on these lands, and I make sure there is ample fodder for them. They are part of a herd that stayed nearby even after the humans who kept them were gone, and when I wish to ride, I summon one of them. I suppose they use the stable from time to time if they wish to shelter from the weather, so I made the necessary repairs to keep it intact. It was beginning to look somewhat ramshackle."

She could imagine. One thing that had fascinated her during these past four-plus years was how quickly buildings and roads could fall into disrepair, and how much effort had to be expended to keep them functional. Sure, back in the day there had always seemed to be road crews and construction crews in various spots around town, working on some project or another, but she hadn't paid a lot of attention to exactly what they were doing.

Now that she'd helped to fill potholes and had been part of a crew that went around Los Alamos and fixed siding and patched stucco, she had a much larger appreciation for the power of entropy.

And she had to admit she was kind of relieved to hear that Abdul had ridden these trails before. True, he was a djinn and therefore could probably get them out of any trouble they might find themselves in, but still, it always helped to have a guide who knew where he was going.

He proved that even more in the next fifteen minutes, because they entered a narrow canyon with a small creek that cut through the center, and soon after that, the soft chatter of the water over its rocky bed turned louder, splashing into the stillness. Sure enough, the canyon terminated in a small waterfall that flowed over the red rocks and down into the streambed, and on its banks, cottonwoods provided welcome shade from the bright nearly noonday sun.

Abdul dismounted and came over to Sarah, then extended a hand to help her down from her horse. She hesitated for a moment—except for that first time when he'd grasped her from the bicep, they had never touched one another—but then she told herself to get over it, that falling while she was trying to climb down from the little mare wouldn't be a very good look.

So she reached over and took his hand, feeling the strength of his fingers as they gripped hers, holding her steady as she got down from her horse. His black stallion had already wandered over to the creek and begun to drink, and the blood bay mare followed as soon as she knew her rider had gotten safely down.

"Thank you," Sarah said. Abdul had let go of her as soon as she stood on solid ground, so it seemed pretty clear that he hadn't been looking for an excuse to touch her.

"You appeared as though you needed the help," he replied. Again, even though she couldn't see his expression, she got the feeling he was smiling as he spoke.

"It's been a long time," she said lightly. "But I'm sure I'll get the hang of it eventually." She paused there so she could look over at the waterfall, at the way the dancing water caught the sunlight and shimmered like a scatter of diamonds. "This is gorgeous, though. Thank you for bringing me here."

"I am glad you like it," he said. "I discovered this place when I first surveyed this land and thought it a good destination, especially on a warm day such as this one."

Yes, it was warm. Not hot yet, although Sarah

thought it might get there later this afternoon. Even so, she was glad of the hat and the sunglasses Abdul had given her, although she guessed they might look a little ridiculous in combination with her blue silk tunic and trousers.

Well, she wasn't here to put on a fashion show. The outfit was more practical than she'd first thought, and it certainly didn't seem as if her companion...her captor...cared what she looked like.

"I suppose you could live here for a thousand years and never get tired of it," she remarked, and his head lifted toward the sky, where a trio of hawks circled high overhead.

"Perhaps," he said. His voice sounded almost doubtful, as though he wasn't quite sure of his answer. "It is a land of many interesting corners and nooks and crannies. That is why I often go riding, even though I have other ways of surveying this part of the world."

Meaning, she supposed, that he could take to the sky and fly like some kind of oversized bird. A raven, she thought, considering he never seemed to wear anything except black from head to toe.

"How long have you been here?" she asked, and his hooded head swiveled toward her.

However, he didn't reply right away, and Sarah wondered if she'd overstepped somehow by asking such a question.

When he spoke, though, his tone sounded friendly enough.

"Not so very long," he said. "Only a week, although I explored this territory before that, just to make sure this was truly the place where I wanted to settle."

A week? She thought of all the changes he'd wrought in the landscape. No human could have accomplished so much in such a short amount of time, but she knew you had to put aside normal measures when you were dealing with djinn and their apparently limitless powers.

Still....

"You chose this place? I thought the elders made the decisions as to who lived where."

Or at least, that was what she had heard. Since she'd gotten all her knowledge secondhand...often thirdhand...she had to admit it probably had some decent-sized holes in it.

Once again, Abdul didn't answer her right away, and she worried all over again that she was asking questions that bordered on rude. Maybe she should have just kept her mouth shut the way she had at breakfast and during dinner the night before, but she couldn't help being curious about him, about why he had come to Ghost Ranch out of all the other locations on the planet.

And oddly, even though he was keeping her on the property against her will, she thought she kind of liked talking with him...when he was willing. There was something old-fashioned and almost charming about the way he spoke, the way he interacted with her. She'd never met anyone like him before.

Well, of course you haven't, she thought then, her inner voice touched with some irritation. *He's the first djinn you've ever encountered.*

Still, she thought it might be a little more than that.

But then he said, "It is true that the elders usually are the ones to decide upon these land grants, so to speak. However, I have rendered some invaluable services for them, and that is why they allowed me to select this place as my home. I wanted land around me, and peace and quiet."

His tone was so neutral as he spoke that it was impossible to tell whether he was throwing some shade on her for intruding on this sanctuary he'd created for himself. Sarah told herself not to be so paranoid, and that if he really hadn't wanted to interact with her, he could have kept her locked up in her room rather than taking her horseback riding or having lunch on the veranda.

"A thousand acres is definitely a lot of land," she remarked, and now he chuckled.

"True enough," he said. "And now that it seems our horses have drunk their fill, perhaps we can continue with our ride."

Yes, the mare and the stallion had turned away from the creek, although water still dripped from their muzzles and even wetted the ends of their long manes. Sarah wondered how much farther into the hills Abdul intended to take her, then brushed the worry aside. After all, they were utterly alone together whether they were up on a riding trail miles from the highway or back at the house, so what difference did it make?

"Sure," she replied with a smile. "But first, you need to help me back on that horse."

Chapter 9

"THERE WAS ABSOLUTELY NO SIGN OF Sarah Wolfe?" Miles asked, and Lindsay shook her head.

"None at all. Right, Carson?"

"Right," he said. His expression was troubled, although Lindsay couldn't help thinking he was probably more worried about what the town council would say about him leaving his companion behind than fearful that something awful might really have happened to Sarah.

As soon as they'd gotten back to town, Lindsay had picked up her walkie-talkie and contacted her husband, then asked him if he could get in touch with the rest of the council so they could meet at City Hall and decide what to do next. Brent Sutherland must have already been there on some kind of business, because he was waiting in the conference room when she and Carson showed up, and Miles and Shawn and Nora arrived soon afterward.

"I knew this was a bad idea," Shawn muttered, and Miles frowned at him.

"There was absolutely no reason to believe either Sarah or Carson would run into any trouble in Abiquiu or Ghost Ranch." He fixed Carson with a piercing look, the kind Lindsay knew meant he wasn't in the mood for any bullshit. "Did you see anything strange at the lake?"

"No," Carson replied immediately. Now he looked a little more relaxed, as if he realized he was back on firmer ground here. "I hiked around and stayed in an abandoned RV that first night. Worst thing I saw was a couple of coyotes, but they took off as soon as I shone a flashlight at them."

"See?" Miles said, although the word was directed at Shawn Gutierrez, and not at the man who'd just spoken. "That sounds perfectly normal to me."

"Well, *something* must have happened to Sarah," Nora put in. "She's always been very responsible—shows up for her work assignments on time, is always there if you need someone to pitch in for a special project. I can't believe she'd forget when she was supposed to show up."

Lindsay had to admit that did sound very out of character for the woman. No, she didn't know her very well, but on the occasions when Sarah had been assigned to work in the lab, she'd always been there right when she was supposed to be, and had labored over repairing devices or whatever other tasks she'd been given with a good eye for detail and not a lot of idle chitchat with the other people who were working at the same time.

Honestly, she wasn't sure whether anyone had known Sarah very well.

"We'll have to go take a look," Brent said. "Take one of the four-wheel-drives, get up there and see if we can figure out what happened. She could have fallen and broken a leg, or worse."

That same sort of terrible scenario had entered Lindsay's mind as well, but she kept hoping the situation might not be quite so dire.

Before she could speak, though, Shawn said, "Or we might still be dealing with djinn here. I don't know if it's the best idea for us to go barging in there with a truck and a search party. Yes, we need to find her and get her out of there, but we also should be cautious."

"Then we'll send in a drone," Brent said, and Lindsay blinked at him.

"We have drones?" she demanded. "Since when?"

"One of our gleaning crews found a couple in the basement of a house in Española," Shawn replied, not looking too put off by her tone. "We've been experimenting with them, trying to get used to how they work, since none of us here had ever flown one."

"And you didn't think about mentioning this to me?" she returned. "We could have sent drones in to scout that country rather than risking several of our people."

"Now, Lindsay," Brent said, his tone doing its best to be consoling, "we just found the things a week or so ago, and we didn't see the point in bringing them up until we had a better idea of how to work with them. Anyway, these aren't commercial or military drones—they can't fly for miles and miles. Even if we use one of the drones to look for Sarah, we'll have to be nearby and fly it in from the highway, something like that, especially since we'll need to rely on the drone's wi-fi to communicate with it since there's no cell service anymore."

Some of her annoyance subsided at hearing these limitations.

Some.

"Okay," she said. "Then it sounds to me like we need to take one of those drones and fly it into Ghost Ranch so we can have a look around before going in on foot. If Sarah fell down a hillside or something, we'll have a much better chance of seeing her with the drone."

Miles steepled his fingers and tapped them against his chin. "I suppose that might work."

"It should," Shawn said. "And I'll fly the drone, since I'm the one who's been practicing with it the most. Even with the roads north of La Chuachia mostly gone to shit, we should still be able to get to the entrance to Ghost Ranch in a couple of hours in my Tundra."

"Then you get the drone and meet me back here," Lindsay replied, and Miles's eyes narrowed behind his glasses.

"I'm not sure if it's a good idea for you to go up there—" he began, and she shook her head.

"I'll be fine," she said, in tones quelling enough that he got the hint. This was not the place or time when she wanted to announce her pregnancy, but if Miles kept acting like a helicopter daddy, someone was going to figure out something was up.

"She will," Brent said. "Because I'll go with them, and if Shawn spots Sarah with the drone, then he and I will be the ones to go in and get her. Lindsay can wait in the truck."

Miles glanced from Brent to Lindsay, and she fixed him with the kind of stare she always used when she needed to let him know she was a big girl and could handle things on her own.

To her relief, her husband didn't offer any further protests, instead saying, "That sounds like a decent plan."

"But you should all have a quick lunch before

you go," Nora suggested. "An extra fifteen minutes isn't going to make much of a difference one way or another."

Lindsay wasn't so sure about that—a lot could happen in fifteen minutes—but she had to admit to herself that whatever the reason for Sarah's disappearance, the critical event had probably already taken place. Besides, it wasn't as if they could blink themselves to Ghost Ranch djinn-style and immediately get to work. No, they'd have to bump their way along some pretty crappy roads to get there, and that would take time.

"All right," she said, knowing there wasn't much use in protesting. "Let's all meet back here at 12:30."

The group got up from the table then and headed for the door. As Lindsay went with them, she found herself hoping this wouldn't all turn out to be an exercise in futility.

Their ride ended up taking the greater part of three hours, but Abdul thought that wasn't too much of an inconvenience, especially after they'd ended up in another canyon he knew about, one with another creek, albeit one that bubbled up from a secret little spring rather than being fed by snow melt from a far-off mountain range. There, he'd conjured himself and Sarah a picnic lunch and several camp chairs, and they ate their noon meal surrounded by cottonwoods and sycamores and oaks, and were serenaded by lively little finches and sparrows and other birds whose names he was just beginning to learn—siskins and chickadees and the gorgeous jays whose plumage shaded from deep black on their feathered crests to brilliant blue along their wings and bodies.

Sarah had seemed happy enough to eat outdoors, especially after Abdul also summoned feed bags for the horses, who began munching immediately after their lunch appeared.

"It does seem like you can ride out here forever," she said, and then took a bite of her sandwich, a tasty concoction of a croissant filled with chicken salad that he thought was the perfect thing to break their fast.

"Perhaps not forever," he replied. "But certainly for many hours. However, after we eat, we will take a trail that leads us back to the house. For your first ride, it is better that you not be in the saddle all day."

She nodded, mouth lifting in a rueful little smile. "Yes, I can already feel it in my legs. But that's okay. It's been wonderful to get out and see so much of the countryside."

Although Abdul knew he was not the best at reading people, he thought she was telling him the truth and nothing more. Certainly during their ride, he'd looked back several times to see her glancing at their surroundings with interest, and noticed the way she smiled with delight when she noticed a new wildflower or species of bird.

All the same, he knew it was time to head home after they ate. It would not be very kind to make her positively bow-legged after spending most of the day in the saddle.

Even as that thought went through his mind, he wanted to shake his head at himself. Sarah was his prisoner, after all. What difference did it make if he ended up causing her some physical discomfort?

Somehow he knew it did matter, even if he did not quite want to admit such a thing.

Not yet.

The rest of their lunch conversation was innocuous enough, though, with both of them commenting on the scenery and the wildlife, and not so long after that, they were back in the saddle and winding their way down out of the hills, going toward the house. Once again, Sarah had accepted his help in getting back on her horse, and even now, he thought he could sense the pressure of her slender fingers against his, the way she seemed so wonderfully alive in a way he couldn't quite articulate to himself.

It is only that you have had very little contact with anyone at all, he thought as they slowly zigged and zagged their way down the hillside. *That is why this seems so strange.*

A logical enough explanation, although he was not sure whether that was the entirety of the matter.

Well, he would worry about it later.

Once they were back at the house, he showed Sarah how to remove her horse's tack and how to rub down the mare so that she would not suffer any ill effects from their extended ride. During all this, the human woman's expression had been slightly skeptical, as if she wondered why they needed to go to all this effort when he could simply snap his fingers and have both their mounts properly groomed and cared for.

Perhaps it was foolish, but it was a ritual he had come to enjoy. It made him feel more connected to the animals, made him more appreciative of the way they labored to provide him with one of his few forms of entertainment.

"But you will probably want to rest until dinner," he said after he'd lowered the mare's saddle to the fence near where they stood. Now that they were done, he would blink the thing into the stable, but he saw no reason to do that until Sarah had gone back into the house.

She didn't protest. "Yes, putting up my feet and reading for a while sounds like a good idea. That was a marvelous ride, though. Thank you again."

A quick flash of a smile, and then she headed inside the house, as natural as though this was already an established routine for them. In a way, he supposed it was; Sarah had clearly come to accept her situation here, and he had not glimpsed even a single sign of her wishing to escape.

Perhaps she was beginning to see that, while she might not have her freedom, her existence at Ghost Ranch was much more comfortable than the one she'd left behind in Los Alamos.

Odd how her presence, rather than annoying him, was something of a comfort. She might ask a probing question every once in a while, but mainly she seemed content to live in the moment, to enjoy the beauty of a waterfall in a hidden canyon, or to smile at the sound of a goldfinch chirping from a nearby tree branch. Because he had never spent any time around humans, he had no idea whether this was normal for them, or whether Sarah Wolfe was something of a special case.

He wanted to believe the latter. Otherwise, he would be forced to reexamine his actions of the not-so-distant past...and wonder if he had truly done the right thing after all.

A strange buzzing sound made him glance upward. Through the trees, he detected an odd object, shaped rather like a cross, with four miniature propellers whirring away in the air.

Abdul would never have said he was entirely

familiar with human technology, and yet he thought he knew what the thing was.

A drone.

Piloted by humans, of course, and clearly sent here to spy on him. Or perhaps not him in particular...no mortal save Sarah even knew of his existence, and even she had no real knowledge of his true nature...but to investigate Ghost Ranch, and most likely try to discover what had happened to their missing explorer.

That was one piece of information he would never allow them to have. If they learned of his presence here...worse, if they somehow managed to learn the truth about him...then he knew he would never have a moment's peace.

His fist clenched, and in the next instant, the drone exploded in a miniature ball of fire. It would not do to have its shrapnel fall here where Sarah might see it, so he immediately blinked the remnants of the little spy machine out of existence.

Only just in time, for a moment later, she emerged from the house and shot him a questioning look.

"What was that?"

He'd already determined it would be best to feign utter ignorance. After all, the evidence of the explosion was already gone.

"What was what?"

Sarah glanced around, but he knew nothing

had changed during the intervening few minutes after she'd gone inside, except that the horses had already wandered off down the hill, presumably on their way to forage in the pasture next to the stable.

A frown pulled at her delicate brows. "I could have sworn I heard something go *bang.*"

"Well, there is certainly nothing like that out here. Perhaps," he suggested, "it was the icemaker in the freezer. It can sound somewhat explosive at times."

She still looked puzzled, but it appeared she was willing to accept his explanation, for she gave a shrug and said, "I guess that was it. Sorry to bother you."

"It was no problem," he said politely, and she gave him a hesitant smile before going back inside once again.

No, it was definitely not a problem.

He would not allow it to be.

"What the hell?" Shawn stared down at his phone, which he'd been using to steer the drone.

Lindsay sent him a worried look. Shawn Gutierrez was not the kind of guy to explode like that unless he had a damn good reason.

"What's the matter?"

"I don't know," he replied. "But the drone was

there one minute, transmitting images...and then it just wasn't."

"Did it run into something?"

Shawn didn't quite roll his eyes, but he looked like he wanted to.

"No. There was nothing to run into. It was in an open area, moving toward a house I'd spotted. And then...nothing."

Lindsay and Shawn and Brent were all in Shawn's big pickup truck, which he'd parked at the entrance to Ghost Ranch. It felt awfully conspic-uous sitting out in the open like that, but because there wasn't another soul around for miles and miles, she knew her feeling of unease was purely visceral and nothing that was actually based on reality. At any rate, the facility itself was located several miles away down a very rough dirt road, so there wasn't much chance of anyone—or anything —sneaking up on them.

"Let me see," she said, and Shawn only shook his head.

"There's nothing to see," he replied, holding up his phone so she could see the screen.

Sure enough, it was now utterly black, which hadn't been the case a few minutes earlier. The two men were in the front seats while she was in the back, but the whole time Shawn had been control-ling the drone, he'd done his best to position his phone so she could mostly have a good view of what was happening.

Not that she had a very good frame of reference, since she'd never visited Ghost Ranch in the before times, so she had no idea whether what she'd been looking at was the same old, same old, or whether something had changed here over the previous four-plus years.

And neither Shawn nor Brent had been here, either, so they were all kind of flying blind. The only thing she'd been able to tell was that there didn't seem to be any sign of Sarah Wolfe anywhere in the area.

Judging by the scowl Shawn currently wore—a departure from his usual sunny expression—he wasn't too happy about his new toy going *kaput.*

"I could have sworn I saw something down there," he said as he set his phone on the console that divided the two front seats.

"Like what?" Brent asked.

"I'm not sure," Shawn replied, and his gaze moved to the phone, even though the drone had obviously stopped transmitting and there was nothing to see on its screen. "There were trees in the way, but it still looked like something was moving beneath them."

"Maybe some kind of animal," Lindsay suggested. "A goat or a horse or something. Lots of them running wild these days."

That was for sure. They had their own herds of sheep and goats and cows in Española, but there were far more that still roamed around the countryside, fending for themselves.

Shawn looked dubious, but it seemed as if he didn't want to argue. No, he only said, "That could have been it. Still doesn't explain what happened to the drone."

"It must have malfunctioned," Brent said. "I guess that's not so weird, considering how long it had been sitting when we found it. Maybe something in the wiring or the electronics went bad, and it just needed some more flying time before it totally failed."

"I suppose so," Shawn said, but then his gaze moved to the empty landscape beyond the lodgepole gate that framed the entrance to the ranch. "Still, I can't shake the feeling that someone did that on purpose."

"You mean a djinn?" Lindsay asked. She guessed her expression now was as skeptical as Shawn's had been a moment earlier. "No one's ever heard of any djinn settling out here."

A shrug. "Maybe not. Is it something we can check on?"

"Sure," she replied, since she knew finding out whether Ghost Ranch was occupied by a djinn should be easy enough. "I can radio Julia and Zahrias when we get back to Los Alamos."

"Then we might as well get going," Shawn said as he began to reach for the ignition button.

Brent stared at him. "Aren't we going to go in and look for Sarah?"

While that might have been the right thing to do, something about Shawn's previous line of questioning made Lindsay wonder if there was a lot more going on here than met the eye. Never in the world would she have said she was remotely psychic, and her hard-headed engineering background made her a great foil for her scientist husband...but the thought of venturing into Ghost Ranch right now with only Brent and Shawn for backup made chills run up and down her spine.

"Eventually," she said. "But I think Shawn is right on this one. If there really is a djinn lurking somewhere on the ranch, we can't just walk in there like we own the place. Look at what happened to the drone."

"A djinn might not have had anything to do with that," Brent argued.

"Or they could have had everything to do with it," Shawn returned. "I don't want to stir up something we can't handle."

For a few seconds, Brent didn't say anything. His jaw was set, and Lindsay knew he hated the idea of abandoning Sarah there without even attempting to go in and find her.

On the other hand, drones didn't usually blow

themselves up in the middle of a clear sky...if that was even what had happened. The drone was too far away for them to have had it in their line of sight, so it might have simply lost power, dropped like a stone, and broken apart on impact.

Mechanical failure didn't give her the creepy crawlies like this, though.

"We'll come back for Sarah," Lindsay said, keeping her tone gentle.

"But first, we need to figure out what's really going on out here."

Chapter 10

SARAH SUPPOSED IT WAS POSSIBLE. AFTER all, it had been years and years since she'd heard a properly functioning icemaker. No one used them in Los Alamos, not when they required so much energy and water. People had learned to have "iced" tea that was only cooled in the refrigerator, and although an exception was made around the Fourth of July so everyone could have ice cream, all the ice was made in kitchens with newer and better freezers than the one in her townhouse's kitchen.

Still....

She went over to the fridge and opened the freezer compartment, then peered in. Yes, there were definitely cubes in the icemaker, and she supposed a batch of them could have dropped just as she was starting to lose herself in the book she'd been reading.

And after all, why would Abdul have any reason to lie to her about something so innocuous?

Absolutely none. Besides, they'd had such a pleasant day so far that she didn't want to walk back outside and start giving him the third degree about the odd noise that had disrupted her reading time. Better to let it go.

She picked up her iPad, but instead of returning to her room, she sat down on the couch in the great room so she could see the landscape outside and enjoy the soft breezes blowing through the space. The walls of the house were so thick that they acted as an excellent insulator, which meant she doubted the place would need any real air conditioning except on the very hottest of summer days...and those had been fewer and farther in between in the world after the Dying, when the climate slipped back into a more normal weather pattern.

Abdul didn't seem ready to make an appearance, though, and she wondered what he was up to. If he were a regular human, she might have said he was busy carrying the saddles down to the stable, which she thought was located on the other side of the low promontory where the house was situated. But a djinn could just blink all the horses' tack wherever he wished, so she doubted he would waste his energy on such a simple chore.

Or maybe he wasn't coming back inside

because she'd decided to plant herself here rather than in her room, and he was avoiding her.

Sarah wasn't sure she liked that possibility, especially after they'd spent such a pleasant couple of hours together.

Wait...was she actually annoyed at the thought that Abdul might not be completely entranced by having her around?

That was just nuts. All right, he hadn't thrown her in a dungeon and shackled her to a wall or anything, but she needed to hang on to the simple fact that she wouldn't be in this house at all if he hadn't compelled her to stay here.

The front door opened then, and she blinked and immediately forced her attention back to the iPad in her lap. If asked, she couldn't have responded with a single coherent detail about the page she was supposed to be reading, but Abdul didn't have to know that.

"You are enjoying your book?"

Again, all politeness. She wondered if he was being deliberately pleasant to lure her into some kind of Stockholm syndrome situation.

Or maybe he'd decided there was no point in acting like a jerk.

"Yes," she lied. "I hope you don't mind me sitting out here. I just figured since you said I had the run of the property—"

"It is fine," he said hastily. "I can see why you

would want to be out here, since the view is so pleasant."

That it was. Actually, as the afternoon had worn on, thunderheads had begun to build up, so near that she thought this time, they might get a real light show instead of a few clouds that dissipated after sunset. Sitting here, she'd have her best chance of seeing something fun.

"But I also wanted to ask if you had any preference for our evening meal," he went on. "I think I would like to make something from scratch."

Sarah blinked again, then set her iPad on the coffee table. "You cook? I thought—"

"Many djinn simply conjure their food, it is true," he said. "But there are those among us who like to do it the old-fashioned way, to use a human phrase. It can be a pleasant occupation to pass the time."

She'd never been too much into cooking, mostly because with school and running to auditions and squeezing in rehearsals and everything else, she barely had time to order takeout. And her father had never seemed to mind, mostly because he worked such long hours and was rarely even home when dinnertime rolled around.

However, she thought she could see why some djinn might want to take up cooking. They were so long-lived that they had a hell of a lot of hours to fill.

And she had a feeling that putting together a favorite recipe would be much more fun for them, partly because they could easily conjure up any missing ingredients or have the garlic chop itself, or whatever.

While it might have been amusing to ask for something really complicated, like beef Wellington or Julia Child's bourguignon recipe, Sarah thought that might be a little petty.

"You can choose something," she said. "I'm not super picky. About the only thing I won't eat is snails."

Was that a glint of dark eyes within his hood?

Probably not; the thing did a remarkably good job of hiding his face, so much so that she wondered if he'd cast some sort of enchantment on it to prevent any observers from seeing even a hit of the features within.

"I think we can avoid snails," he replied, and there was no missing the flicker of amusement in his voice. "But I will ponder this for a while."

After making that comment, he headed down the hallway that, she assumed, led to the main suite and whatever other rooms were located in that wing of the house. She hadn't ventured there yet, mainly because she already felt as though she was skating on thin ice and didn't want to annoy him and be banished to her room once again.

Instead, she picked up the iPad and did her best to focus on the words on the screen.

"'Ghost Ranch'?" Julia Innes repeated, sounding puzzled. "No, I'm pretty sure there aren't any djinn out that way."

Dylan had been down for his afternoon nap when Lindsay got back to Los Alamos, so she figured that was the best time to reach out to Julia and Zahrias to see if they could shed any light on the deepening mystery of Georgia O'Keeffe's former home. Miles stood nearby, listening, although it seemed as if he didn't feel the need to jump into the conversation, not when he hadn't been on the expedition that had gone to that very spot a few hours earlier.

"No one?" Lindsay responded. Maybe the drone's sudden radio silence really was thanks to mechanical failure and nothing else, and yet she still couldn't help thinking something else must be going on here. "That is, I know most of the djinn have been settled in their homes for years now, but there's no chance that someone might have come there recently? It would explain a lot."

"We cannot say for absolutely sure," came Zahrias' deep, somehow smoky voice. "I can ask the elders. If one of your people truly has disappeared there, I believe further investigation is required. Because the elders are the ones who decide who lives where, then it makes the most sense to go to them directly."

"That would be great," Lindsay said. "None of us are really sure what's going on, but with Sarah Wolfe missing and now our drone disappearing for no reason, we can't help thinking it's more than just a coincidence."

Julia came back on the line then, sounding brisk and confident. "Well, whatever's going on, we'll just have to hope the elders clear it up. If they come back and say that no one is living there, then you can go in and search more thoroughly. In fact, I'm sure we could get a couple of our people to go along to help out. Air elementals can cover a lot more ground than us regular folks on foot."

That was a generous offer. More and more, there had been open cooperation between the community in Los Alamos and the djinn/mortal group in the state's former capital, but still, this wasn't a matter that affected the people in Santa Fe at all. Sarah Wolfe was none of their own. Yes, they'd jumped in when Isla Dunbar went missing, but in that case, they'd been fairly certain that a djinn was involved, even if they hadn't pinned down the true culprit right away.

This thing with Sarah...it was just a mystery.

"We'd appreciate that," Lindsay said. "It could turn out she just wandered off and lost track of time, but that doesn't sound like anything Sarah would do."

"We'll get to the bottom of it," Julia replied. "Hang tight, and we'll get back to you as soon as we can."

A little squawk from the speaker seemed to indicate that the other woman had hung up, so Lindsay put down her handset microphone and looked over at her husband.

"I guess that's it," she said. "Now all we can do is wait."

After some ruminating and reflecting on all the various human dishes he'd consumed over the years, Abdul decided to make a large pot of cassoulet. Perhaps it was something Sarah had eaten before and perhaps not, but the hearty concoction of beans and sausage and chicken sounded like a fitting end to a day that had involved some exertion.

Besides, the clouds that had been slowly creeping northward for the greater part of the afternoon had now reached Ghost Ranch, and it seemed as if they might get a thunderstorm or two. It would be good to have the hearty dish with some wine as the rain fell outside.

So he summoned all the ingredients and busied himself in the kitchen. Sarah realized what he was doing at once and set aside her iPad so she could ask him if he needed any help, but he told her no, he had everything in hand.

Which, obviously, was the truth. He could have snapped his fingers and summoned the meal, but he enjoyed doing it this way. However, he wasn't above using his powers to make sure the garlic was minced fine and the onions chopped into precise quarter-inch pieces.

Soon enough, the concoction was simmering on the stovetop, and he went to look out the window.

"Do you think it's going to rain?" Sarah asked. She'd once again put down her tablet and had risen from the sofa, although he noticed she stayed a ways back, as though she didn't want to intrude by coming too close.

"Probably," he replied. In fact, he thought it was a near certainty, what with the way the clouds had now covered almost all the sky, how he could feel the way they were heavy with rain, pulsing with electricity just waiting to be unleashed. "It is a good thing we did not go for a sunset ride, for I am almost certain we would have been soaked by the end of it."

"Good thing," she said, then brushed a hand against the tunic she was wearing. "I think I'll change for dinner—this outfit smells a little too much like horse."

He hadn't noticed, but then, she wasn't standing close enough for him to sense such an odor emanating from her clothing. Tone neutral, he said, "If you think so."

She chuckled. "Oh, I know so. I'll be back out in a few."

A brief pause as she leaned down to retrieve her iPad from the coffee table, and then she headed out of the room. Abdul watched her go, and couldn't help wondering what she would select to wear for that evening's meal. The shimmering teal tunic and pants that would bring out the unusual greenish-blue hues in her eyes, or perhaps the white dress, the one that was utterly simple when hanging but he guessed would be spectacular when worn?

Not that he should even be thinking about such things. He had conjured the clothing because it was beautiful in its own right, and he had always liked to surround himself with beautiful things.

Even if he could not see such beauty in himself, he could at least have it around him at all times.

No point in thinking about Sarah's clothing, not when he still had work to do. The cassoulet bubbled gently on the stovetop, and time would turn it into the delectable concoction he had envisioned for their dinner. Now he needed to focus on making some crusty rolls to go along with it, as well as determining which salad would be best as an accompaniment.

He did not want to analyze too closely why he wanted to make sure this meal would be perfect.

Sarah surveyed the wardrobe Abdul had given her, trying to think what would be the right thing to wear to dinner. That white dress with the tone-on-tone embroidery around the neckline was gorgeous, but although she couldn't tell for sure what he was making for dinner, it looked as though it was some kind of fancy stew, and she knew one splash from her spoon on the bodice of that dress and it would be all over. And all right, she guessed that his djinn magic would fix any kind of stain that occurred, but still, she didn't really like the thought of sitting there for even a couple of minutes with a big blotch on her dress.

But there was one that was similar, also sleeveless and with some embroidery on the bodice, but it was a dark green, something that seemed much safer for slurping soup or stew or whatever they were having. Like almost everything he'd summoned for her, it was also made of silk, and felt cool and airy as she dropped it over her head once she'd discarded the tunic and pants she'd worn for most of the day.

A quick touch-up of her face, and she brushed her hair to get all the tangles out. On the ride, she'd pulled it back into a ponytail so it wouldn't be in the way, but it still needed some work to get it nice and shiny again.

Too bad Abdul hadn't provided any bobby pins or clips or anything she could have used to pull it up and out of the way. Sarah supposed it was all right to leave her hair loose and simple like this, and yet the dress was just fancy enough that it seemed to call for a little extra effort.

Well, she didn't have any jewelry, either, except the silver earrings she'd worn this whole time. Back at her townhouse in Los Alamos, she had the antique bohemian garnet ring she'd been wearing when she fled Albuquerque all those years ago, but she rarely put it on these days. It was a family heirloom and had supposedly belonged to her great-grandmother on her mom's side. Sarah couldn't know for sure, since that ancestor had been long gone by the time she came along, and she hadn't been old enough when her mother had died to have gotten the whole story.

She didn't want to think about that, though.

That tragedy was far back in the past and didn't have any bearing on her life now.

Whatever that life would turn out to be, considering how Abdul hadn't said a single word about letting her leave and she still hadn't come up with anything remotely resembling a decent plan for getting out of here.

When she emerged from her bedroom, the main part of the house was filled with amazing smells, delicious aromas that made her stomach want to growl even though she thought she'd had a decent enough lunch. The table was set as well, with simple, heavy stoneware in a soft sage green that went well with the other natural tones in the house.

Candles flickered on the tabletop, set in unadorned iron holders, and they also shone from the heavy mantel of twisted juniper that adorned the fireplace.

Was Abdul trying to impress her, or did he only think that a meal like this deserved a little extra effort?

Probably the latter. Sarah couldn't come up with a single reason why he should care at all what she thought.

Just as soon as she entered the living room, lightning flashed, illuminating the dark valley below. A few seconds later, thunder rumbled, strong enough that she thought she could hear the sconces rattling on the wall.

"That was close," she remarked.

Abdul had been standing at the kitchen counter, tossing some greens in a large wooden bowl, but he paused then and glanced over at her. "Yes, it was," he said. "Strong enough that it might have disrupted the power here if we still needed to worry about such things. Luckily, we do not."

Because his djinn energy was keeping the lights going and powering the gas stove. For all she knew, this house might have had solar panels on the roof, but solar wouldn't do anything to make the gas oven work.

"Dinner is almost ready," he went on. "Perhaps you would like to choose some music to listen to?"

"'Music'?" she repeated. As far as she'd been able to tell, there didn't seem to be any kind of sound system here.

Maybe he smiled under the hood. "There are speakers concealed in those shelves over there," he said, pointing toward the built-ins that surrounded a truly enormous TV attached to the wall. "And there is also a unit that will allow you to hook up your iPad to it."

Perfect. Since Abdul had already provided enormous libraries of music on the tablet he'd given her, there must be something on there that would work as a good background for their dinner.

"Got it," she told him, and headed back into her bedroom so she could fetch the iPad. Soon enough, she had it hooked up to the Bose system that was so cleverly concealed inside the built-in, with a sort of wicker covering on the cupboards that held the speakers so you couldn't see them but sound could easily escape.

Now all she had to do was figure out what to listen to. With all her focus on musical theater—with a foray into opera one summer when she was trying to decide on the best use of her voice—she had never paid much attention to what was popular. Anyway, playing Taylor Swift or Sabrina Carpenter or Billie Eilish didn't seem like the right thing to do, not on a stormy evening when she was sitting down to dinner with a djinn.

Among the literally hundreds of playlists on the iPad, she found one that appeared to be a mix of Russian composers, Rachmaninoff and Tchaikovsky and Rimsky-Korsakoff. She started that one going, making sure the volume wasn't turned up too high so she wouldn't have to worry about getting blasted out of her seat if it launched into the *1812 Overture* or something similarly bombastic.

Luckily, the first song sounded as if it was from Rimsky-Korsakoff's *Scheherazade,* lush and lovely... and maybe a little too on point for a meal she'd be sharing with a djinn, but she couldn't worry about that now. Instead, she headed over to the long table in the dining area and hovered there for a moment, not sure whether she should offer to help with anything.

"Dinner will be on the table soon," Abdul told her, effectively forestalling any inquiries along those lines. "You may go ahead and sit down."

Well, at least that would stop her from standing here awkwardly, not sure what to do. She pulled out a chair and seated herself, and placed the heavy cream-colored linen napkin from her place setting on her lap. A basket covered with an identical napkin and with a plate of butter next to it seemed to signal the rolls were already on the table, so all Abdul had to do was bring over the bowl of salad and the heavy enamel-over-iron Dutch oven full of the stew he'd made, and then he sat down as well.

"I assumed you would like some wine," he went on. "If not, I will summon something else for you to drink."

Maybe some people would have counseled her to stay completely sober, but oddly, Sarah thought she was safe enough with Abdul. If he'd had any designs on her, he'd had plenty of opportunities during the time she'd been with him for him to do whatever he wanted. Getting just the mildest of buzzes sounded like as good a way as any to end the day.

Besides, although she hadn't been anything

close to an expert on wine, she knew enough that a meal like this probably deserved something more than a glass of water.

"Wine would be great," she told him.

Without comment, he reached for the bottle and laid a finger against the neck. At once, the cork pulled itself out, far more quickly and smoothly than it probably would have emerged if he'd used an ordinary bottle opener.

Sarah couldn't help grinning. "Nice trick."

"Sometimes it is better for us to use our powers," he said as he poured an inch or so of dark wine into her glass.

"I suppose so."

He tipped some wine into the glass in front of him, then inclined his head toward the basket of rolls. "Please, help yourself."

Clearly, no toast would be forthcoming. Sarah didn't really know why she'd expected one, except that the times she'd gone over to friends' houses and they'd made special meals, there had always been some kind of salutation before they started eating.

Then again, what would they even be celebrating? Abdul was holding her against her will—even if she had to admit her prison was a fairly luxurious one—and she was an interloper who'd intruded on his solitude. While she couldn't defend what he'd done, she also had to admit she wasn't entirely blameless here.

So she unfolded the napkin and plucked a roll from the basket, then helped herself to some salad, since the bowl sat close to her place setting. Afterward, she handed the salad to Abdul, who set it down so he could dish up some of the delectable concoction inside the friendly spruce green Dutch oven.

"What is it?" Sarah asked. She recognized plump white beans and sausage and shredded chicken, but she didn't think she'd ever seen the actual dish before.

"Something called cassoulet," Abdul replied. "From France, I believe. It is something I had once long ago."

She wanted to ask if he'd eaten the dish here on Earth all those years in the past, but something stopped her. It was true that djinn had been coming and going from this plane for millennia, sampling human food and music and more, but— even though she couldn't really say why she got that particular impression—she had a feeling Abdul had not been among those who'd made this world their vacation spot.

Maybe a fellow djinn had described the dish to him, and he'd decided to make it for himself.

The fragrant steam wafting up from her plate

smelled amazing, though, so she picked up her fork and scooped up some.

Oh, yes, that was wonderful, hearty, and rich and a blend of flavors that didn't fight with one another at all, but worked together to make something much more than the sum of its parts.

"It's incredible," she said, and his hood tipped toward her again. Not for the first time, she wished she could see his face, could know whether he smiled or remained serious, whether his eyes had lit up from her praise.

But his hood dipped low enough that she could see nothing at all, especially since, with night fallen and the only lighting provided by the candles and a few low-wattage sconces on the wall, it was hard to make out the glint of his eyes, let alone anything else.

"Thank you," he said.

Lightning strobed then, but because Abdul was looking down at his plate, it didn't help Sarah very much. Thunder rumbled a moment later. This time, though, she'd been expecting it and didn't even flinch.

Instead, she reached for her glass of wine and sipped. It was also very good—not that she'd been expecting a djinn to serve Two-Buck Chuck or something—but she'd never taken the time to learn much about wine and therefore had no idea whether it was a Bordeaux or a Burgundy, or a cab from California, or whatever.

Despite the thunder and the music in the background, Sarah still thought it was too quiet in here. "Do you just conjure the wine, or do you find it somewhere and bring it here?"

"This one I brought," he said. "It was in the cellar of a hot springs resort not too far from here. Eventually, I suppose, we djinn will have to create it from nothing, once the current stores are used up."

"Or people will make more," she suggested. "I heard that some of the djinn and humans in Santa Fe are starting to grow grapes again. We've also talked about doing that in Española—well, taking over some of the abandoned vineyards in Velarde and Pojoaque—but it's more important for us to grow food we can actually eat, so the idea has been kind of back-burnered."

For a moment, Abdul didn't respond, and Sarah wondered if he was going to make a disparaging comment about the human community in Los Alamos and its various endeavors. Although everything had been peaceful enough lately, she'd heard there were still plenty of djinn who weren't too thrilled that a group of mortals had been able to survive on their own.

But then he said, his tone mild, "I can see why foodstuffs might be a priority," and he steered the conversation in that direction, inquiring as to what dishes were her favorites, listing ideas for meals they could have in the future. As best she could, Sarah kept up her side of the conversation, but something inside her despaired at those words nonetheless.

Exactly how long was he planning to keep her here?

The two-way radio came alive just as Lindsay was pulling a lasagna out of the oven, and she wanted to swear. She'd been hoarding her allotment of cheese for two weeks now, waiting until she had enough to make a proper dish, one based on the meal her mother used to make when she was a kid. True, purists would say it wasn't real lasagna, not when she had to use the Los Alamos equivalent of jack cheese rather than mozzarella and parmesan, but still, she'd been wanting to try it for months.

Oh, well...the thing needed to sit on the stovetop and congeal a little bit before it could be served anyway.

Miles was nearby, since he'd just set the table and was currently doing his best to prevent Dylan from grabbing all the cutlery. With the ease of long practice, he hoisted the boy onto his hip and then went over to pick up the radio's handset.

"This is Miles," he said, and Lindsay set down

the heavy pan she was holding so she could move closer to the little alcove that housed their two-way radio.

"Hello, Miles," came Zahrias' voice. He almost always sounded calm, sometimes a little stern, but there was a note of tension in his tone that Lindsay didn't like very much. "Is Lindsay there with you?"

"Yes, I'm here," she said, leaning close to the handset Miles held so it would pick up her words. "Do you have some news for us?"

"I do," the djinn leader replied, sounding heavier than ever. "But I fear you will not like it much."

Miles's grip on the handset tightened visibly. "What have you found?"

A pause, and then Zahrias said, "I spoke to the elders. As soon as I mentioned Ghost Ranch, they became visibly tense. Then Ibram informed me that neither the djinn in my community nor the people in Los Alamos are allowed to go anywhere near the place, neither the ranch itself nor nearby Abiquiu. When I attempted to discover why they should make such a strange request, they told me that it is business of the elders and that they would speak no more on the subject."

Lindsay darted a worried look at her husband, while his mouth tightened.

"Can they do that?" he asked. "After all, we've expanded well into Española and several of the neighboring communities, and they haven't stopped us so far."

"I fear the elders can do whatever they like," Zahrias said. "If it is their desire that we go nowhere near Ghost Ranch, then we must abide by their wishes." He paused there, the silence stretching out so long that Lindsay wondered if maybe the connection had failed.

But then he spoke again.

"Whatever has happened to your lost young woman, I am afraid you must leave her to her fate."

Chapter 11

Djinn slept, but Abdul did not. Or rather, after he was done exerting himself for the day, he would go to his room and lie down on the bed there so he might rest, and yet that was not quite the same thing as sleeping the way the elementals or their human counterparts did.

Now, though, he could not even close his eyes, but lay there with his gaze fixed on the ceiling, which was occasionally illuminated by brief bursts of lightning as the storm raged on. Water poured from the eaves and no doubt was pooling in the courtyard. No need to worry about flooding, though, not with his powers wrapped around the house and snaking through it as well, ensuring that the climate-control systems continued to function and everything from the roof down to the foundation was as secure as he could make it.

No, it was not fear about the roof leaking or water seeping under the door that kept him so wakeful now.

Unfortunately, it was the memory of Sarah at dinner as she praised the food he had made and talked to him about the wine, or favorite dishes she'd eaten as a child. The way the candlelight had caught in the cascades of her dark hair as it fell around her shoulders, the sweetness of her voice.

The creamy skin of her throat, and the way he could just barely glimpse the curve of her breasts in the low neckline of the silky green gown she wore.

How had she become so distracting, so lovely? He certainly had not thought much of her looks when he first trapped her here.

Then again, she had not been at her best in that moment, hair pulled back into a messy ponytail and her face pale with fear. Over the intervening time, she seemed to have blossomed, to have lost her fear of him.

And while he had thought himself content with unending days alone here, now he was forced to admit that he had enjoyed these few hours with her far more than he had all those long, empty years before he had been blessed with her presence.

In the darkness of his room, he had no need of the hooded robe that shielded him from the rest of the world. An unconscious gesture, one born of long, bitter habit, made him raise his hand to his face to feel the uneven scars there, the ruin he had been hiding since the world was young.

His mouth twisted. What would she think if she were to see the thing he concealed from everyone, even himself?

As beautiful and as perfect as she was, certainly she would recoil in horror.

Not that it mattered, for he would never allow her to see him as he truly was.

It felt somehow wrong to be this cheerful as she got out of bed and headed for the shower. Shouldn't she instead be brooding over her captivity, or doing her best to come up with a workable plan to flee to Los Alamos?

Maybe. For now, though, Sarah thought she'd much prefer standing in the shower and letting the hot water flow over her, enjoying a luxury that had been denied her ever since the djinn had changed the world forever. The storm of the night before was long gone, and when she finally stepped out and grabbed one of the fluffy towels that had been provided for her, she peeked past the curtains to see that the morning was bright and clear, with what looked like new grass already poking up in the yard outside the window.

Absolutely perfect.

The night before, she'd wondered how long Abdul would keep her at Ghost Ranch before he finally decided there wasn't any point in preventing her from returning to her life in Los Alamos. As she'd lain there in bed, feeling just the slightest bit elevated from the glass and a half of wine she'd drunk with dinner, she'd had the traitorous thought that being trapped here maybe wasn't so bad after all. No unending chores, no shabby little townhouse...no pretending she was something she wasn't.

And that was the crazy part, wasn't it? That she hadn't felt any real need to be anything other than herself? Surely she should have been much more comfortable among her own kind, rather than trapped here by a djinn.

Somehow, though, she'd never been at ease in Los Alamos. Not all the way, not enough to completely let her guard down. A few people in her circle knew something of her past—or at least, she'd told them that she'd lost her father right before the Heat and didn't want to talk about it— but they didn't know everything.

No one did.

Abdul had even heard her singing, and after those first few questions, hadn't pursued the matter, as though he'd guessed it was a subject she didn't want to discuss.

Considering how messed up this world could

be, she found herself realizing that the past twenty-four hours had been some of the most pleasant she'd experienced in a long while.

You can't stay here forever, though, she argued with herself as she went into the closet to choose something to wear. A pretty turquoise dress seemed to match her current mood, although she knew she'd have to change if Abdul suggested horseback riding again. *You're not a guest, you're not his girlfriend—you're his prisoner.*

Well, all right, on the surface, that was true. But could you really call it captivity if you didn't possess a burning desire to get away?

Sarah wasn't sure she was ready to answer that question. It seemed a lot better to just go with the flow and see what happened. If she was presented with the most absolutely perfect plan ever to escape Ghost Ranch and get back to Los Alamos, then obviously, she'd take it.

In the meantime, though, she figured she might as well enjoy herself.

Abdul was sitting at the dining table, sipping some coffee, when she emerged from her room. As always, he wore the same black hooded robe, and she had to bite her tongue to keep herself from asking if he'd ever thought about trying something a little more cheerful, like red or bright blue.

Actually, the mental image of him in a scarlet robe, like some kind of post-Heat Santa Claus, was so silly that she had to stop herself from grinning like an idiot. The last thing she wanted was for him to ask what had suddenly made her smile.

"Some tea?" he asked.

He'd remembered that she wasn't a coffee drinker. Sarah didn't know why that realization warmed her so much, except that during the entire time she'd been with Carson, he hadn't once bothered to take note of her preferences, and instead kept trying to urge her to drink coffee because it just made more sense to share a pot.

"Yes, please," she replied, and couldn't help wondering what was going on with Carson at the moment. He must be in Los Alamos by now, but were they trying to come up with a way to locate her, or had they written her off as lost forever?

No, Lindsay and Miles and the rest of the town council wouldn't do that. Sarah had no idea what they were plotting, but she had to believe they would mount a rescue operation at some point.

For some reason, that idea bothered her. Not only because she was finding herself increasingly ambivalent about staying here at Ghost Ranch, but also because she wasn't sure how Abdul would react if he was suddenly confronted by a group from Los Alamos. He hadn't been too thrilled to find her here, and she had to believe he'd be even less happy to have four or five or even more mortals appear on his doorstep.

Stop borrowing trouble, she told herself as Abdul conjured a pot of tea and mug identical to the ones he'd summoned the day before. *They may decide they can't risk losing any more people out here, and that will be the end of it.*

Possible, but not very probable. It wasn't only that she doubted Lindsay and the rest of the group would write her off so easily, but also that they definitely wanted to expand in this direction, and they wouldn't abandon those plans without a damn good reason.

She poured some tea while Abdul sipped at his coffee. Once again, she was struck by how they could sit here quietly like this and not feel the need to fill the silence with idle chatter, could simply allow themselves to be in the moment.

He was the first to speak, though, asking, "Would you like to ride again today?"

Sarah had been thinking the same thing, although she couldn't help wondering if the trails might be a little muddy after all that rain the night before. "Maybe this afternoon," she said. "You know, to let everything dry out."

"That would probably work better," he allowed. "But perhaps there is something you would like to do this morning?"

The idea of having so much free time was still so foreign to her that she had to think about it for a moment. But then she realized that, even though

Abdul had knocked down the guest quarters he hadn't found aesthetically appealing, there was still a lot remaining of the original Ghost Ranch facilities.

"Maybe we could go look at the museums?" she said. "I visited them with my father when I was a kid, but obviously, I haven't been back since then."

"That is a good idea," Abdul replied. "But you should eat something first. Another muffin, like yesterday?"

As tasty as it had been, Sarah didn't think it was a good idea to keep repeating the same thing over and over again, not when she had a djinn right here who was apparently willing to summon her whatever she liked best.

"Not today," she said, and smiled. No, she couldn't see his face, but that didn't mean she intended to hide her reactions from him. "How about a nice big plate of pancakes?"

Somehow, she thought he smiled in return.

Yes, this had been a good idea. As Sarah had feared, there were still muddy spots here and there, and it was probably best that they'd postponed their ride until this afternoon, but they were able to walk from the house along the path that led to the former visitors center and the museums, the first of which contained sketches and paintings by the woman artist Georgia O'Keeffe, while the second, smaller facility showcased artifacts Abdul hadn't been expecting, such as fossils and pieces of pottery, all the interesting items that had been unearthed when O'Keeffe settled on this remote piece of land.

"I had no idea all this was here," he said, and Sarah sent him an inquiring look.

"You didn't?" she replied, a little startled, and added, "I mean, I just figured you explored all these buildings when you first came to live at Ghost Ranch."

"I did not," he said, then paused near a collection of crystals and geodes displayed in a glass case. "That is, while I knew I would need to do something about the museums at some point, I thought it better to address those items of more immediate importance, such as refurbishing the house and improving the landscape."

"You shouldn't do anything with them," Sarah commented.

Although she couldn't see his expression, he couldn't help smiling a little at her bold tone. "Not even strengthen the roofs and clear out all this dust?"

Now she grinned. "Okay, anything that will improve these places, sure. But I'd hate to think of you just...getting rid of them."

Doing so would certainly not be respectful. While djinn in general had little use for humans, the elementals still acknowledged their creative and artistic gifts, talents that they themselves lacked. Abdul was not precisely one of them, but he also understood that to destroy the works the artists had left behind would do no one any good.

"The museums will remain," he declared. "And so will the two chapels, and the labyrinth, and anything else I deem to be of some purpose."

"There's a labyrinth?" Sarah asked then, her eyes shining with interest.

"There is," he replied. "And we can explore it later when the ground is not so muddy. I had no idea you were interested in such things."

Now her shoulders lifted. In these dusty surroundings—for he had not thought to clean this place up before they ventured in here—she looked bright and beautiful and somehow out of place, in that deep turquoise dress that bared her arms, her hair shiny and free.

What would it feel like to have those glossy strands flow through his fingers like the finest silk?

As best he could, he banished the intrusive thought from his mind. Sarah would certainly not allow him to touch her thus, and he knew he should not even be thinking of her in such a way. It was becoming increasingly more difficult to regard her as a prisoner, but he did not know exactly how he should view her.

An honored guest, he supposed.

"Well," she said, looking cheerful, "it's not like I made a habit of exploring labyrinths or anything. I suppose it's just fun that they have one here."

"Then we will definitely go to look at it later," he told her. "Perhaps after our ride, depending on the hour of our return."

"That sounds like a good idea."

They left the matter there and continued their exploration of the museum. Soon enough, it was time to stop so they could have their noonday meal, and they headed back up to the house.

As they went, he couldn't help wondering why it was that he seemed so easy with her, when he had never before been comfortable around another living soul.

The day had warmed up enough that they ate on the table Abdul had summoned on the patio. He seemed fairly mellow, so Sarah couldn't help making the request that had been floating around in her mind for some time.

"Do you think you could conjure me some proper riding clothes?" she asked, and he tilted his head at her.

"Is there something wrong with what you wore yesterday?"

Sarah brushed her hand against her silk dress, then shook her head. "Not exactly *wrong*," she replied. "But I can't help thinking that some jeans and a T-shirt would probably be better in the saddle than something this fancy."

He was quiet for a moment, and she wondered if she'd offended him. What she'd said was only the truth, but if he'd been trying to show her that staying here wasn't so bad by lavishing beautiful clothes on her, then she could see why he might take her request the wrong way.

But then he said, "I suppose you are right. You will find some new clothing for riding in your room—and a sturdier set of shoes."

That would definitely help. At least he'd provided pretty little ballet-style flats and thong sandals rather than far more impractical heels or platforms, but Sarah knew the shoes he'd given her would still fall apart quickly enough if she kept riding and walking on rough ground in them.

"Thanks." She reached for her glass of iced tea and took a sip, adding, "Do you think it's going to storm again today?"

He lifted his head toward the sky. To be honest, it had been something of a silly question, since right now there wasn't a single cloud dotting that entire sapphire expanse, but Sarah knew just as well as anyone else who'd lived in New Mexico for a while—let alone their entire lives—that things could change on a dime around here, especially during the summer when monsoon season started cranking up.

Apparently, Abdul thought the same thing, because when he glanced back down, he said, "I doubt it, but the air is moving quickly, and that means conditions can shift at a moment's notice. Still, we should be safe to ride, and most likely to explore the labyrinth afterward."

Exactly what she'd wanted to hear.

"Then I'll get changed after lunch," she said.

If his expression shifted, she would never know.

"Of course," he replied.

Abdul had expected to be somewhat disappointed when Sarah appeared in the new clothing he'd summoned for her, and yet he had to admit there was something to be said for the way the slim jeans clung to her legs and the scoop-necked T-shirt showed off her curves. Not to the point where she would probably comment on the fit of the garments—he was certainly no expert on such things, but he had noted in those days before the world ended that many women wore clothing that seemed painfully tight—but enough that he thought she looked as beautiful as ever, if in an entirely different way from how she appeared in her silken finery.

True, the low hiking boots he'd also provided would never be commended for their beauty, but he could tell Sarah had a much easier time of it as she swung herself up into the saddle that afternoon. Perhaps it had been better before, when she'd needed his assistance and he'd been able to hold her hand, if only for a brief moment, although it was probably for the best that they had no reason to touch one another.

She had disordered his thoughts enough already.

He had called the horses to the house and saddled them while she was changing, so they were able to leave without much delay. This time, he guided them due north, away from the house and toward a canyon he thought she would like. No waterfalls or secret springs, but a creek did run through the spot, and all was shaded by cottonwoods and sycamores, with multicolored rock faces soaring hundreds of feet above.

"How many places like this are around here?" Sarah asked as she climbed down from her horse. Her movements still weren't entirely graceful, although he could tell she was getting more comfortable about managing such things on her own.

"More than you might think," Abdul replied. He had also dismounted and now led his horse over to the stream so he could drink from the cool, clear water. "It is part of the reason why I decided to settle at Ghost Ranch. I knew that when the weather was fine, I would be able to find many places of natural beauty to explore."

"It's gorgeous." She'd followed along, and her blood bay mare drank from the water as well, obviously glad of the refreshment after the nearly hour-long climb to get here.

He wanted to say, *So are you,* and immediately thrust such a foolish notion out of his mind. Yes, she looked very lovely standing there with the dappled shade from the trees casting dark and light on her rich-toned hair, even in those silly hiking boots.

However, he didn't want to imagine what her reaction might be if he said such a thing, and he knew he had far greater control over himself than that. Some might have said that he had very little control or he would not have allowed him to think such things in the first place, and yet he wanted to believe there was a world of difference between allowing thoughts like those to take up space in his mind and quite another for them to actually leave his lips.

"And thanks for the boots and the jeans," she added. "It was definitely easier to ride in these clothes."

He murmured, "You're welcome," although he knew deep down that she should not have been in a position to request them at all. No, he should have sent her home immediately and not kept her here; he had acted out of anger and fear, and not because he had any reason to believe she would betray him. From everything that he'd seen over the past two days, she possessed an honorable soul.

And yet he knew he was not much in the habit of trusting others. How could he be, when he had spent all his very long life utterly alone?

"Your singing the other day," he said, and immediately she stiffened, face going blank and wary. "Excuse me, but even I could tell that yours is a trained voice. Why is it that you do not wish to use it, or even speak of it?"

A second or two passed as she stared back at him. Not, he thought, like a deer frozen by the headlights of an oncoming vehicle, but more like a wary horse who was deciding which way she should bolt.

Then her mouth turned up in a lopsided smile, and she said, "Why do you wear that cloak and hood?"

Now it was his turn to go stiff. "That is a completely different matter."

"Is it?" she returned. But then she shook her head, and something about her posture softened, as though she'd realized they were not speaking of the same thing at all. "I suppose it's kind of stupid to be so defensive about it. But I've spent all the time since...well, since before...avoiding the whole topic. I guess I just wanted to act as if it had happened to someone else."

"What happened?" he pressed. For the life of him, he could not think of a single reason why she would want to hide such a glorious talent from the world.

Another of those crooked grins touched her mouth. "How much time do you have?"

"I am a djinn," Abdul said. Not entirely true, but trying to explain what he truly was would have taken far too much effort. "I have all the time in the world."

She reached up to tuck a loose strand of hair behind her ear, then glanced about the canyon where they stood, as though she wanted to be sure no one else was around to hear her story. Somewhat foolish, he thought, since the closest people were far away in Los Alamos and her only audience was himself and the two horses, but he told himself he should be patient.

"All right," she said. "I'll tell you."

Chapter 12

THEY WALKED OVER TO A PAIR OF boulders sheltered by a stand of tall oaks. Sarah couldn't be sure whether those oversized rocks had been there a moment earlier or whether Abdul had conjured them so they'd have a comfortable place to sit, but in the end, she supposed it didn't matter so much.

She'd feel much better having this conversation sitting down.

To be honest, she didn't think she wanted to have it all, except...

...except Abdul seemed like the sort of person who would listen to her story without judgment. He was so entirely detached from human affairs that she hoped he would let her tell him what had happened and how she felt about the situation, and wouldn't interject comments about how she had overreacted to things or deliver saccharine remarks about how she had an amazing talent and shouldn't be hiding it from the world.

"I studied music for a long time," she told him. "My father had me take piano at first, but then he realized not too long afterward that I should have a voice coach as well, so I was trained from around the time when I was ten years old."

"What about your mother?" Abdul asked.

A logical enough question, especially since Sarah knew she'd mentioned her father on several occasions already but had never said anything regarding her mother.

"She died when I was three," she said. "I guess she had a hard time when she was pregnant with me, and everyone told her she shouldn't have another child. But she did...and then we lost her and my baby brother at the same time."

When it had happened, of course, Sarah had been too young to really understand what was going on. She'd known she was going to get a little brother and was excited about that, and even though her mother spent a lot of time in bed and had looked pale and tired for what felt like months on end, she'd never, ever thought that when her father drove her mom to the hospital and left his young daughter with her grandmother to be babysat until they came home, that they wouldn't come back at all.

Or rather, her father returned the next day, haunted and hollow, and it had taken a while after that for her to understand that there wouldn't be a baby brother, and there wouldn't be a mommy anymore, either.

"Anyway," Sarah pressed on, knowing if she stopped to think about what had happened all those years ago, her throat would seize up with unshed tears and she wouldn't be able to keep talking. Even now, that shocking sense of loss could hit her at the worst times and take her breath away, despite years of the best therapy money could buy. "It was always just my father and me. He never seemed interested in getting married again, but he wanted to do everything he could to help me develop my talents. Later on, I started getting parts in community theater and even a couple of local TV commercials. Then, right before...."

She stopped there, the words trailing off as she fought that awful betraying tightness in her throat. No way in the world was she going to break down in front of Abdul. Bad enough that she was telling him all this in the first place.

But he'd asked, and even though she hated to dredge up all those past wounds, in a way, she knew she'd feel better once she got it all out, just like sometimes it was better to vomit all up and get it over with rather than trying to live with the nausea and stomach ache.

"Right before...?" he said. His tone was gentle, and she wondered if her story about losing her mother so young had moved him just a bit. Djinn could sometimes show compassion in odd little ways, so maybe he was feeling some sympathy for her despite everything.

"I got my big break," she said. "A revival of *The Phantom of the Opera*—a musical," she added hastily, since she had no idea how much Abdul knew about musical theater or popular culture in general. "It wasn't the lead, because I was just starting out, but I was in the chorus, and I was an understudy for the lead role and would get to play Christine sometimes in the weekend matinees. It was a very big deal for a girl from Albuquerque who'd only performed in local theater. And then...."

Abdul shifted where he sat on the granite boulder. "And then the Heat was unleashed on the world."

Sarah thought that was an odd way to phrase it, since everyone knew it was the djinn who'd let loose the deadly fever, but she wasn't going to argue semantics now. "Yes. After that, it was all about survival. I didn't talk about music, or what I'd been hoping and dreaming for, because it didn't seem all that important compared to just making it from one day to the next. And I stopped singing."

The djinn's hands tightened on his knees,

which were covered in the same heavy black linen that made up his cloak.

Did he switch to wool in the winter? Maybe not; she'd heard that djinn weren't affected by heat and cold the way humans were.

"You sang the other day," he pointed out, and she shrugged.

"I thought I was alone." He didn't respond to her comment, signaling that he'd like her to elaborate. "I began singing again a few years back after I started getting work assignments to go through the empty houses in Española. It seemed okay then because there wasn't anyone around to hear me. I suppose I felt the same way about coming here to Ghost Ranch. The surroundings were so beautiful, and I knew I was alone, so I figured it was safe."

Sarah paused there, wanting to shake her head at her ignorance. All right, there hadn't been any real sign that there was another living soul around for miles and miles when she walked down that dirt road the first time, but she'd definitely been proven wrong there.

"So, that's why you heard me singing," she concluded. "I wouldn't have done that if I'd known you were here."

Abdul regarded her for a moment, still silent. Then he said, "Would you have come at all?"

Good question. Yes, she'd gone to Ghost Ranch understanding that she was expected to scout the area and let Miles and Lindsay and the rest of the town council know whether it would be a good location to expand into, but Sarah knew that if she'd gotten even the slightest hint that the place was inhabited by a djinn, she would have gone straight back to the rendezvous point and let Lindsay know they needed to look elsewhere.

"No," she replied. "I know better than to intrude on a djinn's home."

His hooded head lifted, and she got the feeling he was looking past the hills that sheltered them now, gazing westward to the sprawling adobe house he had made his own.

"Well," he said at length. "I am very glad that you did not know I was there."

———

Sarah's story moved him more than he had expected. Perhaps in the grand sweep of the cosmos, her individual losses were no great thing, but losing a parent at such a young age would be difficult for anyone, and then to be facing one of the greatest triumphs of her life, only to have it snatched away before she could truly experience it?

That was an entirely different kind of loss, one that would leave its own scars.

And a while later, she revealed that her father had passed from an extremely virulent form of cancer only days before the Heat swept across the world. Abdul experienced a strange sense of relief at hearing that, for now he knew that she hadn't lost either of her parents in the Dying. Perhaps the grandmother she'd mentioned earlier was also gone by then, and therefore she had no close relatives who'd succumbed to the fever that had changed the world forever.

Wishful thinking, most likely, for she must have had cousins and aunts and uncles, and of course friends and acquaintances. Sarah would have experienced her own set of losses, even if they were not quite the same as having immediate family members die of the Heat.

He could not wish that away, no matter how much he might have liked to.

Once they were on their horses and headed back to the house, he asked, "How did you practice?"

"Practice?" Sarah repeated, as if not quite sure what he was driving at.

To be fair, Abdul wasn't entirely certain, either, although an idea had come to him when she spoke of singing alone in the empty houses of Española, of using that marvelous instrument of hers so it wouldn't completely wither away.

"When you began to sing again," he said. "Did you only sing songs that appealed to you, or did you do some kind of vocal exercises?"

"Oh, I started with the exercises." Although she was behind him as they made their way down the narrow, rocky trail, he could just glimpse the rueful quirk of her mouth as she spoke. "And I sounded awful. But I ran through every warm-up and limbering exercise I could think of, and then after that, it felt like I was ready to start singing a real song again. Still, it was always kind of haphazard, since I never knew when I'd get a chance to be alone instead of being stuck doing waitress duty at Pajarito's or working at the co-op."

He could see why regular vocal exercise would be necessary to keep her voice in tip-top shape. She had sounded lovely when he heard her two days earlier, but of course, that was after what appeared to have been several years of gradually working back into it.

"And before?" he went on. "Did you practice at home, or did you go to some kind of studio?"

If she thought it strange for him to be following this line of questioning, she hid it well, for she sounded natural enough as she said, "Both. We still had the piano I played as a kid, so I used that to help me get through the exercises. It's always better to have someone else playing, though, so when I worked with my vocal coach, he had an accompanist there."

Better and better. "I see. And how often did you do that?"

"Twice a week," Sarah said. "I could have gone more, but even biweekly sessions were kind of expensive. My dad insisted on footing the bill for everything, but even though I was starting to actually get paid for singing and acting, he wouldn't let me cover any of it."

"Your family was wealthy?"

Possibly not the most tactful of questions, although Abdul guessed that humanity's remnants must now care very little about how much they might have earned in the time before. None of that mattered any longer.

It didn't seem as if Sarah took any offense at his question, for she replied forthrightly enough, "I don't know about 'wealthy.' I mean, it wasn't as if we summered in the Hamptons or anything. But my dad's job paid well, and he worked so much that he never spent his money on stuff like sports cars or boats or even expensive TVs or something. Mostly, I'd just tell him if I needed something for school or my music, and he'd make sure I had it."

An indulgent parent, clearly, someone who did everything he could to make his daughter's life easier. Did he battle his own demons, wondering if he hadn't pressed his wife for another child, then perhaps she might have lived to raise their daughter?

Of course, that was all pure speculation. Abdul had no reason to believe that their second child wasn't one they had both earnestly desired. It was a tragedy, but for humans, tragedy was a way of life.

Still, he could put the pieces together, and it seemed to him that ever since the world had ended, Sarah had had no real way to truly work on her voice, to burnish it back to the way it had been when she thought a shining career lay ahead of her.

He could not wait to assist her with that goal.

So, she'd unburdened herself to Abdul...and he'd been probably the most sympathetic listener she'd had in a long time. And okay, it was true that she'd kept all this stuff to herself and hadn't even tried confiding in anyone in Los Alamos, but still, she had to admit she was surprised by the way he'd gravely absorbed everything she had to say and hadn't told her she was foolish for still grieving over something she'd lost years ago.

Honestly, she hadn't even lost the thing itself, but the promise of what might have been.

She had to admit this was a new experience for her. God knows Carson Mailer had been just about the exact opposite of a good listener, or sympathetic. Or...just about anything she believed she would have wanted in a partner. She'd gotten together with him because she thought he was cute and he seemed interested, and she hadn't stopped to think how they weren't compatible in any way that mattered.

And, what? Did that mean she was thinking of Abdul as a possible partner?

No, that was crazy. He was a djinn and she was a human. While it was true that plenty of djinn were romantically involved with mortals, they'd selected their lovers long ago, back before the Dying.

All right, she was being just a little disingenuous there. It was much rarer, but she'd heard there were some elementals who'd hooked up with their mortal partners much later on after realizing they weren't as indifferent to humans as they wanted to pretend.

Which still didn't apply to her current situation. Abdul might have turned out to be much kinder than she had any reason to believe, but all the deep conversations and glorious horseback rides in the world couldn't hide the ugly fact that he was keeping her here against her will.

Not that she'd tried very hard to escape.

Because I haven't had the chance yet, she tried to tell herself, but those inner words sounded feeble even to her. There had to have been a moment sometime when Abdul had his guard down and she could have bolted. True, he had djinn speed—and flight—on his side, and yet she was forced to acknowledge that he was only one person. If she had somehow come up with a way to fake him out, make him think she'd zigged when she'd actually zagged, she might have had a chance.

As best she could, she tried to keep those thoughts tucked away as she dismounted her horse and Abdul followed suit. Just like the day before, they removed their mounts' tack and rubbed the horses down before sending them off to graze and enjoy themselves for the rest of the day.

Afterward, the two of them went inside. All the windows were open, and a fresh breeze blew through the house, smelling of dry grass and sun-warmed stone. Even though Sarah couldn't exactly explain how, she could have sworn the fresh air felt cooler coming in than it had when she'd been standing outside.

More djinn magic?

Maybe. She'd always been a fresh air fiend, and if Abdul had come up with a way to have the house stay cool even with warm winds from an eighty-degree day blowing through the place, then more power to him.

He asked her if she would like some water, and she said yes. After he poured a glass for her—one he'd fetched from the cupboard and hadn't simply summoned out of thin air—he said, "I have something I would like to show you."

Sarah couldn't help arching an eyebrow at him. Most likely, it was something completely innocent, but still, when someone made a comment like that....

"I think you will like it," he added, and again, she got the impression that he smiled behind the concealing hood.

"Then lead on."

He indicated that she should follow him, and so she did, moving into the wide hallway that led to the wing of the house she hadn't yet explored, the one where she assumed his bedroom was located.

Was that where he was taking her? she wondered, and a little shiver went through her.

They passed a large room that was obviously a library, with built-in floor-to-ceiling bookcases and a trio of tall windows that looked out onto the hill-side below them. Maybe not quite as magnificent as the one in the Beast's castle in the movies, but still crowded enough with books in all shapes and sizes that Sarah thought she should be able to occupy herself in there for a very long time.

However, the library did not appear to be Abdul's destination, since he continued down the hallway, going past several smaller bedrooms that she only glimpsed as they walked by. But then he paused before he reached the end of the corridor —which terminated in a pair of double doors that she guessed was the entrance to the main suite—and opened the door before stepping aside.

224 • CHRISTINE POPE

"I thought this might help you," he said simply.

Sarah peeked inside, her eyes widening. It was a simple enough space, with the same wide-plank oak floors and white plastered walls as the rest of the house...with one very important difference.

In the center of the room stood a black grand piano.

She turned toward the djinn. "Did you...?"

"Yes, I summoned the piano for you. I thought it might help you with your practice."

Her feet propelled her forward, almost as though the piano was some kind of magnet rather than a large, handsome Steinway. She reached out with one hand to trace the inner curve of the cabinet, feeling the smooth, glossy finish beneath her fingertips.

How long had it been since she'd played?

Well, that was an easy enough question to answer. She'd sat down in the living room of the house she shared with her father and picked out the melody to "Twisted Every Way," one of the songs from *Phantom*, as she worked through the notes of the complicated, somehow sinuous melody. Back then, she'd been doing her best to distract herself from the shock of learning that her father was now in the hospital fighting a deadly disease no one had even known he had.

September twenty-fifth. Yes, that was the date.

So...it had been four years, three months, and twenty-six days.

It seemed absolutely surreal that Abdul had brought this piano here so she could practice. Sure, djinn had the power to summon almost anything they wanted, but still...this was crazy, wasn't it?

If for no other reason than she didn't know if she could even allow herself to practice her singing when she knew he could overhear her.

"Th-thank you," she stammered, not sure what else she should say. "This is incredible."

His shoulders lifted. "I was not using this room. It seemed a good idea to provide you with some other way to occupy your time."

Well, at least Sarah could understand his comment about having more space than he needed in this house. She had no idea what had been in here before he decided to snap his fingers and make a concert grand appear, but clearly, it hadn't been anything terribly important to him.

She lifted the lid and touched several of the keys. As far as she could tell, the piano was perfectly in tune.

Because of course it was.

Still standing in front of the keyboard, she moved her right hand so the fourth finger rested on the high E above middle C. Almost unconsciously, she played the first few notes of Beethoven's "Fur Elise," then paused.

"What is that?" Abdul asked. He had approached from the side but still stood a few feet away, as if he knew he shouldn't crowd her.

"It's a piece by Beethoven," she replied. "The story is that he wrote it for one of his music students...or maybe a woman he was interested in. My dad told me that my mother loved the song so much that they decided to have 'Elise' as my middle name."

Abdul appeared to absorb that bit of information, then looked from her to the keyboard where her hands still rested. "Do you know the rest of it?"

The scary thing was, she probably did. "Fur Elise" was a piece she'd played over and over so many times when she was young, Sarah guessed it was still permanently engraved on her brain.

And somehow, playing piano in front of the djinn seemed easier than just standing here and trying to sing while he watched.

"Only one way to find out," she said with a grin, then pulled out the piano bench and sat down.

A moment to gather her thoughts, to remind herself of all the twists and turns in the tricky middle section of the piece, and then she placed her fingers on the keyboard and began to play.

The tempo was a bit slower than it had been written, but Sarah thought it better to be somewhat measured rather than go at breakneck speed, only to trip all over herself at exactly the wrong moment. And while she knew she hit a clinker once or twice, she still couldn't hold back the rush of pride as her fingers stilled on the final A, with the corresponding notes in the lower registers echoing against the blank walls of the room.

She had to admit the acoustics in here were fantastic.

"That was lovely," Abdul said. "It seems you have not lost much of your skills as a pianist."

"Oh, I used to be a lot better," she replied, then rose from the piano bench. "I'm sure if I sat down to play some Chopin, I'd fail miserably. But the piano is gorgeous."

"Then I will leave you to practice," he told her, and Sarah experienced a flare of alarm.

"Oh, I'm kind of tired after riding all afternoon," she said, a protest that sounded weak even to her.

He crossed his arms. Not for the first time, she thought of how his hands were the only thing she could truly see about him, the skin a warm golden brown, his fingers strong and long—better suited to playing the piano than hers, which, while slender, were on the small side and often had to strain to reach some of the more ambitious chords.

If his hands were so perfect, what must the rest of him look like?

"It is not homework," he said, and that flicker

of amusement had returned to his voice. "You may play, or not. You may sing...or not. But to avoid it would only be a further waste of your talents."

After delivering that remark, he inclined his head before walking calmly out of the room and leaving her alone.

For a moment, Sarah only stood there, not sure what she should do next. The coward in her wanted to follow, to go to her room and pick up the iPad and pretend the Steinway wasn't waiting for her on the other side of the house.

But she'd been a coward for far too long, hadn't she?

A deep breath, and then she sat down on the piano bench and paused for a moment.

Well, she'd begun with Beethoven. She might as well continue in that vein.

Head down and focused on the keys, she began to play the first notes of the *Moonlight Sonata*.

Chapter 13

"We're not seriously going to leave Sarah there to rot, are we?" Lindsay asked.

Miles set down his wine glass, blue-gray eyes narrowed behind his silver-rimmed glasses. More than once, she'd wondered what was going to happen when his prescription shifted and he needed some new ones, but so far that particular fear hadn't come to pass.

Good thing, since they had plenty on their plate already.

"We don't even know she's in Ghost Ranch," he pointed out, then reached over just in time to prevent Dylan from sticking his fist into his plate of lasagna.

All right, that was true. The drone hadn't stayed up long enough for them to see exactly what was going on in there, or whether Sarah was on the property at all. Shawn still claimed that he'd seen some kind of movement under the trees near that big house at the top of the hill, but his eyes could have been playing tricks on him, wanting to manu-facture something that proved their lost volunteer was still alive and in the area.

"And we don't know that she isn't," Lindsay returned. "I just hate the idea that we have to stand back and do nothing simply because the elders told us the place is off limits."

"If they don't want us going there, then it's best that we stay away."

Lindsay picked up her fork and put a bite of lasagna in her mouth. All right, it wasn't exactly like her mother's, not without any access to real mozzarella or parmesan, but it was still cheesy and rich and should have been very satisfying.

At the moment, though, she couldn't keep from fretting over Sarah. In all these years, they hadn't lost a single person—well, okay, Isla had been taken by Aamir al-Qadir, but he had ended up falling in love with her, so no harm, no foul—and Lindsay didn't want to start now.

Even if the elders were telling them they needed to back off.

"Technically, they shouldn't have a say in anything we do," she said, and Miles gave her a pained look.

"I suppose that if you wanted to split hairs, then yes, the djinn elders do not command us humans," he replied. Even as Lindsay began to remark that she was glad he agreed with her, he went on, "However, I don't think it's a very good idea to upset them. The djinn are powerful enough, and the elders are an order of magnitude more. I don't think any of us fully comprehend the extent of their powers. We rely on the devices to protect us, sure, but I can't forget how several of the elders were able to ignore them at least partially when they needed to come near here. Who's to say they won't disregard them entirely if we make them angry enough?"

All right, her husband had a point there. No one really knew what the djinn elders might be capable of if they got their panties in a wad...mostly because no one had been stupid enough to do such a thing in the first place. Maybe far back in the mists of time, one of the elementals had challenged their elders, but whatever had happened, it was obvious that they'd maintained their position as the rulers of the djinn.

Was it really worth having the elders descend on Los Alamos in a rage and putting everyone in jeopardy, just to save one person?

Lindsay had always thought of herself as a nuts and bolts kind of person, someone who relied on logic and facts to make decisions. It was probably a large part of the reason why she and Miles got along so well; neither of them was anything close to sentimental.

And that kind of logic would state, in the words of an old *Star Trek* movie she'd seen years and years ago, that the needs of the many outweighed the needs of the few.

That didn't mean she had to like it.

It also didn't mean she wasn't going to still poke at the problem, trying to see if there was some way they could come at it from a different angle.

"Well, what if we don't go to Ghost Ranch?" she asked then. "What if Sarah got lost going to meet Carson, and she's wandering around somewhere by the lake?"

Once again Miles had to pause before he answered, this time to make sure Dylan wouldn't wrap his fingers around a chunk of lasagna and throw it at the wall. Already Lindsay suspected that the little boy indulged in that kind of behavior not because he was acting out, but because he was curious to see what would happen after he experimented with a particular combination of action and reaction.

Like father, like son.

"Carson said he looked for her," Miles pointed out, but Lindsay only shook her head.

"Do you really trust him on that?"

Miles's mouth thinned. Although he hadn't spent as much time around Sarah's fellow volunteer as his wife had, Lindsay could already tell that he'd taken the other man's measure and found him wanting.

"Probably not," he said.

"Well, then," Lindsay replied, figuring that should take care of that.

Miles, unfortunately, didn't seem ready to capitulate. "We both heard Zahrias. He was quite clear that the elders have interdicted not just Ghost Ranch, but the surrounding areas, including the lake and Abiquiu itself."

While she might have admitted to a failure of hearing on that particular point if she thought it would do any good, she still wasn't quite ready to let the matter go.

"It still seemed to me as if the elders were more concerned about Ghost Ranch itself," she said. "And even though none of us truly understands the real extent of their powers, there've been enough instances where they've been ignorant of things going on here on Earth that we know they're not omniscient. I don't see the harm in sending a small search party to Abiquiu Lake to take a look around, just to be safe. If it turns out they don't find anything, then okay, we'll just have to accept that we may never learn what really happened to

Sarah. But I just don't think I could live with myself if we didn't at least try."

For a moment, Miles didn't say anything. His long, sensitive fingers fiddled with the handle of his fork, telling her he was pondering the issue and that it was better for her to remain silent rather than continue to press her case. Instead, she sipped some wine, reached over with her napkin to wipe a smear of tomato sauce off Dylan's cheek—he made a face but didn't try to pull away—and waited for her husband to respond.

"All right," he said at last. "I'm still not sure this is the intelligent thing to do, but I suppose we can feign ignorance if we're caught. Who did you have in mind for the search party?"

Lindsay knew better than to volunteer, not when she was in the precarious early weeks of her pregnancy. Even if she hadn't been pregnant, she understood that she wasn't the best person for this kind of mission anyway. While she wasn't completely an indoor girl, she also knew she wasn't much of a hiker.

No, they needed a couple of people who could get in there and get out quickly, and leave as little trace as possible behind.

"Shawn, definitely," she said. Having him go was something of a risk, just because he was a valuable member of the town council, but at the same time, he was the outdoorsy type who did twenty-mile hikes for fun and was also good at hunting and fishing. Not that she thought he'd need to bag a deer on this trip or anything close to it, and yet he could live off the land if necessary. "And probably José Padilla," she added, a Native American man who was also in his early thirties like Shawn, and who'd been part of the Isleta pueblo just south of Albuquerque before the world went to shit. He'd demonstrated his tracking abilities before, and she couldn't think of anyone else who'd be a better companion to Shawn Gutierrez on a mission like this.

Miles set down his fork. "They would make a capable team. We can contact them in the morning."

For a second or two, Lindsay thought about protesting the delay. But then she realized it was already past six o'clock, and by the time the two men were outfitted and ready to go, night would be falling. Much better to wait so they could set out first thing in the morning and have a full twelve hours of daylight for their search.

About all she could do now was hope they'd be able to bring Sarah home.

At dinner, Sarah had thanked Abdul for the piano again, but he noted that she seemed distracted, as if

236 • CHRISTINE POPE

she was doing her best to determine how much of her past inhibitions she was willing to let go so that she might begin to truly work on her voice again. Yes, the house was large, but even so, he guessed he would be able to hear her no matter where he went.

That would not be a problem for him, of course; he looked forward to listening to her sing again, even if she was doing something as simple and pedestrian as practicing scales. Her piano skills were excellent, so he didn't think she would have too much trouble accompanying herself.

And yet....

She'd made that stray comment about having an accompanist when she worked with her voice coach. Would it not be much better for her to not have to play as well, and to instead have someone at the piano while she sang?

Probably. But while Abdul could claim many gifts far beyond those most djinn possessed, even he could not summon a human who played the piano out of thin air. He could travel with one, of course, and for a wild moment, he considered pushing his way past the devices that protected Los Alamos and the surrounding countryside so he might take someone to accompany Sarah as she practiced, but that was a foolish notion at best. He had no idea whether anyone in that enclave of humans could play anywhere close to as well as she...even if he knew he was fully capable of gritting his teeth and ignoring the debilitating effects the devices would surely have on him.

Now, though, as he lay in bed and stared up at the darkened ceiling above, an even wilder idea occurred to him.

What if he played for Sarah?

On the surface, of course, the notion sounded absolutely ludicrous. He had never played a piano or any kind of musical instrument, for he, like the djinn, did not have any predilection toward creative pastimes. But he was unlike the elementals in many other ways, and he wondered now if he might be able to summon the necessary skills to do such a thing. After all, he would not be interpreting the music, attempting to put his own stamp on it, but would only play in the manner that Sarah asked him to. She would be the one determining whether to speed up in one section and slow in another, or to grow soft or loud to convey a certain type of emotion.

The more he thought about it, the more the idea appealed to him. In this way, he could make himself indispensable to her, and she would have even less desire to leave Ghost Ranch. He noted she had said nothing on the subject the past couple of days, but that could have been because she knew her pleas to leave would fall on uncaring ears.

But this—he thought this a very good plan indeed. Because he did not need to sleep, he could summon another tablet and some headphones so he would not run the risk of waking her, and he would spend this evening listening to piano music and piano exercises.

And yes, also the melodies from the musical that was supposed to have been her opportunity for success in the theater. Surely she would wish to sing those pieces again.

He smiled in the darkness.

Tomorrow could not come soon enough.

When Sarah got out of the shower the next morning, she paused, towel wrapped around her as she tilted her head to one side.

Was Abdul playing music on the sound system in the living room?

No, that didn't feel right. Her room was down just a short hallway from the main part of the house, while this seemed more muffled, more distant.

And it sounded a lot like....

She held herself still, listening intently.

Was that "Think of Me," Christine's opening aria from Phantom?

A piano arrangement, but she supposed that wasn't too strange, as various pieces from the musical had been reimagined as everything from piano solos to full-on rave dance extravaganzas. But then she heard the music pause and start over again midway through, as if whoever was playing hadn't been satisfied with their performance and wanted to make sure they got it right.

No recording would sound like that.

But...it couldn't be what she was thinking. That was impossible.

Well, only one way to find out.

She finished getting dressed, combed through her damp hair one more time, and emerged from her bedroom. Yes, the music was louder now...and it definitely seemed as though it was coming from the wing of the house where Abdul had conjured a piano only the day before.

The door to that room was pulled partway closed, but since it wasn't locked, she assumed it would be all right to enter. As soon as she was inside, she saw that Abdul actually was sitting on the piano bench, hooded head bent close to the keyboard as though to make sure he didn't miss a single note.

"I didn't know you played," she said once she was a bit closer, and immediately, his fingers stilled on the keys.

"I did not," he replied. "Or rather, I did not until this morning."

Her eyes widened, and she came to stand by the side of the piano so she could get a clearer view of the keyboard. She wasn't sure what she'd been expecting—that he'd installed some kind of weird player piano setup?—but all she saw was his hands resting on the keys.

"You just...taught yourself how to play?" She knew she sounded incredulous, and thought she had every right to be. After all, djinn supposedly had all kinds of crazy powers, but she'd never heard of them just deciding to play an instrument and mastering it in less than the space of a day.

Okay, he hadn't completely mastered the piano, or she wouldn't have heard that bobble she'd detected a little while earlier. But still, it was incredible that he'd been able to play with that level of skill.

And that didn't even take into account what she'd heard through the grapevine in Los Alamos, that djinn might have collected human art and listened to human music, but they didn't have any real inclination or ability to create it for themselves.

"I thought it would help you with your vocal practice if you had someone to accompany you," Abdul said. "It is not as if I expect to play at Carnegie Hall."

Even that very mild quip made her smile. No, what she'd heard so far wouldn't have made Martha Argerich or Yuja Wang quake in their boots, but Sarah thought her djinn companion might turn out to be a very serviceable accompanist.

If, of course, she gathered enough courage to actually sing in front of him.

"Maybe not," she said. "But you sounded great. And I think it would help to have you playing rather than trying to accompany myself. Right now, though, we should probably have some breakfast before we get started, don't you think?"

At once, he got up from the piano bench, saying, "A very good idea. I would not expect you to practice on an empty stomach."

And he led her off toward the kitchen, asking if she would like eggs and toast, or perhaps something lighter so she would not have to wait so long to digest before they came back to the piano room to work. Not sure whether she should be amused or utterly stressed out, she told him that fruit and toast would be fine, and not so long afterward, they were seated at the dining room table and having their morning meal.

The whole time, her brain kept trying to come to grips with the odd reality that Abdul had apparently acquired the gift of playing the piano overnight...and the inevitable realization that very soon, she would have to sing in front of him.

No matter what.

"Stick close to the lake and the highway," Miles said. Lindsay could tell he still wasn't too happy about contravening the elders' orders and sending out a search party anyway, because his mouth was tight and every inch of his lean form seemed to indicate he would much rather be somewhere else.

Or maybe he just looked that way because he wanted to be in his beloved lab and not here in City Hall, giving instructions to Shawn and José.

"Yeah, we know we need to stay away from Ghost Ranch," Shawn replied. Unlike Miles, he appeared utterly relaxed, clad in a T-shirt and jeans and hiking boots, a full backpack resting on the floor next to him. A few feet away, José Padilla, maybe a year or so older than Shawn and several inches shorter, was similarly clad and also didn't seem too worried about the expedition that lay ahead of him.

"Although it sounds as if that's the one place our girl might be found," José remarked, and Miles crossed his arms.

"We don't know that for sure," he said, sounding waspish. Most likely, he wasn't too happy to be making Lindsay's arguments for her, and she decided that was probably a good place to step in.

"We don't know anything," she said reasonably. "That's why we need you to go take a look. It's very possible that she got a late start and went looking for Carson and maybe got lost."

"If that's the case," Shawn pointed out, "don't you think she would have tried to get back to the highway and kept going? Yes, it's kind of a slog when she'd have to walk all the way to Española instead of getting a ride starting in La Chuachia, but still, she would have made it here by now."

"Not if she got lost enough," Lindsay countered. "It's not like that's familiar territory to her, even if she did visit Abiquiu when she was a kid. If she was out of walkie range, there wouldn't have been any way for her to get in contact with Carson."

José frowned. His black hair was slicked back into a tight ponytail bound with a leather thong, and with his broad shoulders and thick biceps, he definitely looked like he'd be able to handle almost anything they encountered.

Well, except for what might be hiding in Ghost Ranch.

Whatever arguments he'd been about to offer, though, Shawn effectively forestalled them by saying, "I suppose we'll find out one way or another. We should get going—the sun's up already, and it's just going to get hotter as the day goes on."

True enough. The weather had been fairly mild so far, and they'd even gotten some rain the night before last, but Lindsay had also noticed that the days were trending warmer as they approached the solstice. At least Shawn and José were going to drive the whole way rather than hike the latter half of the journey. Shawn had insisted his truck could handle it.

"And if something goes wrong, I know how to put her back together," he'd added, patting his Toyota Tundra's fender.

Since he'd been working on and off in the community motor pool for nearly five years and had regularly wrenched on vehicles long before that, Lindsay had known he was only speaking the truth. And she had to admit that driving would be a lot faster.

It might also attract more notice, but they'd all decided it was a risk they'd have to take.

"Yes, better to go now," Miles said, and the little group moved out of the lobby of City Hall where they'd met, and into the parking lot where Shawn's Toyota sat waiting.

The two men were traveling light, so it only took them a moment to toss their backpacks in the extra-cab's rear seat. Then Shawn lifted his hand in a wave.

"We'll be back as soon as we can."

"No more than two days," Lindsay warned him. "If you haven't found any sign of Sarah by then, I doubt you ever will."

"Two days," Shawn promised, and he climbed

into the driver's seat even as José also got into the truck. "Piece of cake."

He closed the door, then started the engine. A moment later, the oversized truck was pulling out of the parking lot and onto Trinity Drive.

"It will be okay," Miles said, and touched her arm. "Let's get to work."

Chapter 14

THE MOMENT HAD COME. SARAH STOOD next to the piano and watched as Abdul seated himself on the bench. He looked at her expectantly, and she swallowed.

Why did something that had once come to her as easily as breathing now feel like utter torture?

Because you're doing it to yourself, she thought. *Abdul went and somehow taught himself to play the piano overnight, and you're sitting here and stressing about singing a basic scale in C?*

All right, she was standing, not sitting, but the point remained.

And it wasn't as if he'd never heard her sing before. Not like this, not only a few feet away from where she stood, but still, that particular horse had already left the barn.

"We'll do some scales first," she said. She

sounded extremely matter-of-fact to herself, but she knew that was only her way of trying to manage her nerves. If she could make the whole process seem like it was no big deal, then maybe she could get past the awful mental blocks she'd built for herself. "You know how to do scales, right?"

In answer, Abdul reached out with one hand and played a simple scale starting on middle C. "Like that?"

"Exactly," she said. "Each time, go up a half step. You know what that is, right?"

Again, he responded by playing the note in question, this time a C-sharp. "Yes?"

Despite the anxious butterflies dancing around in her stomach, she couldn't help flashing him a smile. "Yes. So let's get started."

He touched middle C again, probably to remind her of how it sounded.

Not that she needed the assistance; she might be rusty, and she might not have formally practiced for years and years, but she still had more than a decade of running through these exercises on a daily basis under her belt. Besides, she'd always had perfect pitch, had been able to sing a note that was exactly right even without the help of a piano.

A breath in, not too deep yet, since she only needed enough to support her as she ran up the scale and back down again. All the same, she wanted to wince when the first note left her lips—

not because it was pitchy or sour or even badly supported, but because it sounded too clear, too loud.

And of course she wouldn't be able to get a read on what Abdul was thinking, thanks to the way that damn hood fell so far over his face, hiding everything.

Even Christine had been able to see the Phantom's reactions better than this, since his mask had only covered half his shattered visage.

She couldn't help being grimly amused by that comparison, although she had to admit her situation wasn't quite the same as Christine Daaé's. It might be true that Abdul had kept her here against her will, just as Christine had been held in the Phantom's lair for days, but no one could ever accuse the djinn of being a mad musical genius, not when he'd only begun to play the day before. He would never write an opera for her—would never sing with her.

But what he was doing was being a decent accompanist, and that was what she needed to focus on now.

They moved farther and farther up the scales until she was singing an octave above where she'd started. Once upon a time, those high notes would have been easy, would have floated free from her vocal cords without even a thought, but now she could feel how rusty she was, how even during the times when she'd allowed herself to sing in those empty houses in Española, she hadn't done much that had really tested her range.

Well, that was why she was practicing now.

Another exercise, one where she didn't sing the entire octave, but only slid up five notes and then back down, again moving higher and higher, and this time she could almost feel the way her voice grew stronger and clearer, the highest notes seeming to come right out of the top of her head rather than emanating from her throat.

"Okay, that's enough warm-ups," she said, and paused. Abdul had been playing a piece from *Phantom* earlier, but she wasn't sure she wanted to go there quite yet. That musical was fraught in all kinds of ways she didn't want to think about.

No, better to return to some of the tried-and-true standards, the songs her vocal coach had started her with before they moved on to musicals and even some opera.

"Do you know 'Caro Mio Ben'?" she asked, feeling a little ridiculous. True, it was part of the standard classical repertoire, but there was nothing about practicing with a djinn accompanist that felt at all standard.

"No," Abdul replied. "That is, I listened to a great deal of music last night, but it was mostly from musicals because that is what you said you sang."

True enough. But if he could conjure just about anything she needed, from a pair of jeans to a saddle for her riding horse, then she didn't think summoning a simple book of sheet music should be too difficult.

Assuming he could even read music. From what she'd been able to tell so far, it seemed more as though he'd been playing by ear.

"There's a book of sheet music called *24 Italian Songs and Arias,*" she said. "It's kind of standard for anyone studying voice. It has a manila cover with green printing. Any chance you could get that for us to work with?"

He nodded. "*Italian Songs and Arias.* That should not be a problem."

And a moment later, that very same book appeared on the piano's music stand. Sarah couldn't help startling a little, even though by now she thought she should have been a little more used to the way Abdul could make objects appear out of thin air.

However, she tried to seem matter-of-fact as she reached over and flipped the pages to get to the piece in question. "Can you read the music?"

He didn't reply right away, but instead leaned forward, as though to absorb what was printed on the paper. Another pause while he turned the page, apparently so he could scan the entire piece, and then he went back to the beginning.

"It does not seem too difficult. The notations correspond to the music I have been studying for the past few hours, so I think I should be able to follow along."

That in itself was remarkable enough, but Sarah knew she needed something more than an accompanist who merely "followed along." No, she needed someone who could take cues from her while also realizing that he needed to hold up his side of things.

"Why don't you play it through once, just to be sure?" she suggested. "It's not like we don't have the time to go through it over and over again if necessary."

"True."

He placed his hands on the keyboard, but again he hesitated, as if allowing himself to scan the notations one more time before he got started.

But at last he played the opening chord, and moved through the rest of the piece—which, admittedly, was a slow one, and not anything too complicated—without making a single misstep. When he was done, he glanced up at her, as if looking for her approval.

"That was great," she said. "You're a natural."

He chuckled at that comment. "I am not sure I would say that. But music appears to be highly mathematical, and that means it has a structure I can grasp quite easily."

That it was. Sarah had never approached music that way, because she was far more interested in the emotional impact of a piece than the complex calculations involved in writing it, but even she knew about music's direct correlation to mathematics.

"Well, let's give it a try," she said. Even as she spoke, she realized that she'd have to be the one to dissect her performance, to tell Abdul when they should stop so she could go over a phrase again, whether to shift emphasis or decide on where she thought was the best place to pause and take a breath. That should have been her voice coach's job, but because he'd been lost with so many countless others during the Heat, there wasn't anyone left to do this for her.

All the same, she thought they'd go through the song once without stopping, just so she could refamiliarize herself with the piece. After that, she could start tearing it apart.

She nodded at Abdul. "Go ahead, and we'll see what happens."

He had already thought her voice beautiful. But after nearly two hours of working on that one Italian song with her, he realized she was also a perfectionist. By now he'd lost count of the times she'd made him stop and back up so they could repeat a particular phrase over and over, with her trying one tiny variation and then another, doing whatever she could to make her singing both technically flawless and full of emotion at the same time.

Oddly, the process felt almost exhausting to him—he, who had never been physically tired in all his very long life. However, if Sarah could keep at this without flagging, then he would do no less.

After all, practicing with her had been his idea in the first place.

Eventually, though, she sent him a weary smile and said, "That's probably enough for now. Want to break for lunch?"

He did. Sitting there and playing had been more of an exertion than he'd expected, and his stomach told him it was now well past the noon hour, and they probably should have stopped to eat long before this.

"On the patio?" he asked, and she nodded.

"I could use some fresh air."

They went outside. While he was often fine with preparing his meals, there was no way in the world he would exert himself now, not when they both needed to eat as soon as possible. Instead, he summoned a pitcher of iced tea and a salad fresh with mandarin oranges and chicken and almond slivers, a dish Sarah dug into almost as soon as it appeared in front of her.

"How did you know this was exactly what I needed?"

"Because it was what I needed as well?"

She looked up from her plate then, a smile touching her full mouth. Today she had been in such a hurry to come out and see what he was doing in the music room, she hadn't bothered to put on even the faint cosmetics she wore at other times. However, he didn't think she needed them, not when both her lips and her cheeks were flushed with happy color, an obvious byproduct of their time spent practicing.

Yes, he thought some part of her was beginning to come alive again, and he could not help being cheered by that.

"Maybe so," she said. "You did an awesome job accompanying me today. Sorry about all the fits and starts."

At times, it had been somewhat frustrating. Then again, he'd also found himself fascinated by all the nuance she'd drawn out of the simple piece, the way it sounded so completely different when they'd finished than when they'd begun. Up until now, he had been a consumer of music and nothing other than that, and he knew he would always be grateful to her for showing him how it could be so much more.

"There is nothing to apologize for," he told her. "This was practice, not a performance. It was very educational."

Her nose wrinkled as she reached for her glass of iced tea. "I suppose that's one word for it. All the same, it's not like we have to go at this day and night. If nothing else, my voice will need time to rest and recuperate. So, what should we do this afternoon?"

Something warmed in him at how she'd so casually said "we," as if it was understood that they would spend the afternoon in some kind of shared activity rather than going their separate ways until dinner. Not so very long ago, he would have laughed at the idea that he needed any kind of companionship...let alone human companion-ship...to fill the empty hours.

Now, though, he could only be glad that Sarah seemed to enjoy being around him just as much as he enjoyed being around her.

"Perhaps we could explore the labyrinth?" he suggested. "We did not have enough time yesterday after we got back from our ride, but you did say you wanted to see it."

"I do," she said at once. "That sounds like a great way to spend some time outside. If," she added with an ominous glance up at the sky, "the weather cooperates."

As they had for the past several days, clouds

had begun to gather to the south and east. However, Abdul guessed they were still far enough away that they should not interfere with his and Sarah's visit to the labyrinth, an excursion that should not take them more than an hour or so.

"It will be fine," he replied.

She seemed to be content with that reassurance, because she only nodded and returned to her salad.

He did so as well, glad that he had come up with a way for them to spend even more time together.

Now all he had to do was continue to make her happy.

The labyrinth was larger than Sarah had expected, stretching at least a hundred yards across, if not more. This wasn't a maze out of some English garden—or like the crazy obstacle course in that one Harry Potter book—but rather rows of rocks carefully laid out in the sandy soil. She would have thought it would be easy enough to find her way out without any tall bushes blocking the line of sight...and then she realized navigating through the complex pattern was a lot trickier than she'd first believed.

"Have you been through this before?" she

asked Abdul after they had to go back to the beginning for a third time.

"I have," he said in the grave way of his, the one she thought was more charming than she wanted to admit to herself. "But I did not want to give away the secret."

"If we keep going around and around like this, I might have to wheedle it out of you," she replied with a grin.

How she wished she could see whether he smiled in response!

But, as much as she'd wanted to play Christine Daaé, there was no way in the world Sarah would copy the actions of the musical's heroine by reaching out to pull back Abdul's hood. Whatever his reasons for concealing himself, she needed to respect them... even as she found herself wondering more and more exactly why he felt the need to hide in such a way.

He shook his head. "I am afraid I don't bend to wheedling."

No, he probably didn't. On the other hand, he'd acceded to almost every request of hers...save the most important one of all.

Not for the first time, her traitor brain whispered that it might not be so bad to stay here. Beautiful scenery, an accommodating companion...the chance to practice her singing as much as she wanted.

Put that way, it sure sounded as though she'd landed in clover, even if she doubted that Abdul's reasons for keeping her here had been all that benign.

At least, in the beginning.

"Then I suppose I'll just have to figure it out for myself," she said, doing her best to keep her tone light.

She returned her attention to the labyrinth, scanning the maze of little stone pathways. A few feet from where she stood, there was a small opening, one she hadn't noticed before.

"Let's go that way," she told Abdul, pointing.

"Lead on."

They passed through the narrow gap between the rocks, and this time, she was pretty sure she'd set them on the correct path. The walkways twisted in and around one another, but she realized as long as she kept turning left, they would make it to the center of the labyrinth.

Which they did a few minutes later. It was an open area a few feet across, with gravel laid in the pattern of a many-rayed sun. Over the years, the design had begun to wear away, but it was still recognizable enough.

As if to counter the sun pattern beneath their feet, a cloud passed overhead, dimming the light. Sarah looked up and saw that the thunderheads that had been massing to the east had already begun to drift this way.

Actually, they'd done a lot more than just drift. Now the sky was clear enough to the west, but all around them, the day had already started to darken.

Thunder rumbled, and she glanced over at Abdul. "Maybe we should head back."

He inclined his head toward the stormy sky. "Probably a good idea."

They'd only retraced a few yards of their steps before the landscape lit up with a brilliant flash of light, and thunder growled almost immediately afterward.

How close was that? A mile?

Most likely, not even that.

Definitely not the kind of conditions where you wanted to be outside with at least a five-minute walk to get to any kind of shelter.

Another flash, and then rain began to pour down on them, plastering Sarah's hair to her skull and already beginning to soak through Abdul's heavy linen robe.

Not a single word, but he grasped her by the hands and pulled her to him. She let out a shocked gasp, and the world around them disappeared for a vertigo-inducing second before they re-emerged in the much more comfortable surroundings of the living room.

"That was crazy," she said, reaching up to push a lock of wet hair away from her forehead.

"It was," he replied. "My apologies for our precipitous departure, but I thought it better to get us out of the storm. Even a djinn does not much enjoy getting struck by lightning."

No, probably not. Sarah looked down at her sodden clothing—even as she noticed that somehow Abdul had already either dried his robe or exchanged it for a new one—and said, "I should probably get changed."

"You should," he agreed. "Perhaps you would like some hot tea or chocolate?"

Maybe hot chocolate on a June afternoon was sort of crazy, but right then, it sounded delicious.

"Hot chocolate would be perfect," she said. "Be back in a minute."

She hurried off to her bedroom, where she peeled off the soaked silk tunic and pants she'd been wearing, and exchanged them for one of the dresses Abdul had provided. It had three-quarter sleeves and might turn out to be too warm if the sun reappeared at some point, but right now she felt chilled all over and wanted to be comfortable.

A minute to blot her hair and comb it through, and then she returned to the living room, where Abdul already had a pair of big mugs filled with hot chocolate sitting on the coffee table.

"I did not know whether you wanted marshmallows," he said. He had been waiting on the sofa and obviously expected her to sit there as well.

They'd never been seated so close before, but she told herself that he'd already taken her by the arms, so sitting down a foot away from him honestly didn't seem like that big a deal.

"Marshmallows would be great," she replied. She'd had cocoa this way a few times after coming to live in Los Alamos, but eventually, the marshmallows had disappeared, just like so many other items that couldn't be easily replaced with the resources and technology the survivors there had on hand.

At once, the surface of both cups of hot chocolate bobbed with miniature marshmallows. Sarah reached out to lift the mug to her lips and took a sip that included one of the soft little white pillows of rich, sugary goodness.

That was probably the best marshmallow she'd ever had, creamy and not as sweet as she'd expected, and the hot chocolate was the same way, dark and satisfying, tasting like it had been made with the real stuff and not some powdered junk out of a can.

"This is amazing," she said. "I don't think I've ever had a better cup of hot chocolate, not even at this fancy place in Santa Fe I visited one time."

"I am glad you like it," Abdul replied.

Lightning flashed in the storm-darkened room, and the thunder that pounded a second later was so loud, it sounded as if it must have been directly overhead.

"Good thing we came inside when we did," Sarah remarked.

Abdul sipped from his mug of hot chocolate, then inclined his head. "Yes, this storm is quite a violent one. That was why I thought it better to whisk us away at once."

"Definitely a good call." For some reason, she couldn't quite ignore the way she seemed to still feel the pressure of his fingers on her wrists, gripping them tightly so there would be no chance of her slipping away while they traveled in that instantaneous but still scary djinn fashion. "I could say I'm surprised it blew in so quickly, but weather in New Mexico is like that."

"Yes, I am beginning to understand that one should not take it lightly." He set down his mug and gazed out the picture window that overlooked the valley below. With the rain coming down like this, you could only see about a hundred feet at best, and Sarah knew that the washes and creeks they'd explored over the past couple of days must be filled to the brim already, raging and rushing as they made their way down to the Rio Chama.

She remembered how Abdul had told her that he'd only been here for a week or so, which explained why he wasn't yet familiar with how these summer storms could come out of seemingly nowhere.

"Well, no harm, no foul," she said, and he cocked his head at her.

"I beg your pardon?"

It seemed that, while his English appeared to be near-perfect, he still had some trouble with human idioms.

And honestly, she couldn't say for sure where the phrase had even come from.

"I think it's a baseball thing," she explained. "When the pitcher throws a ball and it goes outside the foul lines, then it's a foul. But the saying is more like, nobody got hurt, so it's all good."

"Interesting."

He picked up his mug of hot chocolate and drank again, and Sarah did the same. Although she supposed it could have been awkward for the two of them to be sitting here like this, somehow she didn't mind at all. No, she kind of liked knowing he was right there, ready to protect her no matter what.

Which, she told herself immediately, was stupid. She could manage just fine on her own and didn't need anyone—let alone a djinn who happened to be holding her prisoner—to keep her safe.

But still...he'd immediately leaped into action once he knew how real the danger was, standing out there in the storm. Sure, she could have hurried up her strong, independent ass and bolted for the house, and yet there was no guarantee she would have made it inside before one of those lightning bolts decided she was an excellent target.

Although the two of them had shared plenty of moments when they were both quiet and didn't feel any need to speak, right then, Sarah thought the silence seemed a bit too awkward.

Or maybe that was just her realizing that she was thinking a bit too kindly of Abdul than she probably should.

"And this is just the beginning of monsoon season," she went on, knowing the words were coming out a little too fast but not sure how to stop herself. "It usually really starts to crank up in July and August, and it's just barely June now."

He set down his mug and got up from the sofa, moving toward the window. The rain still poured down and thunder still rumbled, although the seconds between lightning flashes and echoing rumbles seemed to be increasing, a sign that the storm had begun to move away.

"I like these monsoons of yours," he commented. "The skies in the otherworld never did anything like this."

"The otherworld," Sarah ventured. "That's where the djinn lived before they came here, right?"

"Yes," Abdul said. "It is a place that never

changes. Or rather, while the colors in the sky may shift and boil, there is nothing like terrestrial weather there. It simply...is."

She picked up her mug of hot chocolate and made her way over to the window. Not too close to Abdul, but near enough that they wouldn't have to carry on their conversation from across the room.

"I can see why this would be better," she said. Rain streamed down the windowpanes, and wild winds caught at the cottonwoods and oaks that ringed the house, but all that frenzy only served to make it feel even cozier inside. This was partly why almost everyone she'd ever known—whether back in her old life in Albuquerque or among the survivors in Los Alamos—looked forward to this time of year. The storms were a break from the unrelenting heat of summer, a way to remind themselves that cooler days weren't too far off.

Abdul continued to gaze out the window for a moment, apparently watching the way the rain streamed down in sheets and turned the brick-paved courtyard into a shallow lake. Then he shifted so he looked at Sarah.

"Yes," he said. "This is much better."

Chapter 15

WAS THIS DESIRE? THIS ACHING NEED TO be with her, to see her, to hear her sweet voice, whether she was speaking or singing?

Abdul found it difficult to say, for he had never experienced such emotions before. He only knew that every moment he spent with Sarah, he felt simultaneously more alive...and yet more frustrated...than he ever had in his very long life.

She knew nothing of him. Only the public face —well, the public hood—that he allowed her to see. She did not know what he had done, how he was an utter walking horror, both inside and out.

Very much like the Phantom from her beloved musical, except that tormented genius had not borne a burden even one-thousandth of what Abdul carried from day to day.

Sarah had not guessed any of that, of course. No, although she had been reluctant to practice at first, now...after she'd drunk some lemon water to clear the dregs of hot chocolate from her throat... she seemed eager to return to the music room to use the rest of the afternoon in more vocal exercises. Some time to warm up, and now she moved on from the first Italian song they'd practiced to an aria from an actual opera.

Listening to her sing was like watching a long-caged bird finally take flight and fly free on the wind. At the same time, he thought he understood what she had meant when she'd said earlier that hers was not a voice for opera. It was lighter, sweeter, possibly not designed to carry to the farthest reaches of a concert hall with no need for artificial amplification.

And that, he thought, was why he loved it all the more. Her voice was like her, clear and brilliant and pure, and while he was gladder than he could have ever believed that she had somehow stumbled into his life, at the same time, he could not help wondering how a creature of such shimmering loveliness would react if she ever she learned of all the darkness he hid in his soul.

She must never find out, of course. So far, she had not seemed inclined to pry when he steered their conversations away from subjects he thought might be troublesome, and he must do whatever he could to ensure their situation remained much the same. It seemed to him that she was happy here, happy to practice when the mood took her or to ramble through the countryside when she desired some fresh air.

Or to sit next to him on the couch and not even flinch when he reached for his cocoa...or when he'd taken hold of her arms to rescue her from the storm.

It had been harder than he'd thought to release her once they were safely inside the house, for an impulse had taken hold of him, one that told him to draw her closer, to press his mouth against hers.

Such a thing could never happen, of course. It was one thing for the djinn to take their human lovers, their Chosen, and quite another for a being such as he to even dream of kissing a mortal.

And yet, he could not quite dismiss the notion from his mind.

That night, they shared a quiet meal; the rain still came down—which Sarah told him was unusual, as these storms usually did their work and moved on—although the thunder had mostly died away except for a distant rumble from time to time. They spoke of riding again if the ground wasn't too muddy, and more vocal practice. Commonplaces, of course, but that was fine with him. It was enough simply to have Sarah there, to hear her speak and to watch the candlelight gleam in her unusual blue-green eyes.

Or at least, it was almost enough.

Now more than ever he wished he could truly sleep, that instead of lying here with his gaze fixed on the ceiling, he might lose himself in even an hour or two of blessed oblivion, leaving aside all the burdens and worries of a very long life. Instead, though, something tugged at the outer edges of his consciousness, something that told him all was not as it seemed.

He frowned into the darkness, searching for the source of the wrongness.

That was it. A pair of intruders, wandering around the perimeter of the lake some five miles distant.

Surely they must have come in search of Sarah.

At once, he sat up in bed, angry blood racing through his veins. He could not help being angered by their temerity, for he had no doubt that if they had gone to the elders for counsel, they would have known that Ghost Ranch and its environs were strictly forbidden to mortals.

And yet, there they were. Abdul could not get any real sense of the intruders, except that they were two in number and male, but that was enough.

He pushed back the covers and got out of bed,

summoning his hooded robe to ensure he was properly concealed. On the other side of the house, Sarah slept soundly.

She would never know that he had left for a moment to handle some necessary business.

An eye blink brought him to Abiquiu Lake, where he paused to take his bearings. The landscape here was just as sodden as the one he had left behind, and he guessed the pair of interlopers were not passing a very comfortable night.

And yes, there they were, in a tent set up in one of the lake's former campgrounds. This close, he could sense the repelling field emanating outward from the device they must have hidden somewhere in their tent, but while its presence was an annoyance, it could not cripple his powers the way it might block those of a regular djinn.

A large truck was parked nearby, and yet Abdul could tell the two men slept in the tent rather than taking shelter in the truck's cab. It would perhaps have been drier in there, although he doubted they would have had enough room to stretch out.

The truck gave him pause, but only for a moment. While he had no idea where the men lived in Los Alamos—and he could not have sent the vehicle there even if he wanted to, thanks to the devices that protected the human settlement—he could at least blink it back to the border of the protected lands, well away from here.

A snap of his fingers and the bloated vehicle was gone. Unfortunately, he could not deal with humans in quite the same way, although he thought what he had in store for them was not anything they would soon forget.

Wind surged, sending his black robe fluttering...and wrapping the tent around the two men who had sheltered within, forming a sort of cocoon they could not easily escape. That same gale caught the tent and sent it into the air, whisking them away from the campground and following the course of the Rio Chama until Abdul knew it would deposit them close to the truck he had disposed of just a moment earlier.

There. If that did not send a message to stay far, far away, then he would just have to come up with something much more forceful the next time.

The walkie-talkie crackled to life. As usual, Lindsay had it with her at the lab, since it was the only way anyone could easily get in touch with her unless they wanted to drop everything and come see her in person. A few feet away, Miles lifted his head from the piece of Millerite he had placed under a microscope. As far as they'd been able to tell, the odd mineral discovered on the Miller farm in Cedar Crest would never provide enough long-lasting protection from the djinn to become a viable alternative to the devices he'd invented, but that didn't mean he didn't intend to keep working with it.

"Lindsay?"

Shawn Gutierrez's voice, cracked and hoarse and barely sounding like him.

At once, she set down the touchscreen she'd been holding and hurried to pick up the walkie. "Lindsay here. Are you all right?"

"Well, we're alive," Shawn said dryly. "So I guess that's better than the alternative. But I can tell you for sure that someone—or something—doesn't want us anywhere near Ghost Ranch. It grabbed my truck and then José and me, and dumped us just outside the protected zone. José has a broken ankle, and I've got a dislocated shoulder. And the truck won't start, so we need someone to come and get us."

Lindsay stared down at the walkie-talkie she held. What the hell had just happened?

What happened is that you ignored what Zahrias was trying to tell you, and now two of your men are hurt, she scolded herself.

But she would have plenty of time for self-recriminations later. Right now, the important thing was to get Shawn and José back to Los Alamos.

"Where are you?" she asked. "We'll get someone out there right away to pick you up."

"About a half mile north of La Chuachia, just past mile marker 143."

"Got it," she said. "Hang tight—we'll be there as fast as we can."

She set down the walkie-talkie, only to see Miles regarding her with grim gray eyes.

"You're not going."

"I am," she said. "It's my fault they're in this situation in the first place."

Although she knew her husband was not one for public displays of affection—or even not-so-public ones, since they were currently alone in the lab—he came over and took her hand, then pressed a kiss against her cheek.

"We're not going to talk about 'fault,'" he said. "What we're going to talk about is that this is still a potentially dangerous situation, and you're ten weeks pregnant. Brent and I will go."

Lindsay wanted to argue, but she knew Miles was right. Shawn and José were near the edge of the protected territory, not in it.

And that meant whatever had deposited them —and Shawn's truck—in that spot might still be lurking somewhere near, just waiting to pounce when the rescue party showed up.

"You'll take a device with you," she said, and Miles smiled.

He knew as well as she did that her comment was her way of saying she wouldn't protest...but she'd make damn sure her husband was as safe as possible.

"Of course," he replied, as though that was a given.

And it was. No one left the protected zone without one of the glassy little cubes in their possession.

He squeezed her hand, then reached for the walkie-talkie and shifted the channel.

"Brent?" he said a moment later. "Miles here. It looks like we have to go on a little rescue operation. Meet me at the lab with one of your trucks."

Abdul seemed in an unusually good mood this morning, although Sarah couldn't say exactly why. Maybe it was only that the storms of the day before were now well and gone, and the day outside was bright and fresh, the grass and the trees looking greener and lusher after their soaking.

And while the ground had to be muddy, they'd already planned to practice first and go riding later, so there was no reason to believe the trails wouldn't have recovered by the time they set out on their horses, especially with how rocky much of the soil was around here.

He offered her an omelet, and although she didn't usually eat something that heavy for breakfast, she decided to go with it today. Singing expended a lot of calories, and riding would use up some more, so she thought maybe Abdul knew what he was talking about.

Also, it wasn't something heavy with sausage and cheese, but a frittata lush with roasted bell peppers and onions and just a kiss of parmesan, so she thought that was all right.

In fact, it was so glorious outside that they had their breakfast on the patio. A few puddles remained from the previous night's storm, but because the table had been placed under an enormous sun sail, that part of the courtyard was dry.

"What did you want to work on today?" Abdul asked as she reached for the bowl of sliced strawberries he'd placed next to her plate.

Sarah had been thinking about that very topic as she washed her hair this morning. It had been good to dive back into the songs and arias that had been the bread and butter of her vocal training, but she knew her voice was better suited for musical theater than opera. And while she at first thought that maybe she'd play it safe and choose something from *Beauty and the Beast,* since she'd also performed in that musical...even though she knew Belle's story was fraught as well...she decided it was probably better to really face the music, so to speak, and return to the work that she'd never been able to sing in public.

"Oh, something from *Phantom*," she said casually. "Since I heard you playing 'Think of Me' the other day, it's not like you'd have to learn something new. Does that work?"

"Very much," Abdul replied. "I'm glad to hear you're ready to sing those pieces."

He didn't say anything more than that, but it was enough. In a way, Sarah was relieved to see that he didn't seem inclined to ask her to elaborate, to explain why she had decided now was the time to go back to the musical that had meant so much to her.

To be fair, she wasn't sure if she could have adequately explained the change of heart even to herself. Maybe it was that she felt oddly safe here with Abdul, and if she crashed and burned, or began to sing and then decided she couldn't go on, she somehow knew he wouldn't press the issue or try to convince her to work through her mental blocks.

No, at most he would probably ask if she wanted to switch to a different piece, or maybe suggest that she should take a break and go outside for a walk or something. After all, he wasn't her coach, a person who knew he needed to press and challenge her, only someone happy to see her doing anything at all with her voice.

"It's a plan, then," she said, glad that she sounded so steady.

The real trick would be seeing if she remained that steady once she began to sing.

Abdul still found himself somewhat surprised that Sarah had decided to practice a piece from *The Phantom of the Opera,* but he hadn't asked any questions. Perhaps he was being overly fearful, but he couldn't help thinking that if he'd been too inquisitive, she would have shut down and decided to go back to something safer.

And it was true that he'd already played the song she had chosen, so it wasn't as though they would have to waste any time while he quickly taught himself something new.

When she walked over to the piano, she had her chin up, as if she was inwardly schooling herself to maintain control no matter what happened. He had heard the song—had listened to the original recording, which he'd summoned to his audio library, as well as a piano solo as part of his preparations—and yet he still found himself growing tense as she positioned herself in the curve of the instrument and took a breath. Today she wore the white dress he had provided for her, and he thought she had never looked so lovely as she did right then, with her dark hair providing a contrast to the pale garment, her posture proud and oddly vulnerable at the same time.

"*Think of me,*" she began, and her voice was breathy, hesitant.

Abdul frowned inside his hood...even as he reminded himself that the original song had begun in that very same way. Christine Daaé, unsure of herself, being thrust into the spotlight before she thought she was ready, despite her tutelage by the Phantom.

And then her voice swelling as she gained confidence, just as Sarah got her wind now, the sound carrying clear and pure to every corner of the room, hair falling like a skein of dusky silk down her back, color flaring along her high cheekbones. Abdul's fingers paused on the keyboard so she could sing the final cadenza on her own, rippling up and down the scale until ascending to the double high A, a note that could have come out in a screech but instead was clear as a bell, reverberating throughout the space, until she ended with that final triumphant "me," just as he hit the final chord at the same time.

The sound died away, and for a moment, she only stood there, breasts rising and falling as she seemed to absorb what she had just done.

Bravi...bravi...bravissimi.

Abdul thought of the Phantom's praise for his pupil following her bravura performance, but he knew better than to utter those words aloud. The last thing he wanted was for Sarah to think there was anything remotely parallel about their circumstances.

Even if he knew there were far more resonances than he cared to admit.

"I can see why you were cast in the role," he said, and Sarah turned toward him, eyes shining, cheeks still flushed.

"Thank you. I—" She broke off there, as though she wasn't quite sure what she'd intended to say next. "I guess I needed to know whether I could still do it."

"Clearly, you can." He paused for a moment, wondering whether he should elaborate, then decided against it. If he pointed out that it was a tragedy the world had been deprived of hearing her sing, then she would only revisit the circumstances that had prevented her from doing such a thing, and he did not want her thoughts to linger on the Dying...or the reason why it had happened. Doing his best to sound neutral, he added, "Would you like to run through it again?"

Because while he thought her performance had been perfect, he also did not doubt that she would find something to nitpick about it.

As he'd expected, she nodded. "I think it's a good idea. Let's start with the part where I begin with, 'think of August.' I'm pretty sure I can do a better job with my breath control in that passage."

So they returned to the section of the song she'd indicated and ran through it several times. From there, they moved on to the cadenza. He had thought it perfect, but she wanted to cover it two, three, five times until she judged every note to be exactly where she wanted it to be.

At last, though, she stepped up to the bench where he sat and said, "Okay, that should do it for today. Thanks for being so patient with me."

He hadn't thought of it as being patient, but more being able to drink in every second he spent with her, every moment she sang and he could listen to the power and purity of her voice. Although he'd never been intoxicated—his body would not allow him to be affected by alcohol—he had to believe this was something like being drunk, to have the world feel as though it was somehow lighter and brighter, that all the weight of his grief and anger and guilt had been lifted, simply because she was there.

Of course, he could not allow her to know anything of what he had been thinking. No, she must only believe that he was pleased with the work she had done this morning but was now perfectly content to stop and have lunch, and then go for an afternoon ride.

If he could continue to make her think she was

of very little consequence to him, then perhaps she would never be frightened away by the force of his desire.

———

Both men looked bruised and haggard, José Padilla with his ankle in a cast and Shawn Gutierrez with his left arm in a sling. Miles and Brent had picked them up at the mile marker they'd indicated, then brought them back to Los Alamos. Despite his injuries, Shawn had been upset about having to leave his truck behind; Brent had taken a look under the hood, determined the cause of the problem was a blown fuel injection system, and promised to get it fixed once he was able to find the parts and have the truck towed to a garage in Española that they'd been using as a satellite motor pool location.

Now they were all sitting in the conference room at City Hall, where they'd been joined by Nora Almeida. With the entire town council in the room, Lindsay hoped they'd be able to get some answers as to what exactly had happened to the two men.

"We're not sure what it was," Shawn said. "We didn't really see anything."

"Nothing at all?" Miles replied, voice sharp. "How could you be dropped some fifteen miles from where you started without being able to see a single bit of what was happening to you?"

José made an impatient gesture. "There was this crazy wind that came out of nowhere. I mean, the weather had been rough that afternoon, lots of thunder and rain, but things kind of died down after sunset. But then we heard some kind of weird popping sound—"

"That we think was probably the truck getting zapped out of there," Shawn cut in, and the other man gave him an annoyed look.

"Yeah, maybe it was the truck. Anyway, the next thing we knew, this wind came along and blew down the tent, and then somehow it got wrapped around us and we were flying through the air—"

"You were *flying?*" Lindsay asked. Maybe it had been rude to interrupt José like that, but she was having a hard time believing any of this.

Shawn started to shrug, then winced, remembering too late the arm that had just recently been popped back into its socket, thanks to the first aid delivered by Ellen O'Dell, Los Alamos' resident nurse practitioner. "Well, maybe 'hurtling' is a better word. It's not like we were controlling any of it. But something wrapped that tent around us and then basically threw us fifteen miles."

For a moment, no one spoke. Miles's eyes met hers, and Lindsay gave a very small shake of her head.

None of this made any sense. She knew that djinn could do some crazy stuff, but she'd never heard of any of them pulling a stunt like this one.

Then again, they weren't necessarily dealing with your regular garden-variety djinn here. If the elders were the ones who'd drop-kicked Shawn and José some fifteen miles or so, then Lindsay supposed all bets were off...even as she really didn't want to consider the implications of the elders acting in such an openly hostile manner

Nora's plump, friendly features were troubled. "I understand why you thought you needed to try again to find Sarah," she said. "But after what happened last night, I don't think we can risk it anymore. Who's to say what might happen if we keep sending people to rescue her?"

Not anything that Lindsay wanted to contemplate. Everything she'd heard about the djinn elders seemed to indicate they were a calm, measured group whose biggest failing was standing back and choosing not to interfere even when a lot of the people involved might have preferred a little assistance. For them to do something as crazy as bundling José and Shawn up in a tent and then tossing them more than a dozen miles seemed very out of character.

On the other hand, if there was one thing she'd learned about the djinn over the years, it was that they were full of surprises.

"We're not going to keep sending people," Miles said, his voice flat. Although he much preferred to let everyone on the town council have an equal say in the decisions they made, there had been several occasions when he'd used his position as first among equals—as the man who'd created the invention that had kept them all alive for so long—to lay down the law.

"Whatever's going on with Sarah Wolfe, she's going to have to rescue herself."

Chapter 16

EVEN THOUGH SARAH HAD ONLY BEEN AT Abdul's house for three days now, they'd already fallen into a sort of routine. Practice in the morning—maybe extending into the afternoon, depending on how she felt about where her voice was that particular day—and then some kind of outdoor excursion, whether a trail ride like this one, or their exploration of the labyrinth the day before.

Today, a strange lightness had settled over her, as if some part of her recognized that nothing about this was going to change and she might as well make the best of it. Not that doing so was terribly difficult, considering the way her djinn captor had done everything he could to make her stay here as comfortable as possible.

And she'd sung *Phantom* again. True, the easier

of Christine's solo pieces—she still didn't know for sure whether she would be able to get through "Wishing You Were Somehow Here Again" without at least choking up, let alone sobbing outright—but still, that was a massive mental hurdle she hadn't believed she'd ever be able to clear.

With Abdul's help, though, she'd made her way through "Think of Me," had even been able to summon the detachment to identify the problematic passages and run through them again and again until she was able to sing them to her usual perfecting standards.

That was a leap she couldn't ignore...and she doubted she would have ever gotten there if it hadn't been for Abdul's support.

Today there wasn't a single cloud in the sky, so she didn't think they'd have a repeat of the afternoon before, when pouring rain had chased them out of the labyrinth. In a way, Sarah was a little sorry about that. Somewhere deep down, she knew she wouldn't mind if he took her by the hand again...or even did a little more than that.

But he'd been all business the entire time, so she understood he would only be her accompanist and cheerleader, and she had to be okay with that. If he'd cared about having a human partner, a Chosen, then he would have selected someone way back when the decision was made to inflict the

Heat on the world, and he would have joined the other conscientious objectors in Santa Fe or one of the other djinn/Chosen communities scattered around the globe.

She told herself it was fine. In a lot of ways, this was a dream existence for her—no unending mindless work, the ability to practice as much as she liked and to spend the rest of her days out in nature or reading or whatever else seemed to be the best use of her time at any particular moment.

Even though she knew she was content...for now...she couldn't quite stop herself from wondering why no one from Los Alamos had ever come looking for her.

It seemed his removal of the two interlopers from the campground at Abiquiu Lake had done the job, because the days that followed were quiet, with no sign that anyone else from Los Alamos intended to come sniffing around, looking for their lost explorer.

And Abdul had to be glad of that, because it meant he was free to spend this time with Sarah, listening to her voice blossom even further like a rose opening its petals to the sun, or to wander the countryside with her, sometimes on horseback, sometimes not, depending on their mood on any particular day.

He had even decided that it would be good to have her help in the kitchen, so now they gathered there with the ingredients he assembled for their evening meals, and she assisted with chopping or stirring or whatever else might be required. She always seemed willing to act as his sous chef and appeared content with his explanation that he enjoyed being more hands-on with these sorts of tasks rather than using his powers to do everything.

All in all, the two of them had achieved a domestic harmony he thought many might envy, but underneath it all was still the gnawing worry that one day she might discover the truth about him, and the careful façade of amity and goodwill would collapse like the house of cards he knew it to be.

"What did you do all day in the otherworld?" she asked that night at dinner, and he set down his fork and gave her a startled look.

"Why do you ask?"

Her shoulders lifted. That night she wore a dress in a deep mulberry shade that enhanced the green in her eyes and made her skin seem to glow. Every day he saw her, she seemed more beautiful than the last, but perhaps that was simply because he learned a little more of her with every moment they spent together.

"I suppose I was thinking about all the things we've been doing here," she replied. "My singing practice takes up a lot of time, and you wouldn't have been doing anything like that in the other-world, right?"

"No," he said. "We djinn were not much for artistic pursuits, although there were some who took on the difficult task of bringing plants from this world to that one, and expending a good deal of effort on keeping them alive."

"Because the air isn't the same."

Abdul had told her that during one of their previous conversations, but he was cheered to see she remembered the detail. "Precisely. But for many of us, we spent a great deal of time constructing our palaces and then redoing those sections of them that no longer suited us, or which perhaps we had grown weary of. It was a pursuit that could occupy a great amount of time."

A nod. That night, they had made a bounty of Indian dishes, a task that had required the dirtying of many pots and pans and bowls, and now she pushed at the chicken korma on her plate while she seemed to contemplate what he'd just told her. Then a smile touched her lips.

"No wonder you wanted to remodel this place as soon as you moved in."

"I did," he said. "The footprint of the house

was well enough, but I changed the kitchen and the living spaces to more closely suit my needs."

"All with the snap of a finger."

"Or only an intention," he responded. "It is not necessary to perform a physical action to get the reaction we require. It is enough to merely think of a thing."

Yes, some djinn did like to snap their fingers or wave a hand to accomplish that which could be affected by thought alone, but although he indulged himself from time to time, Abdul generally did not waste his energy on such outward shows.

Then again, he'd never had anyone around to witness him calling material items into being, so there had been no reason to perform as though he had an audience.

For some reason, Sarah's smile broadened. "It's too bad you didn't reveal yourselves back before. I can just imagine some of the HGTV shows you could have starred in—*Djinn Makeover*, or *Djinn House in an Instant*."

Abdul had no idea what HGTV was...or, more precisely, what it had been...but from the context, he assumed she was talking about some sort of television channel. And while he knew that none of the djinn would have been foolish enough to make their identities public back then, he had to admit the idea was somewhat amusing.

"Unfortunately," he said, "we can now only think of what might have been."

Some of the cheerful light went out of her eyes then. "Yes, I suppose that's what a lot of people do these days."

Damn it, he should have paid more attention to what he was saying. The last thing he wanted was for Sarah to start thinking of what the world might have been like if the djinn hadn't intervened and everything had gone on as before.

It would have continued on a headlong course into oblivion, he thought, but he knew now was not the time to speak of such things.

Thinking it best to steer their conversation in other directions, he said, "But even though this house pleases me well enough, there is still a great deal I would like to do to the grounds."

"Oh?" Sarah said. She now appeared a little brighter, as though she, too, was glad to avoid stepping into such fraught territory. "I thought what you did down by the visitors center was all the improvements you planned to make."

"No, that was only the beginning, nothing more. I thought I would create an herb garden and perhaps a kitchen garden as well, so I might grow a good deal of what I need. Perhaps roses and more trees, and grass, too. This part of the world in general does not support large lawns very well, but

I know I can summon whatever water might be required to keep them thriving."

Her brows lifted. "Really? So...you're a water elemental?"

Right then, he wanted to curse himself for his carelessness. The entire time she'd been here, he'd made sure not to do anything in front of her that would point to him having a particular kind of elemental talent over another and had only used the sorts of powers that any djinn possessed. He certainly did not want her to guess that he controlled all of the elements because he was not precisely a djinn in the way she thought of them.

However, he also had gathered that her knowledge of the djinn was limited at best, and had only been gleaned from conversations with her fellow survivors, not from any of the elementals themselves or even observing them in person. Because of that, he guessed he should be able to obfuscate easily enough.

"That sort of calling of water is something any djinn can do," he replied, evading her question. "It makes gardening much easier."

"Got it," she said, then paused, her expression growing thoughtful. "I wouldn't have the garden be too manicured, though. The country around here is so wild, I think the yard surrounding the house should have a certain wildness to it, too." When he didn't comment right away, she hurried on, "I mean, it's just a suggestion. You should do what you want with it."

Because she looked concerned that she might have overstepped, Abdul knew he needed to immediately allay her fears.

"It's an excellent suggestion," he said. "One I will definitely consider when I begin work on the garden. Perhaps tomorrow, if the weather is fine."

"That sounds like fun," she replied with a grin. "As long as you don't want me out there digging holes or something."

The last thing he would ever do was expect that kind of manual labor from her. It was one thing to companionably chop vegetables together in the kitchen, but he would not ask her to perform tasks that might harden her pretty hands or allow her to get burned from too much time in the sun. Already the small cuts and scrapes and rough spots on her fingers from her work assignments in Los Alamos had begun to fade, and he wanted that trend to continue.

"No digging holes," he said. "But you may counsel me on the colors of roses you prefer, and let me know if there are any other flowers you might like."

"That I can do," she replied. Now something about her expression grew sober, as though she'd just realized that making these sorts of plans together meant he intended to keep her here at

Ghost Ranch for a very long time. But then she seemed to gather herself, adding, "I am very partial to irises."

Something they wouldn't be able to plant until the autumn...and wouldn't appear until the following spring.

Yes, it seemed she was beginning to understand that her tenure here would be of quite some duration.

Eight days. When Sarah awoke the next morning, she realized this was the eighth time she'd opened her eyes to this room, the eighth time that she'd understood she was a captive in Abdul's house.

All right, she didn't feel much like a captive anymore, but still, their conversation at dinner the evening before had laid bare the reality that she wouldn't be going anywhere anytime soon.

Or ever.

The problem was, she honestly didn't know what she was supposed to feel about that.

As she got out of bed and headed into the shower, she thought of the original version of *The Phantom of the Opera,* the one written by Gaston Leroux. She'd read it as part of her preparation for playing Christine, figuring it couldn't hurt to go back to the source material to get some extra insight into the character. Quite a few of the differences between the book and its theater adaptation surprised her, but what really jumped out was how long Christine had stayed in the Phantom's underground lair when he kidnapped her from the stage of the opera house. It was a detail that had been kind of glossed over in the musical version, but in reality, she'd been down there for a full two weeks.

Back then, Sarah had only wondered what the heck the two of them had done during all that time. Now she realized there was quite a bit you could do to while away the hours spent with your captor...well, as long as he was of a musical bent.

However, she wasn't sure if "musical" was the best way to describe Abdul. He'd acquired the skill of playing the piano because he'd realized he needed to do so to accompany her while she practiced. It wasn't as if he spent hours in the music room composing his own works, or working out the fingering on Chopin's *Fantaisie Impromptu in C# Minor*, a piece known for its fiendishly difficult notation.

She wasn't sure what she should think about that. In a way, it would have been a lot better if he'd been musical all on his own, because at least then she would know he wasn't playing merely to better serve her needs.

But she'd been going with the flow for the past week-plus, and she knew she'd better continue to do so for the foreseeable future. Questioning Abdul's motivations for being so utterly of service to her didn't seem like a very good idea; otherwise, she'd have to make herself think about where all this was going to end up.

She also couldn't let herself brood over what was happening in Los Alamos, how worried they must be. It seemed clear enough that she wasn't going anywhere, and fretting over their reaction to her disappearance wouldn't change anything.

Instead, she took a long, hot shower, and then, because she knew they'd be working in the garden today, put on some jeans and her hiking boots and a loose, gauzy shirt that breathed but would still give her some protection from the sun. No, it wasn't as glamorous as most of the other outfits Abdul had provided, but it would do for their planned activities.

No response that she could see when she entered the living room and saw him standing at the kitchen island and sipping coffee, but then, she hadn't expected one. It still frustrated her that he hid his face, preventing her from getting a good read on all his reactions, although she knew better than to ask him to remove the hood.

Unlike dinner, which he always seemed to want to do the hard way, he summoned their breakfasts each morning. Today he asked what she would like, and she told him she'd like a breakfast burrito with bacon and lots of cheese.

Utterly fattening, of course, but even though she knew she wasn't going to be digging holes, she figured she would still be standing around a good bit and maybe helping to plant roses and herbs and whatnot, so she figured the extra calories shouldn't be too much of a problem.

To her surprise, Abdul conjured the same meal for himself, remarking, "I had heard of these breakfast burritos, but I have never had one. This seemed like as good a time as any to rectify that lack."

"You're in for a treat," she told him. "They're delicious. Also, since they were invented in New Mexico, it's only fitting that you should start eating them."

"Breakfast burritos came from here?" he asked. "I did not know that."

"Well, it's the urban legend, anyway," Sarah replied. "I suppose they could have first appeared in Texas or Arizona or California, too. But New Mexicans were always into their food, so I can see why someone might have come up with the idea here."

"Interesting," Abdul observed, but he didn't ask any further questions.

Probably a good thing, since the story was one she remembered her father telling her in high school, and she'd never found the need to follow up with some research, not when she had so many other more important matters clamoring for her time back then.

But the burritos he summoned were delicious, filled with fluffy scrambled eggs and crisp bacon and lush cheddar cheese, along with just enough green chile to make them fun and spicy without having her tongue on fire for the next half-hour. And after they were done, they headed out to the open area behind the house that served as its yard, although, since it wasn't fenced, Sarah didn't know for sure how much of the land Abdul planned to develop.

She should have known he would take care of that before he did anything else. Not even a wave of a hand, but as she gazed out at the scrubby grass and occasional spiny cholla cactus, a split-rail fence appeared out of nowhere, closing in what she thought was maybe an acre or so of land. It wouldn't keep out any marauding coyotes, most likely, but at least it defined the area he wanted to work.

"The herb garden over there," he said, pointing to the patch of land immediately behind the kitchen, and at once it was neatly tilled, with basil and thyme and rosemary and other plants she didn't recognize growing in tidy little rows. "And then the vegetables."

Just beyond the herbs, another piece of land

became similarly covered in happy, lush plants, tomatoes and zucchini and beans and eggplant, and even several rows of tall corn taking up the rear.

"That was easy," she remarked, and he shrugged.

"I told you we would not be digging any holes."

That was for sure. And who was she to argue, when all those fun veggies and herbs told her she could probably convince Abdul to make eggplant parmesan in the very near future?

"Fair enough," she said. "Now the roses?"

"I believe so." He was silent for a moment, surveying the undeveloped side of the property. "But I think that needs a bit more thought. Some trees, and perhaps a fountain somewhere?"

As he spoke, a line of poplars sprang into place along the eastern edge of the fence, with a couple of sycamores a little closer to where they stood. A gravel path appeared out of nowhere, and along with it, a small water feature nestled beneath the trees that included an artfully constructed stack of rocks on one side to create a waterfall.

"I like that," Sarah told him. "Especially since you can't really see the pond on the other side of the house when you're standing out here. Every place can use a little water."

Even in the desert, where that resource was as

precious as gold. But then, they didn't need to worry about water anymore, not with so few people to use it up, and not with the way the monsoons had gotten so much wetter over the past couple of years.

"I am glad," Abdul replied. "Now we can consider the roses. Which colors would you like to see?"

She almost replied that she loved all of them— her mother had left behind a rose garden when she died, and although Sarah's father had been too heartbroken to tend to the flowers himself, he'd at least made sure to hire gardeners to keep them alive and give them all the love and care they needed. Those roses had grown in a riot of color, red and pink and yellow and white and lilac, but she didn't know if that kind of jumble would work as well here, not with the stark rocks of Ghost Ranch as a backdrop. No, this garden needed something that would blend better with the landscape.

"Red, of course," she said. "And that pretty kind that's sort of cream-colored but has the red along its edges? Yellow, too, and something sort of apricot or salmon."

"That is a good combination," Abdul agreed. He gazed out at the empty space between the water feature and the house, and out of nowhere, rose-bushes appeared, fully grown and laden with blooms in the same shades Sarah had suggested a moment earlier.

Even as dry as the air was that day, their scent seemed to be everywhere, sweet and piercing at the same time. She breathed it in, thinking it had been a very long time since she'd smelled roses like that. A few people grew them in Los Alamos, but most of the town's inhabitants were more concerned with cultivating edible plants and herbs, so there wasn't anything close to a real rose garden there.

"It's wonderful," she said. "And it's going to be so nice to look out the kitchen window now and see all this growing here instead of just dirt and weeds and cholla cactus."

"That was why I suggested it," he replied. "And, of course, there is a great deal to be said for using fresh herbs and vegetables, something that transcends what I can summon for our meals."

She'd heard much the same thing from people who were into gardening in the before times, but she'd always been so busy back then that the thought of trying to grow anything on her own hadn't even entered her mind. They had fresh stuff in Los Alamos, true, although it all went into a communal pot and you could never be sure of what you were getting from week to week. Fresh, homegrown tomatoes were amazing, but she could have happily skipped the lima beans.

"Then we'll need to make something special

with them tonight," she said. "Eggplant parmesan, or ratatouille, or...well, you can probably come up with a lot more ideas than I can."

"Not really," Abdul replied. "I think eggplant parmesan is an excellent idea. And we can make some fresh rolls to go with it, and perhaps a salad with other items from the garden. It is probably good to have a meal without meat every once in a while."

A kind of eating she'd experimented with from time to time during college, thinking it might make her a little leaner and meaner when she was practicing extra hard for an upcoming performance.

Besides, skipping meat tonight would be easy enough after having that amazing breakfast burrito just a little while ago.

"Sounds like a plan," she said. "Should we gather what we need now, or wait until closer to dinner?"

"We might as well do it now," Abdul replied after a slight pause to consider the question. "That way, we won't have to rush when we get back from our ride, and the vegetables can rest on the counter for that short an amount of time, rather than going into the refrigerator."

True—she kind of hated the thought of taking all those lovely sun-warmed veggies and sticking them right in the fridge. They would definitely be able to handle sitting in the kitchen for a couple of hours.

A pair of large wicker baskets appeared then, looped over Abdul's arms, and he removed one so he could hand it to Sarah.

"I'll gather the eggplant, and you can look for lettuce and tomatoes for the salad," he told her.

That was fine—she thought she was probably much better equipped to judge the various levels of ripeness of the tomato plants he'd conjured, rather than try to figure out which of the eggplants was the right one for the parmesan they'd planned.

He headed for the row where the eggplant grew next to some exuberant zucchini, while she moved down to the one where romaine and butter lettuce were flourishing. It wasn't too hard to find a head of each that looked as though it would be utterly scrumptious in a salad, and the grape tomatoes also appeared to be at the peak of perfection, gleaming like jewels among their leaves, so ripe and juicy that if she hadn't still been full from breakfast, she might have started plucking them off their vines and eating them like candy.

Because she knew she'd rather save them for dinner, she dutifully collected a few dozen, nestling them in her basket next to the lettuce. It seemed that Abdul was taking his time with the eggplant, because he had kneeled next to the row where they grew and was inspecting each one carefully, examining it for any imperfections, probably judging its size to determine if it would be big enough to feed the two of them for dinner.

Sarah was already done with the salad ingredients, so she headed over to the spot where Abdul was deciding on the eggplant. Exactly what happened next, she would never be sure, but as she approached him, her foot caught on a rock or a root or maybe just a depression in the ground, and she stumbled, instinctively reaching out to him for support...and somehow catching hold of his robe rather than his shoulder, yanking it down...yanking it away from his face, revealing the ruin on the right side, as though the skin there had been clawed by monstrous fingers and left to knit together unevenly, with only terrible scars remaining.

The basket of lettuce and tomatoes fell from her fingers.

Dear God.

She took a step back, even as he let out a hiss of shock—of despair?—and immediately yanked at the hood to pull it once more over his head.

It didn't matter, though.

The damage was done.

He got to his feet, looking black and ominous against the bright morning sky.

"Well, then," he said, voice as dark and grim as the robes he wore, "I believe it is time we had a conversation."

Chapter 17

HE HAD THOUGHT THIS MOMENT WOULD never come, had believed he would forever be able to conceal himself from Sarah Wolfe. Never mind that all sorts of accidents lurked out there, just waiting to ruin everything.

Which, he thought with some irony, was exactly what had happened.

Now she sat on the sofa in the living room, huddled into one corner, although he had to admit her expression was not one of fear, or of disgust. Then again, the hood now safely hid his face once more, so she was not being immediately confronted by the hideous ruin of his features.

However, she looked more confused than anything else, as though she was trying to make what she had just seen mesh with everything she knew about the djinn.

And when she spoke, that was her first question.

"I thought—" she paused there, then seemed to gather the words as best she could. "I thought that djinn always healed no matter what happened to them."

Well, at least she had not come right out and demanded to know how he could have been made so hideously ugly.

"Djinn do," he said. "Or at least, they always recover from their wounds if those injuries are not so grievous as to kill them. But you see, I am not precisely a djinn."

She sat up a little straighter then, brows pulling together. Once again, he had the sense of someone trying to come to grips with a difficult situation, and not of her trying her best to get away from the monster who had held her here at Ghost Ranch for more than a week.

"But...." The word trailed off, and she tilted her head, considering him as he stood a few paces away from her, far too tense to sit or do anything except remain there, hands clenched into fists at his side. "But your powers are like a djinn's."

"They are," he conceded. "Or rather, they are more than a djinn's, for I can command all the four elements rather than a single one."

Her eyes widened slightly. Today she had dressed in plain, simple clothes, jeans and a loose shirt, obviously in preparation for their time in the garden. However, her still, solemn expression only made her that much more beautiful when contrasted with the ordinary garb she wore, like a queen in disguise.

"Are you an elder?" she asked, and now her voice was hushed, as though she had suddenly realized she had much more reason to fear him than she'd originally thought.

Perhaps she did.

But no—as angry and shocked as he'd been in that moment when he realized her stumble had led to her unmasking him, he knew it had been an accident and nothing more.

Whatever happened, he knew he could never hurt her, not the woman who had brought so much beauty and joy into his life.

"Not precisely," he said. Now it was his turn to hesitate, as he wondered how much he should tell her, how much he should reveal.

Then again, she had already seen his ravaged face. What were his other secrets, compared to that?

Even the very worst of all, the one he had never thought he would confess to another living soul.

"Then who are you?"

"I am Abdul," he said simply. "I have no family name, for there is no one who came before me. Or rather, the elders were here, and I was intended to be something between them and the djinn, not quite one or the other. But the One who created me made a rare mistake, and you see how I turned out. In His mercy, I was not cast aside like some botched experiment and instead allowed to live. You may make your own judgment as to whether that was such a mercy after all, considering I was forever other, forever apart from mortal and djinn and elder."

Was that the glitter of sympathetic tears in her eyes?

"I am so sorry," she murmured, and he made an impatient gesture.

He did not want her sympathy...and he knew he did not deserve it.

"It is what happened," he said, knowing his tone sounded far too harsh.

Should he leave it there? She must have felt something for him, or otherwise, he doubted she would have been so ready to offer her compassion, the gift of her generous soul.

He could remain silent, and perhaps that empathy might grow into something more, something that would forever bind her to him.

But as terrible as he knew he was, he also understood he could not do that to her. He would not allow her to remain here under false pretenses, believing he was the wounded party and innocent beyond doing whatever he must to protect his isolation.

"There is more," he said, and now he knew his voice was a rasp, shards of glass and steel ripping at the words. "There is much more."

She stared at him, but he noticed how she did not flinch, even now that she knew what his hood concealed. Perhaps he should have left it down, now that he no longer had anything to hide, and yet he could not quite allow himself to do that, to abandon the shield that had protected him from the world for so many millennia.

Before she could reply, he went on, "Do you know, Sarah Wolfe, how the Heat came to be let loose on the world?"

Something of the color in her face left her cheeks then, as if she had somehow begun to guess where this conversation was going, but her voice was steady enough as she replied, "A group of djinn released it. No one knows exactly how it all worked, but that's what we've heard from the elementals in Santa Fe."

"No," Abdul said. The time had come, and he knew he had to say this as plainly as he could. "There was no group of djinn. There was only me."

Now she was dead white, her dark brows and deep sea-green eyes looking like black holes in her paper-hued face. "That isn't possible."

"Oh, it is," he returned. In a way, it felt almost good to speak to her now, to relieve himself of the burden he'd been carrying for so many years. The elders knew the truth of the matter, but no one else. "I will admit the destruction of mankind was not my idea, but rather a conversation held among the djinn for many generations. Then, when it became clear that this world would end in ruin if we did not step in, I realized I had the power to stop humanity. I had the skills required to create a disease that would eliminate the threat forever. And so I went to the elders with the plan, and they spoke to the rest of the djinn, and it was determined that they would go forward with this thing —and that those who objected would be able to save someone from among those who were immune. Because you see, I knew there would be a few survivors, no matter how effective the disease might be. The djinn never knew that only one person was responsible—if asked, they would say some group among them had created the disease and disseminated it among the human population —but none of them would ever be able to identify a single person who had been among that supposed group."

Time seemed to stretch as Sarah sat there on the couch, staring at him. Her expression was still not one of horror, but rather of utter disbelief, as if her mind would not allow itself to grasp what he was saying.

He supposed that wasn't so strange. When confronted with such great evil, the natural inclination was to refuse to recognize it, for otherwise, a human's mind might begin to shatter.

They were so very weak, after all.

Sarah's fingers tightened on the knees of her jeans. "You hated us so much?"

The question startled him. He hadn't been sure she'd be able to speak at all, after being confronted by so many terrible truths, but he had assumed the first thing out of her mouth would have been condemnation.

He had earned it.

"I hated no one," he said calmly, which was also true.

"But...you killed billions of people."

Again true.

However, he did not mind being slightly pedantic in his response.

"The *disease* killed billions of people," he said. "I only created it. But I did so because there was no other way to save this world. You were rushing headlong into disaster with every passing year, and the few solutions you came up with to stop the destruction were half-measures at best and would have changed very little. We djinn had to step in, or there would have been nothing left for us to inherit."

Her mouth opened, as though to offer some sort of response, but then she shut it again. Perhaps she had realized that any argument she made would have been a foolish one, because only a fool would have disputed what he had just said. Distasteful, of course, to cause so many deaths, and yet he certainly had not thought of another way out, and neither had the elders, or surely they would have arrived at a different solution to their problem.

Instead, Sarah pushed herself up from the couch, said in a small, calm voice, "I think I need to go to my room now," and then walked away from him and toward the suite he had provided.

He did not try to stop her.

For a moment, Sarah paused at the entrance to the *en suite* bathroom, feeling her stomach churn and wondering if she was about to throw up. But then it seemed to subside, although she still knew she was queasy and off-balance, wishing with every atom of her being that she hadn't just heard Abdul's horrendous revelations.

He was the one who'd done it. There hadn't been some secret lab filled with djinn scientists, part of the mythology of their new world that she and her fellow residents in Los Alamos had bandied about, but only one man.

Or whatever he was. Not djinn, not elder, some kind of strange being with nearly godlike powers and the devil's face.

No, that wasn't exactly right. One side of his visage had been ravaged beyond recognition, but the other showed how handsome he could have been if something hadn't gone terribly wrong during his creation.

As if that mattered. He could have had the face of an angel, but that wouldn't change the terrible reality that it was his mind that had concocted the disease that had destroyed humanity...or that his hands had been the ones to release it.

Her stomach churned again, but since she could tell she wasn't going to actually vomit, Sarah made herself sit down in the comfortable chair by the window. The outside was just as bright and clear as though nothing momentous had happened in her world, and she found herself frowning, wishing that more storm clouds would converge on the house so the world outside could better match the agony in her soul.

Lying on the side table next to the chair was the iPad Abdul had given her. She stared down at it, wondering how someone who could be responsible for so much suffering and death had thought to give her a tablet loaded with music and books and movies, all the things she might need to be more comfortable here. And how could such a monstrous being have taught himself the piano just so she would have someone to accompany her as she practiced her music?

It didn't make any sense at all.

Stranger than you dreamt it, passed through her mind, and she shook her head. Having random lyrics from *Phantom* rattling around in her head wasn't going to solve anything.

She didn't know how they could fix this. To think she'd honestly believed she was developing feelings for Abdul, even while she'd acknowledged that any kind of a relationship with him would have been impossible.

Oh, it was impossible, all right. She just hadn't known *how* impossible.

She pulled in a breath, then another. Doing so might have helped with her queasiness, but she still had absolutely no idea what she was supposed to do now.

It had been one thing to accept her captivity here...and she knew she had mostly accepted it, had been almost glad that she could stay here and regain her voice and live a life of ease...when she thought Abdul was just a garden-variety djinn with an odd fetish about keeping his face hidden from her. Now she knew the secret of his deformity was nothing compared to the real secrets he'd been hiding, that without him, the Dying would never have happened at all.

And he'd been so calm about it, as though he thought if he just explained his reasoning, then she could somehow find the strength within herself to forgive him!

That was...crazy. How could you forgive a person for killing eight billion people?

She knew this was an inner battle many Chosen must also have fought, but Sarah had to believe their situations were entirely different. None of those djinn had actively killed humans... well, all right, except for reaver djinn like the al-Qadir brothers...although they'd been complicit in those deaths. Yes, supposedly the djinn of the One Thousand had protested such extreme measures, and yet they hadn't done anything to stop it.

Could they have?

Probably not, she guessed. They were only a thousand people, far outnumbered by the rest of the elemental population, which she'd heard was around twenty thousand, give or take.

But just standing by and watching a bus go over a cliff wasn't the same thing as cutting the brake lines.

Okay, she told herself, *you need to be logical about this. You've been here for eight days, and Abdul hasn't done a single thing to harm you. If he'd wanted you dead, you'd be dead already. So now you need to figure out what to do next.*

Could she act as though his revelations hadn't had any huge impact on her, pretend that she thought she could go on pretty much as they'd been for the past week-plus?

She was a good actress...but she doubted she was that good.

All right, maybe she should come out of her room and get in his face, let her anger fly and then subside. That seemed a little more realistic, although she still didn't know how she could even allow herself to be in the same room with him without recoiling in disgust.

Not because of his face, but because of what he'd done to the human race.

This was an impossible situation. And she knew part of what roiled within her now was the realization that she really had begun to care for him —the small kindnesses he showed her, the way he somehow understood when she preferred to be quiet and didn't bother her with idle chitchat.

How he'd gotten her to sing again, *really* sing, in a way she honestly thought she never would.

All while hiding the blackest secret a person could possibly conceal.

Was that tight sensation in her throat unshed tears...or just her doing her best to hold down the bile?

Horribly, she thought it might be a little of both.

———

Utter silence from within Sarah's room, which he supposed was better than wailing and screaming and objects being thrown in a rage.

Or maybe it wasn't.

However, he had to admit she did not seem the type of woman to show her emotions in such an unseemly way. Everything about her was a little controlled, a discipline he guessed she had gained during all those years of intense vocal training, all those hours of practice.

Unfortunate that she hadn't been somewhat more controlled when she lost her balance in the garden.

But no, that was unfair. He had known deep within that this day, this moment, would come sooner or later. What he hadn't known was how she would react to it...and how he would react to her reaction.

Some part of him wanted to knock on the door, to go to her and try to explain. However, he guessed such a gesture would be futile. He had given his explanations, such as they were, and there was little else he could do.

For while he had his reasons, he knew there was no excuse for his acts. Not really.

Only the survival of this world, he thought, but he couldn't say for sure whether even that was enough.

Lacking anything else to do, he went back outside to the garden and made his way to the row where Sarah had suffered her fateful stumble. The basket she'd been carrying lay on the ground, with the lettuce and grape tomatoes it had been holding now scattered here and there, and he bent to retrieve all of it, then went ahead and selected one of the eggplants as well before he added it to the other vegetables in the basket.

Sarah could remain in her room for as long as she wanted, but sooner or later, she would need to eat.

At some point, she'd picked up the iPad and returned to her book, since she didn't know what else to do. The clock on the table told her that lunchtime had come and gone, and even though the world stayed light for a long while at this time of the year, she knew dinner was approaching as well.

Earlier this morning, she would have thought she could never eat again, but now she knew she was hungry. There had been a pitcher of water and a glass in her room, so she hadn't been too thirsty, and yet she found herself wondering if Abdul intended to let her sit in here without food as a sort of punishment for walking away from him.

That didn't seem like something he would do, though. Even though he'd committed the worst crime that anyone could possibly commit, she still couldn't quite believe that he was all right with letting her starve.

Then a soft knock came at the door, and she heard his voice.

"Sarah? I was hoping you might come out and have something to eat."

Well, the invitation settled that question. The one that immediately followed, though, was whether she had the strength to sit down at a table with him, knowing what she knew. From the way he'd just spoken, it seemed obvious enough that he didn't intend to bring a tray to her bedroom.

And although she knew she'd survive tonight without eating anything—and for quite a while longer than that, as long as she had water—she also knew she couldn't hide in here forever.

"Just a minute," she replied, relieved to hear that her voice sounded quite steady.

"I will meet you in the dining room."

Just like that. But she had to admit she was glad

he wasn't going to loiter outside, waiting for her to appear.

That would have been a little creepy.

She went into the bathroom and brushed her hair, then put on some lip gloss. Mostly, she told herself, because she still looked way too pale, and she didn't want to let him know how much his revelation had devastated her.

Oh, who was she kidding? He already knew, because otherwise, she would have emerged from her room long before this.

Still, that minor bit of primping gave her some much-needed courage, and she thought she looked composed enough as she opened her bedroom door and made her way to the dining room. The table was already set, with a green salad studded with tomatoes waiting there, along with a basket of luscious little crusty rolls and a bottle of chianti already opened and ready to go.

Did he really think she was going to drink with him after what had happened earlier today?

Then again, a little wine might be just what the doctor ordered.

Luckily, his back was to her, since he'd been bending to remove something from the oven when she arrived. She took advantage of his distraction to seat herself right away, and when he turned back toward the table, face once again concealed by his hood and a heavy casserole dish in his hands, she already had her napkin in her lap and had done her best to steel herself for the meal ahead.

"Sarah," he said as he came over to the table. "I'm so glad you felt able to join me."

"I was hungry," she said shortly, lest he get the idea she'd emerged for dinner because she wanted the pleasure of his company.

"Not so surprising, since you did not have any lunch. I did not wish to disturb you then, but I thought it better for you to have something for your evening meal."

He set down the casserole dish, which, as she'd already guessed, contained the eggplant parmesan they'd discussed making earlier, in a time that now felt as though it had been a century ago.

Sarah had to admit the parmesan looked delicious, bubbling with cheese and with a layer of tomato sauce covering the breaded slices of eggplant.

The real question was whether she'd be able to keep it down, despite her current hunger.

However, she maintained her silence as Abdul poured some wine into her glass, then into his. Another moment passed while he dished up eggplant parmesan for both of them, and afterward, she placed some salad on her plate before handing the bowl over to him.

He took it from her with a brief nod, then helped himself to some and set the bowl back down a ways away from his plate. With that settled, he reached for his glass, lifted it, and paused.

"I will not propose any kind of toast," he said. "But I will say that I am glad you decided to eat."

About all Sarah could do was nod. Because she hadn't eaten since breakfast, though, she decided to ignore her own glass of wine for a few minutes and instead have some salad and a few bites of eggplant first.

The salad was crisp and fresh, the tomatoes like little bursts of summer when she bit down. And the eggplant parmesan had to be the best she'd ever eaten, the eggplant itself rich and mellow, its crumb coating baked to perfection, with cheese melting over it and tomato sauce so tasty she knew Abdul must have made it from scratch.

Now the real trick would be keeping it all down.

Her stomach seemed fairly quiescent, though, telling her that everything seemed to have mostly settled now she'd had more time to absorb Abdul's hideous revelations from earlier today. Somewhat more encouraged, she broke apart one of the rolls and spread a little butter on it, and after a few bites, she thought it might be safe to finally drink some wine.

It was rich and fruity but not sweet, a good accompaniment to the food they were eating. For the first time, she realized he'd put music on in the background, quiet classical guitar that kept the room from being dead silent but wasn't at all intrusive.

He seemed to understand she didn't want to talk at first, so at least five minutes or so passed before he ventured to speak again.

"I did not wish to hurt you."

Sarah set down her fork, then shifted so she was forced to look at him.

Then again, what was the point, since that stupid hood hid his face from her and she couldn't begin to see what he might be thinking?

"Take off the hood."

His entire body went rigid. "I do not see the point of that."

"I do," she retorted. "I want to see your face. What are you hiding from? The secret's out, isn't it?"

One long, hideous moment, during which he only sat there, unmoving. The only way to tell he was even alive was the subtle rise and fall of his chest under the heavy black cloak.

Then...at last...he reached up and dropped the hood. Dark eyes glittered at her under straight, angry bars of brows.

"Are you satisfied now?"

"I am," she said, and realized she was telling the truth. Yes, those scars weren't so pretty, but they couldn't hide the long, strong nose or the high cheekbones or the determined chin with its scruff of black beard.

Then again, what difference did it make that he would have been drop-dead gorgeous if it weren't for those scars? He was a monster, right?

He blinked. Yes, his eyes were brown, but in the light from the dimmed chandelier overhead and the flicker of the candles on the table, they also reminded her of a fine amber beer.

"Then I am glad I could accommodate your request."

Without looking at her, he picked up his glass of wine and took a large swallow, followed by another. This might have been alarming to Sarah— the last thing she wanted was to be forced to deal with him if he got drunk—except she knew djinn weren't generally affected by alcohol. They could get a little elevated if they drank enough, but it would take a lot more than a single glass of wine, or even two or three or four.

Whereas she knew she could be affected, which was why she also drank some of her chianti. It was barely enough to blur the edges, but she still thought it helped.

A little.

"So...what now?" she asked, and he glanced over at her, clearly surprised by the question.

"I do not know what you mean."

"I think it's obvious enough," she said. "You

told me what you did, but you've also made it clear that you won't allow me to leave. So, what...did you think we were going to go back to the way things were before this morning? It's kind of hard to forget something like that."

His jaw tensed. As far as she could tell, he didn't seem to be doing much to conceal his reactions...but then she realized he might not even know how. After all, he'd spent a very long life hiding behind that hood. He wouldn't have the same defense mechanisms that most people did.

And as much as she hated to admit such a thing to herself, she couldn't help experiencing just the slightest twinge of pity for him right then. He'd never had anything close to a normal life. Unlike the regular djinn, he didn't have a family. He'd never known anything except hiding away from everyone and everything. Although he hadn't gone into a lot of detail—and although it was still a little hard for Sarah to grasp that the djinn thought of God as a real person Who had had real effects on their lives—it sounded clear enough to her that Abdul had come along after the elders but before the djinn or humanity, and God had suffered him to live rather than cast him aside and start over.

It was kind of a lot to deal with, even for an immortal being with near-godlike powers.

No wonder he hadn't seen anything wrong with wiping humankind off the map.

That wasn't entirely correct, though, was it? When Abdul told her what he had done, he had tried to explain why it had been necessary. She didn't agree with him, not one single bit, but if he'd truly thought he had nothing to apologize for, then she doubted he would have wasted any time on explanations.

"I am not asking you to forget," he said. Although she knew it would have been easier for him to look away, he didn't. No, he kept his gaze fixed on her as he went on, "I am not asking you to understand. I only realized I did not want to keep hiding such a terrible truth from you."

What in the world was she supposed to say to that? She'd never had anyone speak to her in such a raw tone, his half-ruined face pleading with her to understand.

In that moment, she realized how much of her life had been spent in shallow interactions—talking about school, talking about work, dancing on top of the surface with absolutely no mention of all the things moving around in the undercurrent. Life might have been more raw and more challenging since the world changed nearly five years ago, but she still didn't think she'd ever had a true heart-to-heart conversation with anyone in Los Alamos.

Not even with Carson, who was supposed to be her boyfriend.

No, especially not Carson.

And when her father was dying, he'd said he was sorry about leaving her alone, but he'd never talked about his fear and his pain, wanting only to wear a brave face to the end.

For all Sarah knew, he'd been glad the end was coming swiftly, since that meant he might finally be reunited with the wife he'd lost so many years before.

This...this right here...this was the most naked interaction she'd ever shared with another living being.

"But I want to understand," she whispered, knowing somehow that she couldn't allow this moment to slip by, that she had to find the strength to meet Abdul's honesty with her own. "Because I don't. At least...I don't understand how you could do such a terrible thing but still play the piano for me. Encourage me. Take me riding, talk to me about birds and wildflowers and cooking. How you could be...kind."

His hand, which had been resting on the table-top, moved toward her and paused. Without realizing what she was doing, Sarah lifted her own hand from where it rested in her lap and placed it next to his.

In the next moment, his fingers had wrapped around hers, strong, warm, but without applying too much pressure, as if to let her know she could withdraw her touch whenever she wished.

"I had never spoken with a human before," he said, and his voice was also not much more than a whisper, low...pleading. "I had no experience of humans, save the knowledge of what they were doing to this world. When I heard you sing, that day when you came to Ghost Ranch, it was as though I realized for the first time that humanity could be capable of great beauty, even as I also realized that once we had encountered one another, I could not allow you to return to your kind. Later on...." The words trailed off as he wrestled with what he needed to say next, those amber-brown eyes fixed on hers. "Later on, I knew I enjoyed having you here. You brought light into my world that I did not even know I was missing. As the days wore on, I began to realize how terrible my crimes truly were. But even I, with all these supposed gifts I have been granted, cannot undo what has been done. I cannot change the past. The only thing I could possibly do to atone for the great mistake I had made was to be kind to you."

Now at last his fingers tightened, and she could see the way his throat moved as he swallowed.

Sarah knew there was no way her own mind could ever encompass the weight of guilt he must be carrying. It would be easy enough to pull her hand from his and tell him no amount of kindness would ever compensate for the pain and grief he had inflicted on those who had survived the loss of their loved ones...or on all the people who had died, even if their suffering had turned out to be brief, with most unaware of what was even happening to them.

Yes, she supposed it would be easy to meet his obvious pain with cruelty.

But what would be the point in continuing that cycle?

Leaving him to bear his burden alone wouldn't bring those people back, or return the world to what it once had been.

"I won't say it's okay," she said after a long pause, during which she'd done her best to decide on the most fitting way to respond to his words. Abdul's eyes half-closed, and she could almost feel the way his body tensed, bracing itself for the words he thought must come next. "Because it's not. But I can't deny that you've been kind to me. At first, I was chafing to get out of here. As time passed, though, I realized I enjoyed being with you at Ghost Ranch much more than I'd ever enjoyed living in Los Alamos, even though I know I should be grateful to everyone there for the way they've kept us survivors safe."

She stopped there, and she forced herself to meet his gaze. Maybe all this was crazy, but at the same time, the crazy thing would be to ignore the truth that had been staring her in the face for the past couple of days, even if she hadn't wanted to acknowledge it.

A sort of wild hope flickered in his eyes. The Sarah she'd been before she came here might not have recognized it for what it was, but the pressure of his fingers on hers told her the truth.

"I enjoyed being here because of you, Abdul, because of the time we spent together. It's because—"

She had to break off there so she could take a breath. Without it, she might not have had the courage to keep going.

"It's because I'm pretty sure I've fallen in love with you."

Chapter 18

IF IT WERE NOT THAT HE DID NOT SLEEP and therefore did not dream, Abdul would have said he surely must be dreaming now.

Had Sarah Wolfe truly just confessed that she had fallen in love with him, even after knowing the worst of his crimes?

Even after seeing his face?

But no, the touch of her slender fingers against his seemed real enough, and there was no mistaking the rosy flush in her cheeks as she spoke, the way she kept gazing at him, expression almost worried, as though she feared he was going to laugh at the foolishness of a human who would dare to love one such as he.

He was not going to laugh, though. Of course he could not laugh, not when she had just given him the greatest gift possible.

334 • CHRISTINE POPE

The gift of her heart.

"Perhaps I loved you from the first moment I heard you," he said. "I had no conception of love, no experience of it. I only realized as time went on that I wanted nothing more than to be with you, to see you, to hear you. Singing made you happy, so I would be your accompanist. You enjoyed being out in nature, so I endeavored to devise expeditions that would please you. Everything I have done these past few days has been for you, only I was too blind to see the reason why."

She swallowed. But she did not pull her hand from his, or try to look away. No, she continued to gaze at him without flinching, which he thought was quite the show of bravery, considering how ravaged his face had always been.

"And I didn't recognize what was happening, either," she said. "Or if I did, I thought I must be suffering some kind of Stockholm syndrome."

Although Abdul knew a great deal of human history, he did not believe he had ever heard that phrase before. "'Stockholm syndrome'?" he repeated.

Now, she smiled, and something of the intensity of the moment seemed to fade. "Well, I won't pretend that I know everything about it, but basically, it's a way of describing when someone starts to have positive feelings for their captor. I mean, I was trapped here because of you, but instead of coming up with ways to escape, all I could seem to do was think about the sound of your voice or what it felt like that one time when you took my hands so we could escape from that thunderstorm. Things like that."

Color had returned to her cheeks as she spoke, and Abdul wondered if that was because she was embarrassed by her feelings, or simply because some time had passed since she first heard his confession, and she had regained some emotional equilibrium.

But he also knew how much her words had moved him, that all the time his heart had been opening to the idea of loving her...even if he had had no idea that was what was happening to him... her heart had warmed to him as well.

"It seems that fate guided us to be together," he said, and she tilted her head, considering his words.

"Maybe you could call it that," she replied. "I'm not going to lie, Abdul—I know what I feel for you, but I also can't ignore what you've done."

"I am not asking you to do that," he said. This was not how he had wanted the conversation to go, and yet he knew he could not shy away from the hard things, not when so much was at stake. "And, as I said before, I will not make excuses. I suppose it comes down to how you will allow yourself to view my deeds." He paused there for a second or two, then continued as an idea occurred to him. "When the bombs were dropped on Japan during your Second World War, who did you think was responsible for all those deaths? Oppenheimer, the man who invented the atomic bomb? The men who flew the planes on those missions? The government? The American people, who put those people in power? Or would you say it was the Japanese themselves, for not surrendering when the war in Europe ended?"

Sarah stared back at him, wide-eyed. It seemed clear enough she had never considered the question before, which he supposed was not so strange. Those bombs had been dropped sixty years before she was even born, and she certainly would have had no reason to analyze the question of the morality involved...unless, perhaps, she had been assigned to write an essay on the topic in school.

"I...I don't know," she said, her voice now shakier than it had been a moment earlier. "I suppose it wasn't any one person, that there was plenty of blame to go around."

"And I would say this is a similar situation," he replied. "Or rather, while the deaths involved are an order of magnitude greater than those who perished in the bombings of Hiroshima and Nagasaki, the principles are not so very different. I created this plague, true, but I did so because it was something the rest of the djinn wanted. So...are they to blame? Am I? Do the elders hold some responsibility, for they certainly went along with the plan? All it would have taken was a single word, right until the very moment when I began to disperse the disease, and I would have stayed my hand. The Heat, as your people called it, would never have been released. But that word was never given, because it was something the djinn desired. The only ones blameless in all this are the members of the One Thousand, for they saved the ones they could."

During all this, Sarah had continued to hold his hand. Now, though, she released it—if gently—but only so she could knot her fingers around one another, as if that might help her to think more clearly. For a long moment, she said nothing, but only sat there in silence, rosy lips pressed together while she seemed to wrestle with herself.

"I don't think it's my place to forgive you," she said at last. "I mean, that's taking a lot on myself, since I can't speak for the ones who died...or the ones who survived. But I think I understand what you're telling me. There's plenty of blame to go around." Another hesitation, and then she added, "But—but you don't have any plans to hurt the people in Los Alamos, do you?"

The idea had never even occurred to him, so he felt comfortable in replying, "No, of course not. If God saw fit to make them immune—and saw fit to create the scientist who invented the djinn-repelling devices—then I am not one to interfere. Indeed, I rather admire them."

"You do?" she asked, her expression both relieved and a little startled.

"Yes," he said. "For they have shown great ingenuity. They are survivors, and it seems they have learned some of the lessons from the world that was destroyed. I do not think they will repeat the mistakes of the past."

"They won't," Sarah said, and now her voice was firm, confident. "I've seen all the work they've done to make sure the settlement is sustainable, that the things they do and the plans they make are all designed to avoid hurting the environment." She stopped there, sending him a rueful smile. "And since I just realized I've been referring to them as 'they' and not 'we,' I guess that says something about where my loyalties lie."

A cautious hope warmed him then. For a few moments, he was not sure what she intended to say —perhaps to tell him that even though she cared for him, she could not allow herself to truly love someone burdened with so much death and destruction?—but those last words appeared to indicate that she was ready to accept him as he was.

However, he needed to find out for sure.

He rose from his seat, and after a moment of hesitation, she got to her feet as well, her lovely face a picture of confusion.

Did she truly not know what he intended to do?

Never in his long life had he ever kissed anyone. But he understood the mechanics of such caresses well enough.

Now he needed to discover whether he dared to put theory into practice.

He bent and touched his mouth to hers, and although she hesitated for just the barest second—more out of surprise than anything else, he thought—she then twined her fingers with his and leaned in close, lips parting slightly so he might taste her, the sweetness of wine on her tongue, a certain delectable flavor that he thought was hers and hers alone.

The heat that coursed through him was utterly unexpected, shocking as a burst of lightning. He had spent countless millennia schooling his body to utmost control, knowing he would never be able to experience physical contact, and to kiss Sarah now was to remind him of everything he had been deprived of during those long, lonely centuries.

She clung to him as well, body pressed against his, and made a soft little sound as their embrace continued, as if she, too, could not quite understand her reaction to his touch.

A moment later, though, she pulled away as she sent him a lopsided smile.

"Well," she said, "I suppose that answers that question."

Until he began to lean toward her, Sarah hadn't truly understood what Abdul intended to do. But once his lips pressed against hers, she realized this was the only way any of this could have ended.

Well, all right...maybe there was one other way. She could have gotten up from the table and walked back to her room, telling Abdul she would never forget, and certainly would never forgive.

For now, though, she was more than happy to let him kiss her, to open her mouth so he'd know she wanted to deepen the kiss. Her body seemed to practically pulse with desire, and she knew no one's kiss had ever made her feel like this before, as though until this moment, she'd only been half alive. The only other experiences that even came close were the times when she was singing at the top of her form, floating along on a breath that would support whatever note she needed to produce, but that still wasn't the same. Those times, she'd still been alone.

Now...now she was with Abdul, and she knew her entire universe had changed forever.

She began to feel almost lightheaded, so she drew away so she could catch her breath. But she spoke words she hoped would be reassuring, and it seemed they worked, since he smiled down at her as well, his half-ravaged face the most beautiful thing in the world to her.

"You did not mind that?"

They were still holding hands, so she gave his fingers a little squeeze as she replied, just to reinforce her point. "No, I didn't mind, not one bit. That was...amazing."

He bent so he could kiss her again, but gently this time, a quick brush of his lips against hers. "I am glad to hear that," he said. "And gladder still to know that we appear to be of one mind. But...."

The word seemed to slide away into the ether, although Sarah thought she knew what he meant.

"But...where do we go from here?"

She knew where she wanted to go—straight into his bedroom, which she'd still never seen. The sensible part of her brain...which, she had to admit, was almost buried by the part of her that wanted to tear all those flowing dark clothes off Abdul's body...tried to tell her there was no reason to rush into things.

Wasn't it kind of a lot to jump right into bed after only one kiss?

"I will not force you," he said quietly. "This must be your decision."

Her lips twisted into a not-quite grin. "Oh, I'm not worried about being 'forced,'" she responded.

"I'm more worried about not having the self-control to keep myself from jumping your bones right here and now."

Rather than smile in return, he tilted his head at her. "I have not heard of this 'jumping bones.'"

"Getting intimate," she said, even as embarrassed blood flooded her cheeks.

"Ah." He paused for a moment, then went on, "I, too, am desirous of such a thing. On the other hand, we do not need to rush into this. I want you to be comfortable, to wait until you know you are ready."

Oh, she was ready now. But she also realized that Abdul had just unburdened some pretty heavy stuff on her, and going to bed with him right away when she hadn't completely processed everything probably wasn't the best idea.

That seemed to settle it.

"Thank you for that," she said, and moved so she could resume her seat. "Then I suppose what we should do now is finish this food before it gets cold."

One corner of his mouth—the corner on the side that was unscarred and perfect—lifted slightly, and she thought of how much she loved the unevenness of it, how the expression was so uniquely his. "It cannot get cold. That is part of the magic of djinn food. But I understand your meaning."

He sat as well, returning his napkin to his lap. Sarah did the same, and with something of an air of unreality, she picked up her fork and returned to her meal as though nothing had happened.

It had, though. She had kissed Abdul, and he had told her he loved her, and she supposed tomorrow they'd do their best to figure out what that all meant.

His bedroom felt emptier than ever that night, but he reminded himself that he must be patient. While he would have loved to have Sarah lying here next to him, he also knew she was being wise in her attempt to take things slowly. They had all the time in the world.

Or at least, he did. There was no such thing as a Chosen for him, for he had never thought he could give a human his love, let alone expect her love in return. That did not mean he would be forced to watch Sarah grow old and die, of course. No, once she was absolutely sure she wanted to be with him forever, then he would join his essence to hers, and she would be young and healthy and beautiful until the end of time.

That was a conversation they could have later on, however. He had no idea how much she knew about djinn/human relationships, but whatever she knew, it did not exactly apply here. Unlike the djinn, who must abide by the elders' rules, he was subject to no one.

Except, perhaps the Power that had brought him into being in the first place.

And that meant he could have her live here for as long as they wanted even if they did not formalize their relationship, for the elders could not interfere, could not come and tell him that he must make her his Chosen if he wanted to continue in a relationship with her.

Not that he would have hesitated. After that first kiss, he would have gladly bound her to him forever...but he also understood that she needed to come to terms with a great many things. Her feelings for him, of course, but also her reaction to his revelations, how she would need to approach her own way of dealing with the actions of his past.

He thought he knew how that would play out, and yet until she told him for certain, he could not allow himself to have too much reckless hope.

Even though he could not sleep, he closed his eyes anyway, just so he could hold the image of Sarah's lovely face in his mind until he could see her once again.

Sleep was long in coming that night, and Sarah couldn't pretend she didn't know the reason why.

She'd kissed him. Kissed the man who'd kept her here for more than a week.

Much more than that, though.

Abdul was the reason why the world had changed.

Or...was he? Yes, he'd created the Heat, but as he'd told her, he would never have invented the terrible disease in the first place if that hadn't been what the djinn wanted.

So who should she hate?

All of them? None?

She'd always been taught that hate was a fruitless emotion, that it hurt the hater more than the hated. And she'd done her best to live her life that way, not allowing petty feuds and jealousies to blossom into anything more than minor irritations. If someone had asked her five years ago, she would have been able to honestly say that she didn't hate anyone. Not really.

For a long time after the Dying, she'd wanted to hate the djinn for what they'd done to the world and the people around her, but she'd let that go as well as the years passed, knowing she couldn't allow that kind of poison to build in her soul if she truly wanted to move on.

And if she couldn't hate the djinn in the collective, then she couldn't let herself hate Abdul.

No, she knew she loved him. Every instinct she possessed told her how wrong that was, but she couldn't deny what her soul had been trying to reveal to her for the past few days. He was kind and gentle and thoughtful, all the qualities she'd always wanted in a partner and had started to believe she would never have.

How could she hate him, when he'd made her feel alive for the first time in years?

So, all right. She loved him. What exactly did that mean? What was supposed to happen next?

She had no idea. This wasn't like hooking up with one of the djinn. Abdul had made it clear that he wasn't exactly one of them, so she knew she was in uncharted territory here.

But then...this was all new for him as well. He'd never been in love, never had anyone in his life. All those long, long years, he'd been utterly on his own.

In that moment, Sarah knew she would do whatever she must to make sure he was never alone again.

Chapter 19

ALL THE TIME SHE HAD BEEN HERE—WELL, except for that first day, perhaps—Abdul had eagerly awaited the moment when Sarah emerged from her room in the morning, wanting to see her, wondering which item of the clothing he'd provided she would choose to wear.

This morning was no different—or rather, he knew he was especially anxious today, for while he thought they had settled matters between them, he could not quite rid himself of the nagging worry that perhaps she would achieve some sort of clarity in the night, and would come to him and announce that she had examined her soul and had realized there was no way in the world she could ever allow herself to spend her life with a monster such as he.

It seemed those fears had been for nothing,

because she came to him in the white dress he loved so much and immediately pressed her lips against his scarred cheek, as if to let him know that she cared little for such surface things. He set down the mug of coffee he held so he could bend and kiss her in earnest, once again reveling in the sensation of her slender body against his, even with all his heavy clothes creating a barrier between them.

"That's a great way to start the morning," she said with a smile. "Wakes me up better than any caffeine."

"So, you do not need any tea today?" he asked, knowing that he teased her a little.

Her smile didn't dim. "Oh, I think I'll still have some. Routines and all that."

He shook his head. It had felt odd to leave his room this morning without his cloak, clad only in the tunic and trousers he always wore underneath, but he had left the hooded robe aside, knowing that Sarah would surely ask why he felt the need to cover up when she already knew what lay beneath the hood.

But he conjured her customary mug of tea for her, Darjeeling this time, and she thanked him and took a sip. Because the tea was summoned the djinn way and not made by dipping a teabag in a cup of hot water, she did not have to wait for it to cool down to her preferred temperature.

"Are we singing this morning?" she asked.

An amusing way to phrase the question, since she was the one who did all the singing while he merely provided the accompaniment. But he supposed he could see why she'd said it like that, as though she wanted to make sure he knew he was an important element of her practice sessions.

And since he had thought a great deal about how this morning should go—and had decided they should carry on as normal, at least until they decided to do otherwise—he had no problem with immediately responding, "I thought we would. And perhaps we could work in the garden a bit, and then go for a ride?"

She agreed that sounded like a good idea, and, after a bit of back and forth, they both decided on egg white omelets with tomatoes and bell peppers and white cheese, something that would be tasty without being too heavy. During the breakfast that followed, they chatted about what they might make for dinner—it was decided that grilled chicken and more vegetables were a good meal for a summer evening—and discussed further plans for the grounds.

It was all so very normal that Abdul began to wonder if perhaps he had imagined their embraces of the night before or the kiss of greeting that Sarah had given him earlier that morning. But no...from time to time, their gazes would lock, and those rich sea-colored eyes would become an ocean he would gladly drown in. The need and longing were there, clear enough for him to see, and he guessed she was doing her best to return to the time when they had not shared any intimacies at all, was trying to be casual because she feared she wouldn't be able to otherwise keep a tight hold on her emotions.

He told himself that was all right. It was not as if he needed her to declare her love for him every second of the day, and those lingering looks she gave him were enough to express her feelings even if she did not utter anything aloud.

After breakfast—and after they had both taken a quick break to clean their teeth—they met in the music room. He sat down on the bench and gave her an expectant glance.

"So," he said. "What should it be today? More Mozart?"

For she had been practicing an aria from *Cosi Fan Tutte,* something well suited to her pure soprano, and although he thought she had done very well with it, he had known she still wanted to keep tinkering away, getting it closer to her internal idea of perfection.

"No," she said. "I'd like to try 'Wishing You Were Somehow Here Again' from *Phantom.*"

His eyebrows lifted in surprise. Although he was somewhat familiar with the song because of the multiple times he had listened to the musical, wanting to learn it so he could see something of why it had been so important to her, he had also gotten the impression that she was not very eager to sing that particular piece, with its clear message of loss and sorrow.

"You are sure?" he inquired, even as he realized that perhaps hadn't been the most politic question to ask.

Her shoulders set, and her chin lifted. "I think I'm ready."

Although he had only been around her for a little more than a week, he knew it was not wise to argue when she wore that kind of determined expression. "Very well," he said. "Although I would like to play it through once to familiarize myself with the notes. I had thought we were going to work on '*Come Scoglio.*'"

While she didn't precisely relax, something about the set of her mouth seemed to ease somewhat. "Oh, that's fine. It'll help me get into the right head space."

So he thumbed through all the scores he carried in his mind, located the correct one, and launched into the song. It was very lovely, although sad, and he had been secretly hoping for a while that Sarah might wish to sing it, just so he could hear her rendition of the tune.

When he was done, he looked back up at her. "Are you ready now?"

"I am," she said. "Go ahead and start whenever you like."

He played the introduction, and when her voice joined with the notes of the piano, it was as if the music had been distilled into pure sorrow, sweet, but at the same time an ocean of tears pouring into his soul. And when she sang, *"Help me say goodbye"* for the second time, and the note drifted effortlessly into an octave jump that reverberated throughout the room, Abdul realized tears of his own had slipped down his cheeks.

Sarah had remained in the curve of the piano for a moment after she was done, but then she looked over at him and made a sound of dismay. "Abdul, what's the matter?"

"Nothing is the matter," he replied as he lifted his hands from the keyboard so he could wipe the tears from his face. "Or at least, what used to be the matter is perhaps not as painful as it once was. That was beautiful, Sarah."

Her mouth curved in a small smile. "It took a long time to work up the nerve to sing it again. But I'm glad I did."

"I am glad as well," he said, then rose from the bench. Sarah sent him an inquiring glance, and he added, "I do not think you can improve on what you just sang. It seems somehow wrong to go back and pick it apart like you would some of the other pieces you've been practicing."

Her expression turned thoughtful. "I can think of a few places where I'd want to work with it some more, but I understand. Let's just leave it alone for now." She looked down at herself, at the white dress she wore, and her mouth quirked. "If we're going to head out to the garden, though, I'd better change. This thing wouldn't last five minutes out there."

Abdul knew the moment had passed, so he allowed himself a smile of his own. "That would probably be wise. I will meet you in the kitchen."

"Give me five minutes."

She came over to him, went on her tiptoes so she could press a soft kiss against his mouth, and then she hurried out of the room.

As he watched her go, Abdul lifted a hand to touch the lips she had kissed just a moment earlier. It had come so naturally to her, the caress almost casual, as if she understood this was how things would be between them going forward and there was no reason to act otherwise.

He thought he liked it very much.

⸻

Once again, Sarah was much lighter of spirit than she'd expected. Yes, she'd determined that she would sing that bugaboo of a song and get it over with, but once she'd accomplished what had first seemed like an impossible feat, she understood more than ever why it had been so important to her.

All those years, she'd never mourned her father the way she believed she should. Of course, she had cried for him and thought of all the time that had been taken from them—his chance to watch her on stage in a real professional production, the opportunity to hopefully one day walk her down the aisle and see his grandchildren come into the world. All those moments had been stolen by the cancer that had been eating away at him, unknown, for months, but she had barely begun to understand what that loss truly meant before the Heat swept over the world. Afterward, she'd had to think of survival and little else, and even once things stabilized in Los Alamos and the people there began to think they might have something resembling a normal life after all, she'd done her best to push her grief aside. Everyone around her had suffered their own losses, and they hadn't been able to say goodbye the way she had. Who was she to indulge her grief?

So she hadn't, had kept it tucked away in a secret little corner of her soul. And she'd thought that she could never sing "Wishing" again, not ever, because if she did, all the pain and the loss would come pouring out and she'd never be able to bottle it up again.

But that wasn't what had happened. It had hurt to sing those words, lyrics where Christine's loss so neatly echoed her own, but instead of falling down into a ball of mush, somehow giving voice to those sentiments made her stronger by the minute, until at the end, she was bursting with so much energy she thought she probably could have held that high G for hours.

Now she was positively cheerful as she took off the white dress and carefully hung it in the closet, figuring she could change back into it for dinner if she decided she wanted to be a little fancy. It felt good to get into her jeans and another loose, comfy blouse, mostly because she knew she could look forward to some time in the garden, and then they would go on a ride, maybe bring a picnic lunch along since it was still fairly early and it might be fun to eat away from the house for once.

And it felt even better to know she'd be doing all these things with Abdul, the one person in the world who shouldn't have understood her at all but somehow managed to appreciate all her quirks and foibles and odd little angles.

She knew she was smiling as she left her bedroom and headed to the kitchen. As promised, he was waiting there for her, although he was staring out the window with a distracted expression on his face.

"What's the matter?" she asked, and he put his

fingers to his lips and beckoned for her to come closer.

Mystified, she did as he requested...then shook her head when she spied the mule deer doe standing in the middle of their vegetable garden, calmly munching away on some lettuce. Her sides were distended, telling Sarah the animal was probably eating for two.

"There goes our salad," she murmured, and he chuckled.

"I can summon whatever we need," he said, also keeping his voice low. "But because it looks as though she is about to have that baby any day now, she probably needs the lettuce more than we do."

Fair enough. It seemed obvious that Abdul didn't want to scare her off, which meant a change of plans was in order.

"I assume we won't be doing any gardening this morning," Sarah said.

"No, we should leave her to her breakfast. I don't want to frighten her away by coming and going from the house—would you mind if I transported the two of us to the stables instead?"

His eyes didn't quite meet hers as he made this request, and she wondered if he was worried she might think he was forcing things by suggesting they get away from the house using the djinn mode of travel.

No force required, though; she looked forward to holding on to him as they traveled to the stables.

"I don't mind," she said, and stepped closer. "Ready when you are."

A relieved smile tugged at his lips, and at once he put his arms around her, holding her close.

Yes, that was just perfect.

What wasn't perfect was that odd non-space in between here and there, the one that made it seem as though they had crossed some kind of incomprehensible void to journey to a spot that wasn't even a quarter-mile away. However, it didn't last long enough to be utterly nauseating, although Sarah hung on to him for a moment longer so she could get her bearings once they appeared outside the stables.

She didn't see the horses inside, but that was all right—Abdul lifted his fingers to his mouth and did a pretty damn good "come here" whistle, and immediately his big black stallion and the blood bay mare that had become Sarah's regular mount came trotting over, looking perky and raring to go.

"Handy," she remarked, and he only shrugged.

"They were very well-trained horses when I found them."

They must have been pretty young, barely more than yearlings, because right now they looked as though they were in the prime of life. By this point, she was used to putting on her mare's saddle and getting her bridle set up just so, and only a few minutes passed before they were mounted up and heading away from the ranch and into the hills.

Big cottonball puffs of clouds floated overhead, and Sarah wondered if once again they might have rain later this afternoon. That was all right, though —they were getting such an early start that they'd be able to have a good long ride and lunch before they needed to start worrying about the weather.

This was one of their favorite rides, the one that led up into the canyon with the waterfall and the stream that flowed through it. The air seemed a little cooler than it had the day before, and she could tell the horses were cheered by not having to slog through the heat, their tails swishing and their heads up as they reached their destination.

Sarah and Abdul both dismounted and allowed the horses to wander off toward the stream, since they would return just as soon as they were called. The shade under the trees beckoned them, and when they approached the largest of the cottonwoods, she saw that a small wooden table and two chairs had already been set up there, with a picnic basket waiting on the tabletop.

"It's great that you didn't have to make the horses carry our lunch," she said as they approached their picnic spot. "They might have had something to say about that."

"Possibly," Abdul agreed as he unfolded the

cloth that had covered the basket's contents and began setting out plates and napkins and a dizzying array of cheese and meat and fruit. "I hope you don't mind this kind of food. It seemed to suit the day."

Since Sarah honestly couldn't remember the last time she'd had anything remotely resembling a charcuterie board, the setup looked positively amazing to her. "It's perfect," she told him. "I always loved these kinds of picnics."

He looked pleased by her comment, and continued with his setup until at last he pulled a bottle of wine and some glasses out of the basket. She could have sworn there wasn't room for those items in there, but then, this was Abdul she was dealing with. Very likely, he'd summoned the wine and the glasses at the last minute after deciding what would be best to accompany their feast.

And it was all absolutely amazing—the goat cheese, the rich yellow cheese subtly flavored with herbs, the bite-sized pieces of sliced meat and the crusty baguette and the little jar of yummy fig jam. They sampled the various treats and compared notes, and interspersed bites of food with sips of wine, which was a fruity pinot just big enough to stand up to the various flavors but not so strong that it overpowered anything.

Eventually, though, they began to wind down, and Abdul quietly made the leftovers and the basket disappear. Some wine remained, though, so the bottle and the glasses stayed behind.

"You seem content," he said, and Sarah nodded.

"I am. More than content." She stopped there and gazed across the valley, pausing to watch the horses who munched on the green grass and didn't seem as though they had a care in the world. A sort of peace lay over the landscape, one she didn't think she'd ever encountered before, even though she and Abdul had been here several times over the past week or so.

Then she realized it wasn't the world around her that had changed, but herself. The Sarah from a few days ago was a very different Sarah from the one who'd heard the worst from Abdul and knew she still loved him.

Should she be this happy when she knew the truth about him?

Some people would probably say she shouldn't. But if she'd learned anything after the world had changed, it was that you couldn't go back. Making herself miserable now—denying Abdul her feelings, her love—wouldn't suddenly restore all the lives that had been lost.

"I'm happy," she said, and his face lit up.

When he looked like that...when she could practically see the love emanating from him, a glow that would never be quenched...she could forget the scars that marred the right side of his face, could forget everything except how good it was to be with him.

He must have seen those emotions reflected in her expression, because he got up from his wooden folding chair and came over to her so he could take her hands and bring her to her feet as well, with his strong arms going around her and bringing her close, his mouth pressed against hers, tasting of wine and sweet fruit.

Even though this wasn't the first time they had kissed, she still was almost shocked by how quickly her body responded to him, how desire flared through her, demanding, strong as a river in flood. She wanted to sink onto the ground with him, to have him take her right then and there, even with the horses munching on the grass a few feet away and absolutely nothing to protect them from the bare earth.

Abdul must have sensed the heat flaring within her, because he murmured, "I have an idea," and just as quick as that, they were away from the valley with its shady trees and lively waterfall, and inside a room she'd never seen before but immediately knew must be his bedroom, with a large king bed in a frame of what looked like reclaimed wood, heavy and rustic. The heavy terra-cotta-hued drapes were closed to conceal the brightness of the day, and candles flickered on the bedside tables and the long dresser on the other side of the room.

"If you wish it," he said, and she pressed a kiss against his throat, feeling his pulse beat beneath her lips.

"Oh, I wish it, Abdul," she replied. "I wish it more than anything."

He obviously didn't need any more encouragement than that, because almost as soon as she was finished speaking, he caught the edge of her loose shirt and pulled it up and over her head, then fumbled with the clasp of her bra for a second before he got it unhooked and cast it aside to join her shirt. Then his mouth closed on her nipple and she gasped aloud, wondering if he was going to make her come right then and there as a wave of heat pulsed through her body.

Not quite, but after he took hold of her jeans and her underwear and pulled them down at the same time, his fingers found her, probing, and she gasped again, knowing it had been way too long since she'd been with anyone, and longer still since she'd felt like this.

No, forget that. She'd never been with anyone who made her entire body come to life in such a way, had never had anyone whose touch, whose caresses, were so in harmony with what she needed. The climax came fast, and she clamped down on his fingers as the orgasm rushed over her, all heat and tingling darkness and waves of ecstasy that continued to pulse through her even after he'd stopped so he could pull off the tunic and loose pants and boots he wore.

God, his body was magnificent, heavier with muscle than she'd thought it would be, stomach flat and shoulders broad...and he was clearly very ready for her.

A little shiver went through her as she looked at him. He was big, quite a bit bigger than any of the other men she'd been with.

It would be all right. This was Abdul, and she knew he would never do anything to hurt her.

Hoping he hadn't noticed her hesitation, she reached out and took him in her hand, and his eyes closed as he lay against the pillows, breath coming almost in pants.

Had anyone ever touched him like this? Sarah doubted it; he'd lived his entire life alone, had never even shared a kiss before she had come here to Ghost Ranch.

Well, it was time to give him a new experience.

She bent and took him in her mouth, tasted the slightest hint of salt, marveled at the silkiness of his skin while he was so hard underneath. A moan escaped his lips, one that sounded as though it had been ripped from his throat, raw with need...and maybe a little bit of shock.

His hand touched her hair as she pleasured

him, but she could tell he held back, didn't want to put too much pressure on her for fear she might think he was compelling her to continue. No force involved—she wanted to do this, wanted to let him see just how much she loved him.

Needed him.

He came a moment later, and she tasted his seed, taking it down, her own body thrilling with desire at the same time. In the past, she'd done this because she knew her partners had expected it of her, but now, she knew this was all her, every part of her wanting him to experience the act for the first time in the very best way.

When she pushed herself up, wiping her mouth, he stared at her with wide brown eyes that held a mixture of shock and wonder.

"That was...unexpected," he managed, and then out of nowhere, a glass of water appeared in his hand. "But I thought you might want this."

She did, very much. After taking the glass from him, she allowed herself a couple of swallows before she set it down on the bedside table. "Thanks," she said. "It's amazing how you can practically read my mind."

"I am not so sure about that," he replied. "But I very much hope this is what you were thinking about now."

He pulled her to him and their mouths met, hot, hungry, even as their bodies touched and she could feel him hard against her leg once again, as if she hadn't just given him the mother of all orgasms only a moment before.

Clearly, djinn bounced back a lot faster than human men did.

But that was all right, because he pushed her down against the pillows, his mouth trailing along her belly down to her mound, until his tongue touched her and she let out a cry that was almost a scream, all of her thoughts and her need and her love focused on those amazing sensations swirling in her core.

She came only a moment later, her hands caught in his thick, longish hair as she rode out the climax, her breath coming in harsh pants. No time to recover, not really, because almost at once he shifted and she felt him pressing against her entrance.

Yes, he was big, but she was ready for him, her body crying out for him to join with her. He seemed to sense her need, because he pushed in at once.

She wrapped her legs around him, driving him in deeper, and now they were moving together, point and counterpoint, harmony and melody, so perfect, so utterly sublime, that she knew those times before had only been sex and nothing more.

This...this was love, the kind of love she hadn't even known existed. How could she have ever sung of love when everything in her life before now had been a pale counterfeit of what she and Abdul shared?

She didn't know, and it didn't matter. Nothing mattered except the glorious sensations flooding through her body, the way she knew another climax was on its way, bigger and better than even the ones from a few moments earlier.

It burst through her like the light of an exploding sun, shockwaves rippling along every nerve ending, every single atom of her being, even as Abdul also hit the edge and went over it, his heat filling her core, his breath harsh gasps.

They clung to one another for what felt like hours afterward, although Sarah couldn't say for sure how long it had been.

Time didn't matter, though. They were here together, and she loved him and he loved her. Everything else was just details.

He touched his lips to her cheek, a brush of gentle butterfly wings. "You are the most perfect thing I could have ever imagined."

"So are you," she whispered. Scarred and solitary and carrying too much of a burden for too long.

But not alone anymore.

She would never let him be alone.

Chapter 20

ODD HOW THE WORLD COULD CHANGE SO completely in such a short amount of time. True, it had changed when Sarah first kissed him, but now —now that they had made love, had become one for a single ineffable moment that he could never have even comprehended before this past hour— everything was different.

Of course, they had attempted to be natural with one another afterward, had kissed and gone in the shower to clean up, then gotten dressed, but he knew his love for her before had been a weak thing compared to what it was now. It was a bright, hot star burning in his chest, the searing realization that he would do anything...anything at all...to make sure she was always safe and happy.

And that included reassuring her that the horses would make their way home without a problem and that all the picnic items they had left behind would be taken care of. Even though it might have seemed an anticlimax to some, they went out into the garden afterward to collect the fruit and vegetables they wanted for that night's dinner. In a way, Abdul thought that was perfect, because to him it solidified their bond, let both of them know that passion would always be part of their existence, but that it was also all right to do the simple things as well.

Of course, that did not prevent them from returning to his bedroom after they were done in the garden, and for them to explore one another's bodies all over again, in a more leisurely fashion this time, as if they both understood that there was no need for haste now.

Nor was there in their dinner preparation, or in the lovemaking that followed, this time lit not just by candlelight, but by the lightning flashes of a storm that had come in near sunset, bringing with it thunder and sudden rain.

Sarah slept afterward, but of course, he did not require slumber. He lay there for a while, listening to her soft breaths, and realized he was thirsty.

The simplest thing would have been to summon a glass of water, and yet some impulse made him slide out from under the sheets and gather up his pants, although he left his tunic behind. And when he went into the kitchen, he saw at once he was not alone, that one of the elders, Idris, stood there by the island.

Abdul stopped where he was, eyes narrowing. "Are you here to lecture me, elder? For I find that somewhat disingenuous of you, considering how you have taken a Chosen of your own."

The space was dim, lit only by the digital clock on the cooktop, but djinn—or those adjacent to them—did not need much illumination to see well. Idris's expression was somewhat rueful, and his voice sounded even enough as he replied, "No, you will get no lecture from me. We all know that you are not subject to our whims in the way that other djinn are. It is only...have you truly considered what it means to bring this woman into your life?"

It meant coming alive after so many centuries of merely existing, nothing more. It meant being glad to feel the sunshine on his face, to know that the woman he loved cared nothing about his surface scars, for she had somehow looked deep into his soul and seen something worth saving.

"Did you consider that same thing when you made Amber McCoy your Chosen?"

Idris smiled. "Of course I did...and I fought against what I knew was in my heart, for I could not see how it was possible that an elder of the djinn might bestow his heart upon a mortal. But at least I had seen how the djinn of the One Thousand had made it work with their human partners, so I believe I had more context in evaluating the situation than you, who have always lived apart from all others."

No more than the truth, Abdul supposed, and yet he found he did not much appreciate the elder's argument. "This was not something I sought," he said, then paused, eyes narrowing. "How is it that you know anything of what has passed between Sarah and myself when you know better than to interfere in my life?"

The elder's smile remained in place. "It was not that difficult to put the pieces together, especially after Zahrias al-Harith contacted us with concerns brought forth by the survivors in Los Alamos, who were missing one of their own. When we heard she had disappeared somewhere near Ghost Ranch, we knew you must be involved somehow. I will admit, though, that we feared you might have disposed of her outright for trespassing on your lands. However, we were able to detect a human presence here, so we knew she was still alive."

Abdul did not like hearing any of this, although he realized the elders' powers extended even beyond his, and he knew they could hear and see things that no ordinary djinn would ever be able to sense.

"How kind of you to stand back and not interfere," he replied, knowing there was an edge to his voice he could not quite conceal.

"It was not our place to interfere."

He returned, "Are you not interfering now?"

"No," Idris said. "I cannot prevent you from continuing on your current course of action. All I can do is counsel you to be wise in what you do. If you truly love this woman—"

"I do," Abdul cut in as he crossed his arms. "I love her in ways you cannot possibly begin to imagine."

The elder did not rise to the challenge in his voice, and instead replied in the same mild tone he'd already been using, "Does it surprise you for me to say that I am glad to hear it? All the same, it is also necessary for you to be honest with her. You must not conceal what you have done."

"What I did," Abdul said, voice more of a rasp than ever, "was in service to the djinn, and you know that as well as anyone."

"True," Idris allowed. "Still, it would not do for you to keep her ignorant of your past."

How self-righteous he looked standing there, so confident that the only way Abdul could have possibly earned Sarah's love was by lying to her!

Well, he was about to let Idris know that elders were most certainly not omniscient, especially in matters of the heart.

"She knows everything," he said flatly. "I did not hide anything from her, for that would not be fair, or wise. Does this surprise you?"

Judging by the way Idris's eyebrows had lifted at that confession, he was very much surprised, indeed. However, he responded in the same calm tone, "I would be lying if I said it did not. On the other hand, I know you are not one to prevaricate. However, even if this woman is here of her own free will and loves you despite everything, it would not do to forget that she has people who fear the worst has happened to her. Would you really have her stay here without letting them know she is safe? For while I and the other elders have forbidden them to come near this place, that will not stop them from worrying about her fate."

This was not something Abdul had given a great deal of thought to. Yes, the people of Los Alamos had mounted that ill-considered attempt to come in search of Sarah, and yet he had not thought there was any real attachment there. Surely she had never gone into depth about any friends or other people she cared about in the little mountain town.

But he had to admit she might have withheld such information in order to protect them, especially in her early days here when she had no reason at all to trust him.

"This is possible," he said. "And I will discuss it with Sarah when she awakes." He paused there, eyes narrowing, for he realized that he and Idris had been speaking in normal enough tones, and even though the house was large, their conversation still might have been sufficiently loud to rouse her.

"She will not wake," Idris said, and his eyes glinted in the darkness, as though he had guessed at what Abdul was thinking. "I have ensured that she will sleep deeply until morning. This was not a conversation I wished to have interrupted."

"Apparently," Abdul responded, his tone now dry. While he did not much appreciate the elder meddling in such a way, he could see why Idris might have believed such measures were necessary. "But since I have already told you that I will bring this up with her, I do not see any reason for you to press the issue further."

A brief silence, and then Idris inclined his head. "I will not. And although you might not believe me, I wish only the best for you and the woman who has gifted you her heart. Take care, Abdul."

The elder vanished then, and Abdul remained alone in the kitchen for a moment longer, staring at the spot where the other man had just stood. He had given his word, and that meant he would speak with Sarah in the morning.

All the same, he was not much looking forward to that conversation.

A resigned breath, and then he went to fetch himself a glass of water.

Sarah couldn't remember the last time she'd slept this deeply, or for so long.

Must be all that glorious sex, she thought with an inner grin, and turned over to see Abdul watching her, his expression much more serious than she thought the situation warranted.

"Is everything okay?" she asked, sitting up. She'd fallen asleep naked, and her loose hair mostly covered her naked breasts.

Mostly.

His gaze flicked to them, and even though she thought she detected a certain warmth in his eyes, he still looked almost stern as he said, "Everything is fine. But there are certain matters we need to discuss. Go ahead and shower, and then we can meet in the kitchen."

Somewhat mystified, she reached over the side of the bed so she could locate her blouse and panties from the day before and put them on, although she decided it wasn't worth the effort to put on her bra and jeans, not when she was only going to the other side of the house so she could get cleaned up.

As she went, she wondered what in the world could have happened to make Abdul look so grim this morning. He didn't seem angry, though, so she didn't think it was anything she had done.

At least, she hoped it wasn't. She'd gone to

sleep thinking everything in their world was absolutely perfect, and now...

...well, now she wasn't sure exactly what was going on.

If she'd been intimate with a mortal man, she supposed how both of them might have been worried about an unexpected pregnancy resulting from all that abandoned lovemaking. She and Carson had always been careful, even though he'd grumbled about the condoms she'd made him wear.

But that wasn't a problem with djinn. From what she'd heard, they were very deliberate and in control of their reproduction, and she guessed it must be much the same with Abdul, or he would have said something to her.

No, something else was going on.

Luckily, she'd washed her hair the day before, so she skipped that step, instead showering quickly so she could get out and put on a dress, since that didn't take as much time as trying to figure out a top and jeans. Soon enough, she was finished and in the kitchen, where Abdul had already summoned some coffee for himself and a mug of tea for her.

"Thanks," she said as he handed it over. "Now do you want to tell me what's going on?"

For a moment he was silent, staring down into his mug of coffee as though it was the most important thing in the world. "Do you miss your friends in Los Alamos?" he asked abruptly, and she stared back at him, startled.

"Where did that come from?"

"Do you?"

It seemed he'd gotten a bug in his ear about something. Was he regretting their intimacy, and was now trying to figure out if she would rather go back where she came from?

Even though it was a gut punch to say the words, she forced them out anyway.

"Are you trying to get rid of me?"

At once, his expression softened, and he set down his coffee so he could reach out and touch her cheek. "No, of course not. You are more important to me than anything in the world. It is only that I wonder if I am being selfish by having you here with me and away from everyone else you know."

Clearly, it was time to set the record straight. She set her mug down on the island and grasped both his hands in hers. "Abdul, I'm right where I want to be. Maybe we could have handled this differently, but don't you ever think—not for one second—that you're being selfish. If anything, I'm the selfish one."

His brows lifted. "I am not sure that is an accurate assessment of the situation. Why on earth would you believe such a thing?"

"Because—" Sarah paused for a moment to collect her thoughts. Wasn't it selfish to be living here in luxury, utterly happy, while everyone in Los Alamos was working their butts off to keep the community going? She'd always done her part to pitch in while she was there, but she'd also never had quite the rah-rah attitude about being part of the last outpost of humanity, or whatever. That said, she knew she'd left people behind who must be worried about her, even if it didn't seem as though they'd tried very hard to track down where she'd gone. "Because I suppose I screwed up, in a way. I should have done something to let them know I was all right. Then again, maybe it's not something I need to worry about, since I get the feeling they didn't even come looking for me."

His fingers tightened around hers, although he didn't let go. "I fear that is my fault."

Sarah blinked at him. "What are you trying to say?"

At least he didn't look away. No, those amber-ale eyes held hers as he said, "They sent a small search party to look for you. I couldn't risk having them come anywhere near here, so...I removed them."

"You didn't...?" she began, then stopped herself.

Did she even want to hear the answer to that question?

"No, no," he said hurriedly. "They are not dead. A little banged up, I fear, for I was not very gentle. But nothing they cannot heal from quickly enough."

She was going to need a minute to process that one. Ignoring the tea Abdul had gotten her, she untangled her fingers from his and went to sit down at the dining room table. He followed, but not too closely, instead choosing to hover a few feet away rather than crowd her personal space.

Probably a good idea. She pressed her lips together, then looked up at him.

"How long ago?"

He didn't pretend to misunderstand the question. "Three days."

Three days. Definitely before she and Abdul had shared any kind of intimacies...but definitely after she'd begun to have feelings for him, even if she might not have admitted such a thing to herself during that time. Still, she needed to recognize the uncomfortable fact that if the rescue party from Los Alamos had actually managed to make it to her, there was at least a fifty-fifty chance that she might have told them she wanted to stay where she was.

Which meant she wasn't going to let herself be too angry with Abdul. After all, he'd told her at the very beginning that this was his home and he didn't appreciate intruders. He'd only done what he thought he needed to.

"Okay," she said. "Maybe there might have been a better way for you to handle the situation, but I suppose it could have been worse. I just wish there was a way to let them all know I'm okay so they won't keep sending people to look for me."

Abdul was silent for a moment, brows pulled together as he appeared to contemplate the problem. As he'd done yesterday, he'd left off the hooded robe and wore a black tunic and black pants, and Sarah realized she was already barely noticing the scars on the one half of his face, as if her brain had noted them once and decided to move on.

"Then you must go and tell them yourself," he said, and she tilted her head at him.

"You're sending me away?"

Immediately, he came over and pressed a kiss against the top of her head. Even that gentlest of pressure from his mouth was enough to send her blood racing again, and she knew she would never survive if she had to live without him.

"Dearest, of course not. It is only that I think it better for you to go in person and let them know that you have come and gone of your own free will. I will even accompany you, if you wish. The devices will be somewhat of a challenge, but I can manage them if necessary."

His expression was earnest, and Sarah knew he meant every word he'd said.

She wouldn't make him do such a terrible thing, though. While she might not have seen first-hand what Miles Odekirk's devices could do to a djinn, she'd heard it could be pretty bad. And while Abdul wasn't an ordinary djinn, he was close enough to them physically that she knew it still would not be at all pleasant for him to be around them for even a short time.

"You can't do that," she said as she rose from her chair. "I don't want you to. But maybe—maybe you can come with me to the edge of the protected territory and wait for me there. It'll feel better to know you're closer than being all the way out here in Ghost Ranch."

"Of course I will do that for you," he replied at once. "And anything else that is within my power to make the process easier."

He could probably think of quite a few things, considering all the supernatural gifts he had at his command. And while Sarah had to admit she wasn't overly thrilled about going back to Los Alamos, even for a short amount of time, she realized this was a dangling thread that really needed to be tied off. The last thing she wanted was for Lindsay Odekirk—or anyone else—to spend any more time worrying about her than she already had.

"All right," she said, glad she sounded firm and unworried, even though a few nervous butterflies had started darting around in her stomach at the thought of returning to her former home and doing her best to explain what had happened to her over these past ten days.

"We'll go after breakfast."

Chapter 21

IN THE END, IT WASN'T SO VERY DIFFICULT. Abdul could tell that Sarah was not completely happy to be going on this mission but at the same time understood it was necessary. And because they both wanted to get it over with as quickly as they could, he came up with a plan that he thought would work.

They traveled in djinn fashion from Ghost Ranch to the border of the protected territory, not too far from the original place where Sarah had told him she'd begun her original exploration into the lands around Abiquiu and Ghost Ranch. This time, however, she would not be going back on foot, but would instead drive herself to Los Alamos in the pickup truck he summoned for her.

"Not bad," she said with a grin as she ran a hand over the sleek black fender of the big Nissan.

"There are a couple of guys I know who'd kill for one of these, even though we're only supposed to drive electric vehicles in town."

"Then you can leave it for them here when you are done with your mission," Abdul replied. "It is not as if you will need the vehicle after you return from Los Alamos."

Her expression turned thoughtful. "True. I'll let Lindsay know to have someone come pick it up later today. That's who I'm going to talk to," she added. "It makes the most sense. She and Miles are the ones in charge, pretty much, and that way I won't have to go into a bunch of explanations with a lot of different people. They can just get the information out to the community in the way they think best."

Sarah paused there, her expression distant, and Abdul reached over and touched her hand. She'd already confessed to him that, while she had quite a few acquaintances in Los Alamos, it wasn't as if any of them had been truly close friends, the sort of people she would have confided in.

No wonder she didn't feel a strong connection to the town, even though she'd lived there for nearly five years.

"It is a good idea," he told her. "Where will you find this Lindsay?"

A quick flash of a smile, one that felt infinitely warmer than the bright summer sun that shone down on both of them. "Oh, it's the middle of the day. She'll be at the lab. And if she's not there for some strange reason, then she'll be at home. Either way, I can make this work."

That sounded reassuring. It seemed as if the woman Sarah was looking for had a fairly set schedule, and if she was not where she was supposed to be, well, the town wasn't so large that it would be difficult to track her down.

"Then do what you must," he told her. "I will be waiting for you here."

"It's probably going to take a couple of hours," she said, now looking somewhat dubious. "Wouldn't you rather wait for me at the ranch?"

Should he say that he would happily wait for her in this desolate spot forever, if that was what the situation required?

He decided against being quite so bold, although he did lean down and kiss her softly on the lips. "It will be no trouble to remain here. I know you will be as quick about this as possible."

Her eyes locked on his, now warm with the same desire he knew he'd felt even after that very gentle kiss he'd just given her. "Oh, I'll be fast," she said. "No worries about that."

She reached over to touch his hand, then turned so she could climb into the pickup truck's cab and start the engine. Abdul thought she looked smaller than he'd expected, sitting up high in such a way, and for a moment wondered if he should have provided a more modest vehicle for her.

But no, even if she would be traveling through regions protected by Miles Odekirk's devices, there might still be stretches of rough road and places where it would serve her to be driving something sturdy like the pickup truck.

He lifted his hand to wave goodbye, and she rolled down the window so she could return the gesture. After that, though, the truck accelerated, bumping its way along the uneven road, until it traveled around a bend and was lost from view.

Even though he knew exactly where she was going and that she intended to come back to this spot as quickly as she could, Abdul could not quite prevent the pang of worry that went through him as she disappeared down the highway. What if something went wrong? What if Lindsay decided that Sarah wasn't thinking clearly and tried to keep her there in Los Alamos?

Well, if that happened, he would go and fetch the woman he loved.

No matter what doing so might cost him.

Miles had volunteered to head over to Pajarito's and grab a late lunch for both of them, so Lindsay had the lab to herself. She supposed she could have gone with him, except it had become routine for her and her husband to always eat lunch on-site rather than going out and sitting down at the town's only restaurant like a couple of civilized people.

Most of the time, she was fine with being here. At her suggestion, they'd brought in a small bistro set and put it in one corner so they could at least eat at a proper table rather than one of the workbenches, but today, she knew she was out of sorts, annoyed with their continued lack of progress at modifying the devices and at the same time fretting over the continuing mystery of Sarah Wolfe's disappearance. Both Shawn and José were healing fine—well, Shawn was pretty much back to normal, and José, while on crutches, should be back on his feet in another few weeks—so Lindsay knew things could be a lot worse.

On the other hand, they could be a lot better, too.

Or maybe this was all the effects of pregnancy hormones and nothing more. At least she hadn't been feeling queasy the past couple of days. No, she was turning practically ravenous, which made her hope that Miles would be back with their sandwiches soon.

The door opened and she turned, thinking it must be her husband and her long-awaited lunch.

Her eyes widened.

Sarah Wolfe stood in the doorway, expression diffident. On the surface, she didn't look much different from the woman who had disappeared more than a week ago—she was dressed in jeans and hiking boots and a sleeveless cotton blouse—but at the same time, something seemed to have changed about her, since she almost looked as if she was glowing from within despite her obvious uncertainty.

"Hi, Lindsay," she said, casual as though she hadn't gone missing without a trace, as though no one had known what the hell had been going on with her for the past ten days.

"Sarah!" she exclaimed, and got down off her stool so she could go to the door. "Are you okay?"

"I'm fine," the other woman replied. "I just—I wanted to come and let you know I was all right so you wouldn't send anyone else to come looking for me."

The words sounded normal enough, and yet Lindsay thought the situation was anything but normal. "Where have you been all this time?"

"At Ghost Ranch," Sarah said. She hesitated for a moment, as if deciding the best way to go on. "I... met someone there."

"A djinn?" Lindsay asked, although she couldn't think of any other possible reply, not after the elders had warned them off...not after what had happened to José and Shawn.

A pause, one so brief that it was almost imperceptible.

Lindsay noticed it, though, and couldn't stop herself from frowning.

"Something like that," Sarah responded, which wasn't much of an explanation. "He's—he's not like anyone I've ever met. I'll be staying with him there, and I wanted to make sure everyone knew to keep away from the place."

This was sounding sketchier and sketchier. True, Sarah Wolfe looked like she'd just come back from a spa vacation with lots of expensive skin treatments, but if everything was going well for her, why would she need to warn everyone to stay away?

Well, nothing like going straight to the heart of the matter.

"Why not?"

Sarah stared back at her steadily. If she'd been trying to hide something, wouldn't she have glanced away or at the very least done her best not to lock gazes like this?

"Because he values his privacy," she said. "That's why he went to live in Ghost Ranch in the first place. He had no idea we were planning to try settling there."

That sounded almost plausible. After all, the town council had only recently decided to see whether expanding in that direction was even a good idea or not. It wasn't something they'd discussed with the Santa Fe djinn until after the fact, so there was no way anyone else could have even known about their plans.

"'He values his privacy,'" Lindsay repeated slowly. "But he's okay with having you there."

Maybe the slightest tilt of Sarah's head. "Something like that. We've come to...an understanding."

That brief hesitation in the other woman's voice told Lindsay pretty much everything she needed to know. This mysterious djinn or whatever-he-was wanted the rest of the world to be hands-off, but he was absolutely fine with having a pretty human woman around.

And it really wasn't any of her business. If anyone had a problem with Sarah being there with her djinn, that would be the djinn elders, not a mortal woman who was just trying to keep Los Alamos going and knew when she needed to keep her nose out of things.

"That's good," Lindsay said. "But...you're really going to stay there, just like that?"

"I am," Sarah replied. She took a step forward, and something in her expression turned almost pleading. "I know this must look crazy to you— and probably to just about anyone else. But he loves me, and I love him. In the end, what else really matters?"

Lindsay had seen that look before, on the faces of the Chosen in Santa Fe who were head over heels for their djinn partners. Hell, she'd probably worn it herself, once upon a time, back when she thought she was in love with the djinn Rafi...only to realize after he was gone that he'd probably cast a glamour on her so she'd be willing and compliant.

But there was nothing compliant about Sarah's expression now. In fact, there was maybe just a hint of defiance in it, as if she'd known she might come up against some resistance and was now willing to fight the good fight if necessary.

Not much point in that, though, not if the object of her affection was a little something more than a djinn. He hadn't accompanied her on this mission, true, and yet Lindsay knew that the elders could come to Los Alamos if they absolutely had to, even though being around that many of Miles's devices was painful for them. There was no reason to think that Sarah's otherworldly lover wouldn't come in search of her if she was held here.

Lindsay wouldn't do such a thing, however. Sarah Wolfe was a grown woman with her own free will, and even if other people might think she was making a foolish decision, it was hers to make.

"Do you need to go to your house and get anything?" she asked then, and something about Sarah's stance seemed to relax.

She'd obviously guessed that Lindsay wasn't going to throw up any roadblocks to keep her here.

"I already did," she replied at once. "A ring that

belonged to my grandmother. There's nothing else in that house that I need."

She stopped there, but Lindsay thought she understood. Like so many others—like herself—Sarah had run from the djinn reavers in her hometown with pretty much the clothes on her back and not a whole lot more. Some might have wondered why she hadn't acquired some more personal possessions during her time here in Los Alamos, and yet there had always seemed to be something about her that held back despite her outer friendliness, as if she'd never truly allowed herself to become a part of the community.

Which meant she might be making a wiser choice than Lindsay had first thought.

"Then I guess all I can do is wish you good luck," she said.

Sarah smiled then. "I already have good luck. That's why I found Abdul. But thanks." A pause, and she added, "Oh, and I'm going to leave the truck I'm driving at the place in La Chuachia that we used as our rendezvous point. It's a really good truck, but I'm not going to need it after today, and I figured maybe someone here would."

Obviously, a truck conjured by her djinn—Abdul—so Sarah could drive here in style to say her goodbyes. However, Lindsay wasn't about to turn down the gift. While they'd done their best to switch over to electric vehicles as much as possible, they still needed to maintain a fairly sizable fleet of trucks and SUVs to do any real hauling or other heavy-duty work. Having a brand-new vehicle to add to that fleet was welcome news.

Not that a truck would ever replace Sarah, of course.

"We can definitely use it," Lindsay said. "Thank you."

A quick smile, and Sarah turned to go. As she was halfway out the door, however, Lindsay couldn't help calling out a final question.

"Are we ever going to see you again?"

Sarah stopped and appeared to consider for a moment.

"I don't know," she said at last.

He had always known she would return to him, and yet he couldn't ignore the leap of joy in his heart as the big black truck came rumbling down the highway. The sun had risen further as she was gone and now rode high in the clear blue sky. A mortal would perhaps have been hot as they waited here, especially if they had been garbed as he was in his black clothing, but djinn did not suffer from the heat and the cold, and neither did he.

The truck came to a stop, and Sarah climbed out. More than that—she hurried over to him as soon as she was on solid ground and threw her arms around his waist so she could hug him close.

"That's done," she said, and he bent down and kissed her, tasting the sweetness of her lips.

Yes, she was sweet, but sweeter still was the realization that she truly did love him, and had returned of her own volition.

"Lindsay did not try to stop you?" he asked after he ended the kiss.

Those green-blue eyes seemed purer and clearer than anything he had ever seen, clearer than the sky overhead or the rushing waters of the Rio Chama, a hundred yards or so from where they stood.

"Well, I could tell that she didn't completely understand," Sarah replied. "But she didn't press me, and she didn't call for backup to keep me there or anything like that. She had a djinn partner once—he was killed by some rebel djinn years ago—so at least she knows a little about this kind of thing, even if our situations are very different."

Abdul knew something of the rebellion mounted by Khalim al-Usar and his followers. A messy, bloody business. It was unfortunate that Lindsay had lost her partner to that violence...but her past had also apparently provided her with enough context to understand that Sarah was only following her heart.

"Then are you ready to go home?" he asked, and she nodded.

"Very."

They still held one another, so all he had to do was tighten his grasp before they whirled away to the house he had so recently made his, and which now felt truly like home because Sarah lived there as well. He let go once their feet were on firm ground, but only so he would be able to look more deeply into her eyes.

"Now that you have said your goodbyes, we must talk."

A faint furrow appeared between her brows, but she sounded natural enough as she said, "I thought we'd already talked."

"About some things, true." He took her by the hand and led her over to the sofa, where they both seated themselves and she gazed at him, expression partly earnest, partly concerned. "But I want to make sure you know exactly what is to come next."

She continued to hold his hand, saying, "I know how it works for djinn and their Chosen. Is this really all that different?"

"It is, only in that I am not bound by any agreements with the elders." Abdul stopped there, trying to think of the best way to express what he needed to tell her. "I made no bargain to love you. I simply do, nothing more, nothing less. When I commit to you, you will also share in my powers and enjoy unending health and life. But if there ever comes a time when you weary of me, then I will let you go back to your people."

"I could never get tired of you, Abdul," she said, her voice hushed and fierce at the same time. "I love you, and I made the decision to be with you."

Her words warmed him, but at the same time, he wanted to make sure she knew she had choices here. "I am glad to hear that," he replied. "But still, I wanted you to know that you have more freedom than the Chosen do. You are not bound to me for all eternity unless you truly wish to be."

"I do wish it," she said. "I can't imagine a future where I would ever change my mind." She hesitated, although her fingers tightened on his as if she wanted to underscore her words. A garnet ring flashed on her right hand, one he hadn't seen before, and he guessed it must be an heirloom she had recovered during her short visit to Los Alamos. "Thank you, though," she added. "Thank you for telling me."

"We promised always to be honest with one another," he told her. "Even in this...or rather, especially in this. And now, I only want to say that your life is entwined with mine, just as my energy is entwined with yours. All that I have, I freely give to you."

As he spoke, he knew that he had done much the same thing as the djinn when they declared a human to be their Chosen—a small part of his magic went to her, ensuring that she would never fall ill, would never be anything more than the perfectly lovely age she was now.

She stared at him, eyes wide. "Was that...was that it?"

"Yes, my love," he said. "As I said, our energies are joined, and that means you will never get sick again, will never suffer an injury that does not heal almost at once...will never grow old."

A long silence as she absorbed those words, and then she smiled. "That's a lot to take in."

"It is," he agreed. "But you will have all the time in the world to learn how to live with it."

She honestly didn't feel a bit different. All right, a little thrill had gone through her as Abdul spoke, but that was more because she could recognize the solemnity of the moment even if she couldn't exactly pinpoint how.

And yet...here they were.

Are you well, my love? echoed in her mind, and she blinked at Abdul, at his grave, handsome face.

"What was that?" she gasped aloud, and he smiled at her.

You did not know that the djinn speak to their

*partners thus? It is much the same for you and me,
even though I am not precisely one of them.*

Well, there was something. She supposed she'd
heard somewhere that djinn and their Chosen
shared a sort of telepathic bond, but because that
little detail wasn't anything that affected her day-to-
day life in Los Alamos, she hadn't stopped to think
about it much.

I—I guess I knew something about it, she
responded, marveling a little at how easy it was to
slip into this kind of communication. *I have to
admit, it is kind of cool.*

Very. Something in that inner voice changed
as he went on, *But because I am more than a
djinn, I have other talents as well. I thought it
might give you hope to see what I have envisioned
for the people of Los Alamos and the world in
general, just so you will know that you have not
abandoned them, and instead are part of better
times to come.*

And then—well, Sarah wasn't sure she could
ever adequately explain the experience to anyone
else, not when she was having a hard time grasping
it herself, but it was as though she was seeing with
Abdul's eyes. Not the room where they stood, with
its big kiva-style fireplace in the corner and the large
windows that provided endless vistas of the high
desert landscape surrounding them, but of a place
it took her a moment to recognize as Española,

since it was so very changed from what she knew of the town.

On either side of the Rio Grande, which was full of snow melt and moving fast, stretched fields of corn and squash and beans and so many other types of vegetables, all lush and green and approaching their peak. The ugly strip malls and gas stations and businesses that had crowded along Highway 68 were gone, and the road itself was wider, mainly because of a median thick with trees that ran right down the center. More trees lined either side of the highway, providing shade and shelter. Here and there, houses peeked out from among the greenery, but each sat on its own large plot of land, at least two or three acres. North along the river valley, grapes flourished in Velarde and Embudo and Dixon, and to the west, people gathered hops along the banks of the Rio Chama.

Everything was peaceful and lovely and flourishing, and her heart warmed at the vision. This was what they'd hoped for in Los Alamos, even when it seemed as if such a dream would be a very long time coming...if it ever arrived at all.

And beyond that, she saw djinn walking the streets of the mountain town that had been her temporary home, and humans strolling in Santa Fe, and people who seemed somehow in between and who she guessed must be the children of the djinn and Chosen who lived there, offspring who were neither quite one or the other, but a bridge between the two races.

It will be like this all over the world, Abdul told her. *Or rather, the children of djinn and humans will come together to meet and learn from one another, and soon enough, those djinn who thought to live apart will become connected to them as well. It will be a better future for all of them, and as time passes, no one will even remember there was once a division between the two peoples. The devices will be set aside, and all will be able to come and go freely as they wish.*

You really think that? She wanted to believe in such a wonderful vision of the future...and yet she couldn't quite forget the bloodthirsty past of both humans and djinn.

I do. His inner voice was firm, unwavering. *It is the only possible outcome of what occurred before.*

Her fingers stole into his, and she breathed in, glad that he felt so strong, so reassuring.

If he was sure of this perfect future, then she would allow herself to be certain as well.

One question remained, though.

What about us?

This time, that inner visualization was more of a flash that came all at once, rather than something that felt like a movie she was watching. She saw Abdul at the piano as she sang...she saw the two of them laughing in the kitchen as they prepared a meal...she saw them riding into the mountains, accompanied by a pair of friendly dogs that looked like they might be border collie mixes...

...and she saw herself standing in front of the window in this very room, an infant cradled in her arms, as Abdul bent to press his lips against the top of her head. The entire space seemed to float in warm light, surrounding them, and she could practically feel the contentment of their future selves wrapping itself around her, letting her know that all would be well.

"I love you," she said simply. The words needed to be said aloud, she thought, and that was why she had spoken that way rather than thinking them to him.

"I love you, Sarah Wolfe," he said.

"And love will heal the world."

The End

This concludes the Djinn Wars series. Thank you and blessings to everyone who went on this long journey with me!

To see more paranormal romance and urban fantasy titles from Christine Pope, just turn the page!

Also by Christine Pope

THE WITCHES OF MINGUS MOUNTAIN

(Paranormal Romance)

Stolen Time

Borrowed Time

Killing Time (February 2025)

PROJECT DEMON HUNTERS

(Paranormal Romance)

Unquiet Souls

Unbound Spirits

Unholy Ground

Unseen Voices

Unmarked Graves

Unbroken Vows

Unholy Night

THE DJINN WARS*

(Paranormal Romance)

Chosen

Taken

Fallen

Broken

Forsaken

Forbidden

Awoken

Illuminated

Stolen

Forgotten

Driven

Unspoken

Hidden

Written

Given

Mistaken

FAMILIAR SPIRITS*

(Cozy Mystery/Paranormal Romance)

Spells and Spaniels

Cauldrons and Cats

Hexes and Hedgehogs

Charms and Chihuahuas

Runes and Ravens

LATTES AND LEVITATION*

(Cozy Mystery/Paranormal Romance)

Caffeine Before Curses

Muffins After Magic

Pastries and Prophecies

Eclairs and Ectoplasm

Sugar Skulls and Specters

Wedding Cakes and Wishes

HEDGEWITCH FOR HIRE*

(Cozy Mystery/Paranormal Romance)

Grave Mistake

Social Medium

Household Demons

Perpetual Potion

Jingle Spells

Wandering Monsters

Uninvited Ghosts

Prophet Motive

Ballroom Bits

Spell Check

Brew Confessions

Charm School (July 2024)

UNEXPECTED MAGIC*

(Urban Fantasy/Paranormal Romance)

Found Objects

Finders, Keepers

Lost and Found

Finding Destiny

THE WITCHES OF WHEELER PARK*

(Paranormal Romance)

Storm Born

Thunder Road

Winds of Change

Mind Games

A Wheeler Park Christmas

Blood Ties

Healing Hands

Wishful Thinking

Smoke and Mirrors

MISS PRIMM'S ACADEMY FOR WAYWARD
WITCHES*

(Fantasy/Academy Romance)

Misspelled

Dispelled

Expelled

THE DEVIL YOU KNOW*

(Paranormal Romance)

Sympathy for the Devil

Charmed, I'm Sure

A Wing and a Prayer

Wish Upon a Star

THE WITCHES OF CANYON ROAD*

(Paranormal Romance)

Hidden Gifts

Darker Paths

Mysterious Ways

A Canyon Road Christmas

Demon Born

An Ill Wind

Higher Ground

Haunted Hearts

THE WITCHES OF CLEOPATRA HILL*

(Paranormal Romance)

Darkangel

Darknight

Darkmoon

Sympathetic Magic

Protector

Spellbound

A Cleopatra Hill Christmas

Impractical Magic

Strange Magic

The Arrangement

Defender

Bad Blood

Deep Magic

Darktide

THE WATCHERS TRILOGY*

(Paranormal Romance)

Falling Dark

Dead of Night

Rising Dawn

THE SEDONA FILES*

(Paranormal/Science Fiction Romance)

Bad Vibrations

Desert Hearts

Angel Fire

Star Crossed

Falling Angels

Enemy Mine

TALES OF THE LATTER KINGDOMS*

(Fantasy Romance)

All Fall Down

Dragon Rose

Binding Spell

Ashes of Roses

One Thousand Nights

Threads of Gold

The Wolf of Harrow Hall

Moon Dance

The Song of the Thrush

THE GAIAN CONSORTIUM SERIES*

(Science Fiction Romance)

Beast (free prequel novella)

Blood Will Tell

Breath of Life

The Gaia Gambit

The Mandala Maneuver

The Titan Trap

The Zhore Deception

The Refugee Ruse

STANDALONE TITLES

Hearts on Fire (Paranormal Romance)

Taking Dictation (Contemporary Romance)

Golden Heart (Gaslamp Fantasy Romance)

Night Music: A Modern Reimagining of The Phantom of the Opera (Contemporary Romance)

Ghost Dance: A Sequel to Gaston Leroux's The Phantom of the Opera (Historical Mystery/Romance)

Flight Before Christmas (Fantasy Romance)

* Indicates a completed series

About the Author

USA Today bestselling author Christine Pope has been writing stories ever since she commandeered her family's Smith-Corona typewriter back in grade school. Her work includes paranormal romance, cozy paranormal mystery, and urban fantasy, among others. She makes her home in Arizona.

Christine Pope on the Web:
www.christinepope.com

facebook.com/ChristinePopeAuthor
pinterest.com/ChristineJPope
bookbub.com/authors/christine-pope